W9-BMS-469

DANGEROUS
BEHAViOR

DANGEROUS BEHAVIOR

WALTER MARKS

An Otto Penzler Book

CARROLL & GRAF PUBLISHERS
NEW YORK

DANGEROUS BEHAVIOR

Carroll & Graf Publishers
An Imprint of Avalon Publishing Group Incorporated
161 William Street, 16th Floor
New York, NY 10038

Library of Congress Cataloging-in-Publication Data is available.

ISBN: 0-7867-1043-8

Printed in the United States of America
Distributed by Publishers Group West

For Joan Brooker,
who said I could,
and Dr. Robert E. Gould,
who said I should.

Acknowledgments

Thank you—Elaine Kagan for getting on the phone, Gene Young for early guidance, Albert LaFarge for showing me how it's done, the Van Doren family for providing a creative environment, Zoila Wiseman for correcting my Spanish, Michael Mindlin Jr. for sending me to Henry, my attorneys Morton L. Leavy and Susan Steiger for laying down the law, Amy Edelstein for expert detailing, my editor Otto Penzler for bringing out the best in me, Claiborne Hancock, Wendie Carr, and all the good folks at Carroll & Graf, and my agent Henry Morrison for being extraordinary.

Mad, bad, and dangerous to know.

—LADY CAROLINE LAMB
describing Lord Byron

DANGEROUS
BEHAViOR

A cold March wind howled across the courtyard of the Dyckman Manhattan housing project. It was almost sundown, and the cobra-headed street lamps were on. Agnes Rivera pushed her stroller along the sidewalk, toting a heavy A&P shopping bag in her right hand, while struggling to steer the stroller with her left. "I bought too much," she thought, as the grocery bag's twine handle cut into her fingers. "I should've had them deliver."

Her two-and-a-half-year-old daughter began whining again. Agnes wished she hadn't treated the child so harshly at the checkout counter, with everybody watching. But sometimes little Margarita could drive her nuts. Agnes cursed softly, wondering, as she did every day, why the hell she'd ever decided to have the kid and raise her alone. She pulled out a package of Oreos, and tossed it into Margarita's lap, promising to give her one at home if she'd only shut up. The little girl fell silent.

She thought about the hassle at the supermarket. "I'm still young," she said to herself, "and not that bad looking. Is this all life has to offer?"

At the entrance to her ground floor apartment Agnes dug in her purse for her door key. Then, as she inserted it into the lock, a man's forearm slammed across her throat.

"Don't make a sound or I'll cut you."

The gleam of a knife flashed in front of her face. Fear paralyzed her. She spoke in a voice she could not recognize.

"What . . . what do you want?"

"Inside."

"Please. Please don't hurt me. . . ."

"Open the door. And shut up, bitch."

The anger in his words stripped Agnes of all hope. He followed her as she pushed the stroller inside.

The man was wearing gloves to avoid fingerprints. He closed the door and they were plunged into darkness.

Outside, two teen-aged boys scuttled by on skateboards. They wore dark colored sweatshirts with hoods pulled up over their heads. They stopped when they heard a muffled, terrified voice from within the apartment. "Why are you doing this? . . . Please. No. No. Don't . . ."

There was a hideous scream, followed by the sobbing of a frightened child.

The two boys looked at each other. One laughed and began to inhale and exhale loudly. His friend giggled and spoke in an ominous tone, as if narrating the trailer of a horror movie.

"Jason . . . is back."

They high-fived each other and kicked off on their boards. The sidewalk reverberated with harsh scraping sounds as they sped away.

Inside the apartment, the man still gripped Agnes from behind. In the pale light from the window, he could see her limp body; he had sliced open her throat with one swipe of his knife. Blood spurted and oozed out of the woman's neck as he let her slide to the floor.

The little girl in the stroller had stopped crying. She'd torn open the package of cookies in her lap and was chewing on one with a blank expression on her face.

The killer knelt down beside Agnes and surveyed his grisly work. Her open eyes seemed to be staring at him, mocking, belittling. Suddenly the fury in him boiled up once more. With a guttural grunt, he raised the knife and plunged it into her chest. Then he did it again, and again, and again.

Chapter 1

"**Look** directly into the camera."

I stared straight ahead as the lens aperture whirred and clicked.

"Turn to your right, please."

Pivoting on the stool, I tilted my head up to eliminate the slight pouch of flesh below my chin. *A guy's gotta look his best even in a prison mug shot.*

After the photo shoot, a guard escorted me down a dim corridor. I noticed my hands were still ink-smudged from the fingerprinting.

I looked up at the row of naked light bulbs burning in their ceiling sockets. Each bulb was encased in a metal cage, the light itself imprisoned, struggling to escape.

We passed a row of cells. They had metal doors with small barred windows. I knew there were men penned up inside, I could feel their eyes on me. A door rattled violently and a harsh voice called out.

"Hey, ya redheaded pussy. C'mere and lemme ream out yer pretty punk a-hole."

The sucking sound of a wet kiss gave my genitals a panic attack. They shrunk up reflexively.

The guard grabbed my arm, hustled me forward. "Keep lookin' straight ahead, man. 'Round here, you don't wanna be havin' eye contact. Ever."

"If I avoid eye contact," I said, "How'm I supposed to interact with people?"

The guard snorted. "They say guys who do what you do hafta be crazy."

"That's a stereotype."

"All the same," the guard said, "You best take my advice."

"It's not my style."

"Then it's yo' ass."

We descended a cement stairway and emerged through a doorway into a bright sunlit prison yard. It was large as three football fields and surrounded by a forty-foot high concrete wall. The wall, topped by a chainlink fence and writhing coils of razor wire, sent an unmistakable message: Don't even *think* about busting out.

It was a warm summer morning, and I saw about a hundred men, supervised by guards with automatic weapons. Some of the inmates loitered in small groups, others stood or sat alone. A haze of cigarette smoke rose over the yard. A few prisoners were playing catch or exercising. In one area, a bunch of heavily muscled men were lifting weights. Their strained grunts echoed off the high walls, sounding like the first attempts at language by Neanderthal man.

We crossed in front of the bodybuilders. A breeze came up, and I caught a whiff of male sweat. The convicts checked me out like predators eyeing prey. My stomach churned. I decided the guard was right and fixed my eyes straight ahead. *They know I'm not one of them.*

We approached the prison hospital, a bunker-like building with barred windows. When we got to the reception desk, the guard showed the nurse our access passes.

"Psychiatric ward?" she asked. The guard nodded.

The words *psychiatric ward* gave me a feeling of comfort; it was a place I was used to, where I belonged.

The elevator took us up to the psychiatric floor. The guard

punched a keypad on the security door, the lock clicked and we entered. An orderly was pushing a patient in a wheelchair. The patient was handcuffed and leg-shackled to the chrome rails of the chair. As he went by, his face twisted into an expression of rage and he spat at me. I dodged the spittle, then stopped and covered my eyes, pressing my palms so hard into the sockets that I saw only amorphous floaters against a pitch black background.

I thought about the events that had brought me here.

Jesus. Will I be able to handle this?

Chapter 2

The guard marched me down a hall to an open door. A sign beside it read "Dr. Benjamin Caldwell — Director of Psychiatry." Dr. Caldwell was at his desk, puffing on a curve-stemmed briar pipe and glaring angrily at a computer screen. He was an African-American man in his late fifties, with gray hair that was getting thin in patches, and a neatly trimmed mustache. His maroon short-sleeved shirt was a bit tight for his thick torso. He wore polyester pants, hip-hop baggy. When he looked up, the guard left.

"Ah, Dr. Rothberg," he said, motioning me in. "Welcome to the joint."

I'd met Ben Caldwell once before, during my job interview in New York. My application had a recommendation from Dr. Edward Sorenson, Dean for Clinical Affairs at Bellevue Psychiatric Hospital.

Ben had asked me if I was really, as Sorenson said, "a brilliant and gifted technician." I told him Ed was my mentor and given to hyperbole. But I did know my stuff.

He wanted to know why a hot-shot Bellevue resident would want to work in a penitentiary. I said I thought prison was a place where I could do some good.

Ben said he figured there was more to it, but he chose not to pry. After all, I was highly qualified, and besides nobody else had applied for the position.

My new boss turned off his computer and squinted at me.

"What happened to your eyes?" he asked.

"Huh?"

"Your eyes. There's a black somethin' all over 'em."

It took me a moment. "Oh, yeah," I said displaying my ink-stained hands. "From the fingerprinting."

Ben took out a handkerchief. "Lemme see if I can clean you up."

"Where's the men's room? I can . . ."

He got up close to me. "Just hold still." He started dabbing around my eyes. I could smell his pipe-breath. I felt like a bad little boy. Luckily he didn't moisten the hanky with his tongue—I definitely would've lost it.

"Well, that's the best I can do," he said, stepping back. "Now it just looks like you had a rough night."

"Thanks."

"Your office'll be ready tomorrow. It's still being painted. You found a place to live?"

"Not yet. I drove up last night and checked into some No Tell Motel outside of town. I'll look for a place when I get settled."

"My wife's a real estate agent," Ben said. "She's in sales, but maybe she'll know of a rental. I'll ask."

"That would be great."

"Please, David. Sit down."

I sank into a battered leather armchair.

"What'd'ya say we get right to work?" Ben said.

"Sounds good."

Ben shoved a pile of file folders across his desk. "I'm gonna start you off with ten hard-core looney-tunes. I know it's a heavy case load but we're swamped."

"That's no problem. Last year I had twice as many. . . . "

"Believe me. Even working in a big city hospital didn't prepare you for these jokers. It's gonna be on-the-job-training, but don't worry—you can look over my shoulder till you get the hang of it."

I glanced at the label on the top folder. "Victor Thomas Janko. I know that name."

"He made big headlines in the city, fifteen years ago. They called him The Baby Carriage Killer."

"Oh, yes. I remember. . . . "

The telephone rang and Ben answered it. He shrugged apologetically toward me and barked into the phone.

"Look, warden, my group therapy room is like an oven. If you can spend fifty thousand dollars on a new electric chair, you can afford five hundred bucks for a Fedders from the Wiz."

I could see he was going to be a while, so I picked up the Janko file.

A *New York Post* article reported a brutal crime in Washington Heights. Victor Thomas Janko had allegedly stabbed Agnes Rivera while her child watched. The medical examiner found twenty-three knife-inflicted wounds on the woman's body. When the police entered the victim's Dyckman Street apartment, the little girl was in her stroller, and her mother was dead, still wearing her coat. There was no sign of forced entry.

Housing cops in a patrol car had spotted Janko walking away from the building, knife in hand, with the woman's blood all over him. When he was ordered to stop and surrender, Janko simply dropped the knife and sat down on the curb with a dazed look. He was questioned but refused to talk. He was turned over to the NYPD, who also could get nothing out of him.

A *Times* Op-Ed column, "The Insanity of the Insanity Defense," said Janko's public defender had first entered a plea of Not Guilty by Reason of Insanity." But the DA feared the jury might buy it, and Janko would be remanded to a mental hospital, only to be let out on the streets a few years later. So, to protect the public (and also his political future), the DA offered the lawyer a deal. If Janko would plead guilty to Murder Two, he'd get the minimum sentence—

fifteen years to life, instead of the maximum—twenty-five years to life. . . .

"Sorry," Ben said.

"No problem." I replied. "I was just reading about Janko's sentencing."

"Yeah. His fifteen years is up now so he's eligible for parole. That's why I'm giving him to you."

I looked at him questioningly. Ben went on in a matter-of-fact manner. "I want you to evaluate the prisoner and then testify before the Parole Board. The hearing is a week from Thursday."

"Shouldn't his doctor do that?"

"He hasn't received any treatment."

Ben saw my puzzled expression. "We've got a problem here at Vanderkill," he explained. "When it comes to budget appropriations, Albany always plays politics and favors Sing Sing, because they've got the big name. We have about as many prisoners as they do, but we get only half the funding. So for sixteen hundred inmates, all we have is a staff of nine—two shrinks, including you, three social workers, and four nurses. Plus a handful of orderlies and paramedics. So we only treat inmates who really go banana-cakes. Janko hasn't done that."

"So . . . nobody looks after him?" I asked.

Ben struck a match and tried to re-light his pipe but all the tobacco had been smoked. He sucked in only hot sulfurous air and burnt briar.

"Shee-it."

He banged out the pipe on a cut-glass ash tray. "I go over once in a while and check him out," he said. "He's well-behaved, never says much. He's taken up painting. And he's pretty good."

"Any diagnosis?", I asked.

"Definitely nutsy."

"Can you give me a brand name?"

"Well, he's Obsessive-Compulsive and . . . well, you'll see in his file."

"I don't understand," I said evenly. "Wouldn't it be better to do this yourself? At least you've got a little history with the guy."

"David, I've been without an assistant for six months now, and between the clinical work and the administrative bullshit I'm on serious overload. I need you to help tote the freight. This evaluation requires an appearance before the Parole Board, and that takes half a day, which I can't afford. Actually, you don't even have to see Janko. Just launch the Risk Prediction Program, then enter his variables—y'know, age, education, socio-economic status. . . ."

I was getting edgy. "You want me to do a psychiatric evaluation based on what a *computer* says?"

Ben started filling his pipe from a leather pouch. "Yeah. He'll come out in the High to Very High Risk group. Then just tell the Parole Board that in your expert opinion, the prisoner, 'if released, is likely to behave in a manner dangerous to himself or others.' That'll keep him inside for another five years."

"So you're denying a person parole on the basis of a machine's prediction? That doesn't sound . . . fair."

"What's not fair," Ben asserted, "is the state law that says the prison psychiatrist has to make this call. Because the truth is, dangerous behavior can't be predicted. There are just too many complex factors involved."

"Well, we can make an educated guess."

"No. We can only make an uneducated guess. We simply don't know enough about what causes a person to act violently."

"But a computer knows?"

Ben struck a match. "Follow-up studies show that computer predictions are . . . *puff-puff-puff* . . . thirty percent more accurate than shrinks."

"Oh, come on."

"Those are the numbers."

Ben's tone indicated *end of discussion.* I spoke quietly. "I think I should at least interview the guy."

"You want to meet him? Fine with me."

"And if I need a few more clinical sessions to . . ."

Ben cut me off with a waving finger. "C'mon. We gotta do rounds."

When we entered the hallway I felt Ben's arm around my shoulders. "I'm really glad you're here," he said.

It was, I thought, exactly the right thing for him to say and do. And because he knew exactly what to say and do, Ben had the potential to be a real pain in the ass.

Chapter 3

Before we saw Rasheed Harris, Ben filled me in on the patient's history. He'd been taken to the hospital for observation after attempting to hang himself with torn-up bed sheets. When he came in he was deeply depressed and just wanted to end it all. Ben put him on the antidepressant Sinequan, 150 mg per day, and let him rest for a while. After a week, Harris seemed to respond to the medication, and Ben put him into one of the daily group sessions. By the end of week four, Harris said he felt better and wanted to return to the general population. Ben had approved him for discharge, and was now checking him out before he left.

Harris lay on his bed, reading *People* magazine. He was a tall, emaciated black man with his hair in twists. Ben introduced us and then asked Harris how he felt. The prisoner sat up and smiled. "Dr. Caldwell," he said. "I'm real fine. Thanks for helpin' me git my shit together."

Ben nodded. "You been feeling drowsy?"

"No."

"Is your mouth dry?"

"No."

"Any constipation?"

"No," the prisoner said grinning, "Everything be comin' out aa'ight."

A look of suspicion flickered across Ben's face.

"Lemme check your pressure," Ben said, bringing out a blood pressure cuff.

"That's cool," Harris said, offering his arm.

Ben pumped the rubber ball. "130 over 80."

He went to the foot of Harris's bed and picked up his chart. After reading it carefully, he glanced at me with a faint smile on his face. Then he spoke to the prisoner.

"Rasheed. Gimme your condom."

"Say what?"

"Gimme your damn rubber."

"What you talkin' 'bout?"

"Don't be jerkin' me around, muthafucka," Ben shouted. "I ain't no fish."

"I ain't got nothin'," Harris protested.

"Drop your pants and yank it out for me," Ben said. "Or I'll do it for ya."

Shamefaced, the prisoner undid his belt, reached back and pulled a condom out of his rectum. The condom was stuffed with pills.

"Drop that stinkin' shit in the trash," Ben ordered. Harris did as he was told. Then Ben called for a guard.

After the inmate was taken away, Ben explained he'd had doubts about Harris all along. He suspected Rasheed had faked his suicide attempt to get into the psychiatric section and steal pills. Prison, Ben said, is a drug culture and inmates know more pharmacology than your local Walgreen druggist. Harris figured he'd be getting tricyclic antidepressants, which sold for big bucks because they enhanced other drugs of choice—narcotic analgesics and amphetamines. He faked taking his pills and later stashed them up his ass so he could smuggle them out.

"Where did he get the condom?" I asked.

"Vending machine," Ben replied. "It's in the canteen, right between the candy and the cigarettes."

Crash course on prison life.

"How did the blood pressure tip you off?" I asked.

"His readings were the same as the day he got here."

I thought for a moment.

"Of course," I said. "You had him on Sinequan, but he showed no side effects—no constipation, dry mouth, drowsiness, or . . . *low* blood pressure."

"Exactly," Ben said. "He was on a maximum dosage. He hadda have *some* side effects." He gave me a big grin. "You slick, man."

I tried not to look self-satisfied, "One more question, Ben," I said. "What's a fish?"

"What?"

"You told Harris you weren't a fish."

"Oh," Ben said, laughing. "Actually, you're a fish. A new arrival. Fresh fish. Someone who don' know da drill."

Ben started moving toward the door. "Next on our list is Bobby Sanchcz. He's a full-time resident of Paranoia-ville."

"Does he hallucinate?"

"Yeah. He hears voices that get beamed down to him from a TV satellite. These days he says Lieutenant Columbo is telling him what to do."

"Columbo?" I said. "That show hasn't been on for years. He must be hearing re-runs."

Ben laughed. It was the first time I'd heard him laugh. But then, this was first time all day I'd felt comfortable enough to crack a joke.

Ben got serious. "We're watching him very carefully," he said. "Sanchez is trouble."

We went to see Sanchez, who was in bed and appeared to be sleeping.

"*Oye,* Sanchez," Ben said softly. "*¿Está durmiendo?*"

When Sanchez failed to respond, Ben whispered that we'd better come back later. He explained Sanchez was in a constant state of fear, feeling people were planning to kill him. If Ben woke him suddenly, he might panic and get violent. Or maybe he was pretending to be asleep, which meant he didn't want to talk. We left quietly.

Next we visited Nigel Penrose. I recognized him as the guy who'd spit at me from his wheelchair. Mr. Penrose was now calm and amiable. Ben told me he'd just gotten a session of electroconvulsive therapy. Ben asked how he was feeling, and the patient replied in a Mayfair English accent. "After all that electric current passing through my system, I feel *shockingly* good."

Ben said some encouraging words, and we moved on to the group therapy room. The guard who'd taken Harris away was now leaning against the door. He introduced himself as Brian Cacciatti. A large, pearl-handled revolver protruded from a holster on his hip. I told him it looked impressive.

"Six-eighty-six Magnum Plus," he said, patting the gun with pride. "Seven rounds, special order. Any of these wackos act up, I show 'em this. Chills 'em out a lot quicker than intravenous Valium."

When we entered the group therapy room, Ben said he kept the guard stationed outside to give his patients privacy. But he could summon Cacciatti with his beeper if he had to.

"Does that happen often?" I asked.

"Not if I'm doing my job right."

When we sat down, I saw why Ben was pushing so hard for a new air conditioner. This unit was snarling instead of humming, pumping hot then cool then hot then cool air into the room, as if it were having mood swings.

The patients began to straggle in. They took seats on folding chairs in a circle. Ben told them who I was and explained today I'd only be observing.

Nobody spoke. Ben just sat back. The six patients avoided all eye contact. Finally, one man stood up and told everyone else they were assholes. That triggered the action.

The speaker was clearly schizophrenic, his delusional thinking expressed in pretentious and disorganized speech.

"You're all assholes," he proclaimed. "You're pathetic, paltry assholes because of your dispicableness, which has been propagated not only on the premises but also in general."

A morbidly obese guy shouted him down. "I'm onto you, Fart-breath," he said. "I know you're just a mouthpiece for the warden. You and him are in cahoots . . ."

"Oh, please. I'm sick of your tiresome conspiracy theories."

"Ain't no theory. A theory is somethin' that might be true and might not. I happen to know there's a plan goin' on, a plan to get every con in this room feelin' like turds, like we was lower than insects. But lemme tell ya somethin', Fart-breath. Ain't nobody gonna grind me down. Not you, and not the warden."

"What you guys don't realize," a pasty-faced man said quietly, "is we're fucked. Don't matter what we do or say, we're fucked."

It seemed much like the group sessions I'd run at Bellevue. The usual dynamic was at work—the complex mix of hostility, compliance, imitative behavior, humor, rage, and catharsis.

I'd expected the men to act differently because they were criminals. But they didn't. I couldn't tell from watching them which one was a murderer, a rapist, a robber, or an arsonist.

Still, there was one profound difference between them and my Bellevue patients—these men were not *free*.

All the patterns of character—drive, desire, fear, defense—were distorted because they had no control over their lives.

If a man is caged up is he paranoid for feeling his keepers are against him? Is he a pathological depressive because he's despondent? Can he be called phobic because he fears something terrible is going to happen to him?

I'm going to have to change my mind set. And I know it'll take some time to learn how to help these guys.

By the time the group session was over, I'd made myself a promise: *This time I'm going to do things right.*

Chapter 4

After work, I went down to the parking lot and got into my car—
a restored 1972 New York City Checker Cab. When I bought the old
taxi at a Newark car auction it was bright yellow with a black and
white checkerboard pattern around the moldings. Printing on the
door said *50 cents first ¼ mile, 10 cents each additional ¼ mile.*

When I went to register the car, I learned that in New York City
only working taxis can be painted yellow, and if I wanted to drive the
car I'd have to change its color. So the vehicle was now robin's egg
blue. But I kept the checkerboard trim and the price advisory. For
old time's sake.

I got in and savored the aged cab smell—musty with hints of Esso
fumes, dime-store perfume, and nickel cigars. A million fares picked
up and dropped off in the Big Apple.

I left the prison and drove through some dense woods, punishing
my rebuilt suspension on the pot-holed road. Then I turned left and
followed Route 7 leading into town. The view was like a color photo
in an "I ♥ NY" brochure; rolling, verdant mountains rising along
both sides of the nearby Hudson River. About a mile before the vil-

lage, the road widened to four lanes, and I passed a small shopping center. It had a food mart, a sporting goods store, an auto body shop and—my pulse quickened—the yellow plastic arches of a McDonald's. The sign was an eyesore, but I was happy there were Big Macs within driving distance. I scarfed them down so often at Bellevue, the head nurse said the MD on my name tag stood for Mickey D.

The sun was setting behind the mountains when I got to the center of town. Main Street, Vanderkill, looked like Main Street, USA, circa 1930. The business district was a block long. One side of the street was straight out of an Edward Hopper painting, a row of two-story red brick buildings. The amber sunlight turned the bricks orange and created dark, slanted shadows under the cornices and window sills. There were stores on the ground floors, offices above.

Across the street were private homes that had been converted into shops. They had cutesy names like "Perc's" (a coffee house) and "Hair-do-well" (unisex beauty salon). One yellow house with a mansard roof had a sign that said "Vanderkill Obstetrics and Gynecology Center," and displayed the shingles of nine—count 'em—*nine* OB/GYNs. Go figure.

Telephone poles lined the sidewalks, tilting at odd angles, many hung with distribution transformers. The sky above was crisscrossed with power lines, phone wires, and other loose-hanging cords.

No underground cables. Nice. It wasn't the prettiest town in the world, but Vanderkill kept the look and spirit of an older, mellower America.

Ten minutes later I pulled up at my motel. I'd forgotten to take my room key so I stopped off at the office.

The Hospitality Inn was a Mom and Pop operation. Pop was manning the desk. He was a shifty looking twerp with a ferret face. He leaned back in a swivel chair, watching TV—"America's Funniest High Speed Car Crashes." On the wall was a diploma from the American School of Motel Management, with *Ray and Gina Incaviglia* inscribed in Olde English lettering.

"Forgot my key."

"Room number?"

"Seven."

Ray reached in a mailbox and flipped me the key without missing one second of ". . . *on the Pasadena Freeway . . . Burbank cop car in a triple rollover . . . followed by a 360. Nobody was hurt.*"

I walked over to my room, in a row of dilapidated units facing the parking lot. When I reached the doorway, I heard an angry, buzzing sound, and looked up to see the motel's neon sign flickering to life. For a moment it read only "SPITALITY INN." Then the "HO" went on. *Truth in advertising.*

Once I got inside, it felt good just to be in my own space. It was cramped, dingy, and furnished with Salvation Army rejects, but it was okay. I was used to close quarters; back in the city I lived on a small houseboat permanently moored in the Hudson River Boat Basin at 79th Street. I'd bought the twenty-eight foot Sunseeker with money my mom left me when she died. Most people said I was nuts, especially since it was so far away from the hospital. But when I saw an ad for it in *New York Magazine* I couldn't resist. Living on a peaceful river in the middle of the frenetic city I thought was way cool. And it was three blocks from Zabar's and H&H Bagels.

When I left New York, I rented the boat to my boss Ed Sorenson, who lived in Scarsdale and wanted a Manhattan *pied a terre*. I think he really needed it for this psychiatric social worker he was shtuping, but hey.

Ed said he wouldn't be there that much so I could use it when I came to town—just call first.

I took off my jacket. My first order of business was to feed Shelly. Shelly is my pet three-toed box turtle. Well, she's not really mine. She belongs to an autistic kid named Henry Simpkins I looked after at Bellevue. His mom said the turtle was the only thing that made her son smile, so we kept Shelly by his bed. Henry finally had to be moved to Anson/Packwell in Palo Alto for long term care; no pets allowed. I told the boy I'd mind Shelly till he came home. It'd been two years now.

I dumped some Kibbles 'n' Bits into her vivarium.

"Madam, dinner is served."

Shelly poked her head out of her shell and shambled over to the food. She looked up at me with her red-eyed, sharp-nosed face. I scratched my fingernails over her high-domed carapace. She loved that.

I went to the mini-fridge and popped a Heineken I'd bought the night before, then stripped down to boxers and tee-shirt.

I plugged in my laptop and set it on the nightstand. Sitting on the edge of the bed, I began typing up my notes on the day's events.

The process felt alien to me, and after a few moments I realized why. This was the first real clinical work I'd done since Melissa.

I closed my eyes and flashed on her face, her mouth really. Melissa had a way of biting into her lower lip as if it were soft candy. I shook my head. *I am not going to think about Melissa.*

When I finished my notes, I took out Victor Janko's folder. Since Janko had received no treatment at the penitentiary, there wasn't much in his file. At the time of his admission, Ben had done a psychological evaluation of the prisoner.

Janko's personality type is Obsessive-Compulsive, with component of Passive-Aggressive style. Appears quiet and well-mannered, but shows evidence of repressed anger below calm surface. Has potential to act out violently.

There was no mention of psychosis.

The file contained a report on Janko's avid interest in painting, with a notation that two years ago, one of his works had been reproduced in a *Newsweek* article on prison artists.

The only other data was a chart similar to a school report card, rating Janko's conduct over the past fifteen years. He'd gotten all A's. The name of his cell block was listed as Ad Seg. I wondered what that meant.

Each year under *Visitation* there was the word *None*. But in the last year there were regular visits from a Ms. Daisy Leszczynski . . .

Suddenly my mind and body sagged with exhaustion. It had been a long day.

I got up and went into the bathroom, thinking a shower might revive me. In the mirror I saw my ink-smudged eyes.

Oh, swell. I've spent my first day on the job looking like a red-headed Rocky Raccoon.

I took off my underwear and got into the shower.

No soap.

Chapter 5

At noon the next day I was crossing the prison yard with a guard. We stopped at a building that was separated from the main cell block. Its entrance door was made of wooden planks studded with large iron nailheads. It looked medieval.

"Ad Seg?" the guard said. "Oh, that stands for Administrative Segregation, the new bullshit word for Solitary. Solitary Confinement."

Aaron "Stevie" Karp was a veteran of twenty-something years working in the slammer. He said he got the nickname "Stevie" because he idolized Steven Seagal, who played rogue cops that were Above the Law and Hard to Kill. Like Seagal, Karp wore wraparound sunglasses and a meager ponytail that belonged on the ass of a Chihuahua. The area in which he outdid the out-of-shape movie star was his beer-belly. I guessed it was one of those guts that looks soft and flabby but is actually hard as a cast iron soup kettle. This was a phenomenon I didn't understand. Truth be told, I was putting on a smidge of weight myself, and as I furtively pushed a finger into my belly, the flesh gave way like the Pilsbury Doughboy. I sucked in my gut and vowed to switch to McVeggie burgers and start a regimen of daily stomach crunches.

Stevie Karp found a key on his keyring, which was attached by a lanyard to his belt. He unlocked the door.

"Why is Janko being kept in Ad Seg?" I asked.

We entered the building, and began to ascend a metal stairway.

"'Cause from day one he couldn't get along in the population," the guard said. "First of all, his personality's very irritatin'—you'll see what I mean when you meet him. But the main problem was—he was the Baby Carriage Killer."

The guard handled the stairs without effort. My breath was coming in wheezes.

"See," Stevie went on, "killin' a mama in front of her little baby, that goes against inmate morality. Victor took a couple o' kick-ass beatin's, so we decided to transfer him. If somebody whacked Victor, it woulda been looked on like he got what he deserved. Even in Ad Seg, we've kept him in a separate area, away from the other men. He's in a cell that used to be the old Discipline Room."

I was sucking wind when we got to the top. The guard didn't notice. He was giving me a history of the Ad Seg Unit. When Stevie first started working there, he said, the place was dirty, dark, and crawling with rats and roaches; for all attempts and purposes (sic) you could say it was a dungeon. It was called the Hole, and they used to send bad-ass prisoners there for punishment. The threat of sending a guy to the Hole gave the guards some real clout. Nowdays, Stevie explained, there were these namby-pamby regulations, and the building was only used for special cases like Janko, and for guys who were considered too dangerous to be around other inmates.

Still, the guard said, he made sure life in the ASU was no picnic in the park, which was his responsibility as head muckle-dee-muck of the place.

"What's your relationship with Janko like?" I asked.

"Huh?"

"I mean . . . do you like him?"

"He's awright."

"Do you trust him?"

The guard looked amused. "Doc," he replied, "Victor's a con. You can't trust a con. Your con says somethin', he means somethin' else. He does somethin', it's only to *git* somethin' else. He swears somethin's true, you bet your ass it *ain't*."

"You think that's true of every inmate?"

"Look, if it was *you* penned up in this place, how would you act?"

"I have no idea."

"You'd have only two things on your mind," Stevie explained, "survivin' while you were here, and gettin' out soon as you can. Now, in the slams, honesty sure ain't no help in survivin'. And despite what the Bible says—the truth will not set you free."

We were outside Janko's cell. Instead of iron bars, the cell had chainlink across its front like a playground fence. The door was made of the same material; the lock set into a thick steel plate.

The cell had no window. It was furnished with bare essentials: a sink, a toilet, a cot, a chair. Victor Thomas Janko, dressed in a lime-green jumpsuit, stood at an easel, painting. I indicated I'd like to observe Janko before going in.

"He ain't gonna notice us, Doc," Stevie said, not even whispering. "He's in his own world when he's paintin'."

I was surprised by Janko's work. I'd expected some abstract blotches, or angry scrawls, or something primitive like Grandma Moses. But Janko was an expert Photorealist. He was painting a meticulous depiction of a beach scene with palm trees. Part of the picture was unfinished—marked off into grid sections like a highway billboard. Every few moments, he looked over and referred to a blow-up of a beach photograph, also marked off with a grid.

Other paintings lined the floor of the cell, propped against the walls. Each was a tropical beach scene, devoid of people. In one corner were more canvases, stacked in a tall pile.

"Why doesn't he hang his pictures on the wall?"

"He ain't allowed no nails," Stevie replied. "A nail could be used as a weapon."

Victor was working so intensely he appeared to be in pain. His tongue lolled out of his mouth like Michael Jordan driving strong to the hoop.

I was struck by how ordinary Janko looked. He was a short, plumpish man, with straight sandy hair and pale skin. He wore glasses with heavy, clear-plastic frames. His age was listed in the file as forty-three but he seemed younger. His facial features were soft, babyish, almost unformed. From his appearance, it was hard to imagine him committing an act of murderous violence. Then I remembered Son of Sam.

"Yo, Vic," Stevie called out as he unlocked the cell door. Victor Janko ignored us. The guard shouted, "Victor, you got a visitor."

The prisoner put down his paintbrush and turned to us. I stepped forward, "Mr. Janko. I'm Dr. David Rothberg."

Victor nodded and said nothing.

"I'm sorry to interrupt your work."

Victor didn't reply. His face was expressionless.

"Do you mind if I sit down?"

"Oh, sure," Victor said quietly. Then he leaped up grabbing a towel and crossed to the chair.

"There's dust on it, though. Lemme dust it for ya."

He dusted the chair carefully, inspecting for every speck of dirt. Then he stood straight up.

"It's funny," Victor said, "You don't realize how many grains of dust there are in the air, till you see a beam of sunlight. And there they are . . . hundreds and hundreds of 'em . . . floating around like tiny little . . . creatures or somethin'. And then . . . you can't believe you breathe that stuff into your lungs."

He smiled awkwardly. His complexion was so pale I wondered how long it'd been since he'd *seen* a beam of sunlight. "Okay. Thanks," I said to the guard. "You can leave us alone."

"No can do," he said. "Ad Seg regulations. No visitor in a cell without a guard."

"I'm not a visitor. I'm staff."

"That's the rule, Doc. It's for your own protection. Every man here is considered dangerous."

"Mr. Janko doesn't seem to me to be dangerous."

"Don't be too sure," Stevie said, "He does have a shank."

The guard stepped over to the easel and picked up Victor's palette knife.

"That's a palette knife," I said. "It can't hurt anybody."

"It can if he sharpens it."

He demonstrated, honing the blade against the cinderblock wall. Suddenly, he whirled and lunged, slashing and jabbing at me in a mock attack. I jumped back, my heart thumping. Stevie smirked.

"Look," I said, "stand outside if you want. But I need to talk to Mr. Janko alone."

"Unless you got written permission from the warden, I stay." He stood arms folded, an immovable object.

I turned my attention to Victor's paintings.

"I see you're a Photorealist," I said.

Victor didn't reply.

"Are you using acrylics?"

"Oh. You know about . . . art?

"A little bit," I said, recalling a Photorealist Show I'd seen at the Whitney. "Y'know, your technique reminds me of Richard Estes, 'though of course he does city street scenes and you do beaches."

"Have you . . . did you ever hear of Ralph Goings?"

"I . . . believe so."

"He paints ketchup bottles. Heinz 57," Victor said with intensity. "And diners . . . y'know, old fashioned diners? He . . . he's my influence."

"I can see that."

Victor looked away, trying to hide the fact that my interest pleased him.

"I understand one of your paintings was reproduced in *Newsweek*."

Victor's eyes still avoided me.

"You must've been very proud."

Victor shrugged and smiled nervously. I went over to his current painting and examined it closely.

"Don't touch it," Victor shouted.

I pulled away. Victor spoke in a controlled voice. "You . . . you might smudge it."

"This is a very precise process, isn't it?" I asked.

"You're not kiddin'."

"What happens when you make a mistake?"

"Pardon me?"

"What happens if your brush slips?"

Victor's lips moved for a few seconds before the words came out. "I don't let that happen."

"But sometimes mistakes are unavoidable."

Silence. Victor appeared more and more uncomfortable. His eyes took on the blank look of a blind man and he started making soft, tuneless, whistling sounds.

"Is something wrong?" I said.

"Pardon me?"

"Does it bother you to discuss your work?"

"I know why you're here," Victor said abruptly.

"You do?"

"Yeah. Stevie told me—before the parole hearing they always send a shrink. To see if you're . . . okay in the mental department."

"How do you feel about that?"

"Fine."

"So," I said. "Would you like to tell me a little about yourself?"

Victor looked at me vacantly.

"What else are you interested in besides painting?"

No answer. Ben was right about Janko's personality being Obsessive-Compulsive. He displayed the classic preoccupation with cleanliness and order, and also a typical Ob-Com defense mechanism: any time he felt anxious or threatened, he'd clam up.

The prisoner started making the whistling sounds again. He took off his eyeglasses and slid them carefully into his breast pocket. I noticed the frames weren't really clear; they had aged to the color of pale urine. I sat down in the chair and watched him. The whistling made me very uneasy. I've always been amazed by how well Obsessive-Compulsives handle the tension they create by being silent. They can almost always tolerate it better than I can.

I decided maybe a tough question would jolt him out of his withdrawal.

"How do you feel about the fact that you killed someone?"

He stopped whistling.

"Pardon me?"

Pardon me. His favorite evasive phrase. Was it an unconscious expression of his desire to be forgiven, paroled?

"How do you feel about the crime you committed?"

Victor averted his eyes. I pressed him. "Do you feel remorse? Are you sorry for what you did?"

Victor put his glasses back on then turned and stared directly at me. The glazed look was gone.

"Sorry?" Victor said. "How could I be sorry? Sorry is what you say when you bump into somebody. Or when you're like late for supper. But when you take another person's life . . . I mean, that's the worst thing anybody can do. It's . . . a Mortal Sin. And they say I stabbed this lady . . . while . . . while her own kid watched. Does sorry mean anything when you do something like that?"

"What do you mean, they say you stabbed her?" I asked. "Are you saying you didn't do it?"

Victor's eyes closed and opened. "I don't remember," he said in a flat tone.

"What don't you remember?"

"I don't remember . . . killing anybody."

Victor removed his glasses again and lowered his gaze. Once more, he began the strange, whistling noises. I tried to wait him out but it was no go.

"Well, thank you, Mr. Janko," I said getting up. "I'm glad we had this time together."

I signaled Karp I was ready to leave and the guard unlocked the cell door. As I went out, I called back to the prisoner. "So long."

Victor looked up diffidently. "Pardon me . . . Doctor?"

I stopped.

"Are you . . . will you be coming back again?"

"Would you like me to?"

"It's okay with me."

I nodded noncommittally and left with the guard.

Karp stopped at the stairway and turned to me. "Doc," he said, "I think I should tell you somethin'. Victor was lyin'. He was lyin' to you about the murder."

"What do you mean?"

"He knows damn well he killed that lady. He told me about it lots o' times. Like he was boastin' . . . y'know, tryin' to show off what a bad dude he is."

"But why would he lie to me with you right there in the cell? He'd know you'd contradict him."

"I don't know why, Doc. Maybe he forgot he told me. Maybe he forgot I was standin' there. Maybe he figured I'm his friend so I won't rat him out. Maybe he's just nuts."

He paused for a moment. "I'd vote for nuts."

I didn't respond. I started down the stairs, but as I took my first step, Karp spoke. "Doc."

I turned.

"You gonna let him outta here?" he asked.

"It's not up to me."

"Come on, Doc. The man's a model prisoner. Victor is Mister Good Behavior. Plus, his paintin' counts real heavy as rehab. Parole Board got no *basis* keepin' him in here. Not unless you say he's a bad risk. Fact is, Doc, you're all that stands between Victor Janko and freedom."

"So you believe he should be kept in prison?"

"I wouldn't let him out on a bet," the guard said. "Them quiet types are the worst. They can crack without any warnin'. One minute he be fine, next minute he be back carvin' up some woman."

I said nothing.

"Lemme ask you a question," Stevie went on. "Would you be willin' to send your sister or your mother down a dark alley knowin' Victor Janko was lurkin' in the shadows?"

who looked like a black Mister Clean. He was bipolar, in an intense
manic phase. Not only did he speak loud and fast but also in a string
of rhyming hip-hop phrases, accompanied by finger snaps.

"Din't do no felony/ Don't even know da melody/In for twenny/
Help me, Savior/Lemme out on Good Behavior. . . ."

He'd been in before and I checked his chart. Under *Diagnosis*
Ben had written *"Definitely has his Ups and Downs."* Then in paren-
thesis—(*Bipolar 1, Rapid Cycling—for you DSM-IV freaks.*)

He'd been on Lithium. I decided to try an anti-convulsant,
Depakote. They led him away rapping.

"Man be takin' me off da Lith/ Put me on some other shit/ Don't
make me no never mind/I'm manic-depressive so I feels fine . . . I
gon' shine . . . all the time. . . ."

In the afternoon I sat in on another group therapy session. Then I
played chess with Nigel Penrose and he whipped my ass.

At seven I was back in Ben's office, typing up notes on my laptop.
Ben came in and said he was heading home. He showed me a white
cardboard container.

"Kung Pao chicken. I'm gonna heave it, 'less you want some."

I'd been too busy for lunch so I said great. It was cold, but it was
food and I was starved. I chowed down while I finished up.

At eight I quit working. I decided to leave my computer set up on
the desk in "charge" mode. But I had no key to lock the office door.

I went down to the nurses's station. The night nurse was just coming on duty. I saw by her ID badge her name was Kim Cavanagh and
I introduced myself.

"Have you got a key to Dr. Caldwell's office?"

"Sure," she said.

"I'd like to lock it tonight. I'm leaving my laptop."

"I'll do it for you. Have a nice evening, Doctor."

She was kind of pretty. Her face was a bit bland, but probably
because she wasn't wearing makeup.

Bet that's because she's working in this male-infested zoo.

Her day-shift counterpart had less of a problem. She looked like
Nurse Rachit.

I turned and walked down the steel stairway. Karp's footsteps
echoed behind me.

"Listen," he said. "This here's a bad place, Doc, with a lotta bad
people in it. You hang 'round any length of time, that bad gonna rub
off on ya. So you best be careful, hear?"

Chapter 6

The next day my office was painted, but the paint was still wet and the room was fumy. So I worked out of Ben's office.

He asked if I wouldn't mind going into his computer to reorganize his files. I booted him up, took one look and said I couldn't.

"Why not?"

"I can't *re*-organize your files because they weren't organized in the first place."

"Wha'd'ya mean?"

"Well, for one thing—you store all your files on your desktop."

"Sure," Ben said. "Just like I do in real life. Makes it easier to find 'em."

This man who trusts life-and-death decisions to a computer is a closet Luddite.

I spent most of the morning trying to make digital order out of his analog chaos. Then we did rounds together.

Later I signed in a new patient, who insisted I call him Six which was short for 6847-30-31, " 'Cause a number is all I am in this shithole." Six was a beefy African American with a shiny shaved head

Hidden beneath Kim's starched white uniform my practiced eye could discern a righteous bosom.

She was just the type I'd've had a thing with when I was at Bellevue. After I got my MD, I went through a phase—working my way through a succession of nurses, candy stripers, and paramedics. Then I settled down with Bronwyn Silver, a sexy, intelligent X-ray technician. It was good until she started pushing me to sell the houseboat and get a real apartment like a grown man so we could have a regular life. After the breakup she called to say she was marrying an anesthesiologist—"Better hours, higher pay."

Then came the incident with Melissa, and I decided to put my libido on hiatus. For half a year now it'd been just me and Shelly.

"If anything comes up tonight," I said to Kim, "I can be reached at 732-3000."

"Let me write that down," she said, leaning over her desk.

34Cs.

"It's the Bates Motel," I said.

"Bates Mo . . ." She laughed. "Oh, yes, I knew Norman. He was in my high school class—a real mama's boy."

"Actually, it's the Hospitality Inn," I said.

"Over on Route 101? Yeah, it does look kinda spooky. Be careful in the shower."

We made major eye contact and I left.

I crossed the prison yard and passed the fortress-like building where Victor Janko was locked up. I was dying to go in and see him again, but that would mean going against Ben's orders.

Driving back to my motel, I couldn't get Janko off my mind.

"Are you . . . will you be coming back?"

"Would you like me to?"

"It's okay with me."

I'd made a connection. It wasn't much, but it was a start. *If my job is to figure out if Janko is dangerous, how can I just walk away now? I promised myself I would do things right at Vanderkill—do all I could to help my patients. And the moment I walked through Victor's cell door, he became my patient. He's not just some convict automatically to be labeled a menace to society. He's a person, a troubled person, with a ton of psychic baggage.*

What kind of life did he have now? Fifteen years in solitary, with almost no human contact? How did his confinement affect how he saw the world, the way he behaved towards me? He must've been disturbed before his imprisonment so being here could only have exacerbated his emotional problems. . . .

I'd just stopped at a traffic signal when the aura struck. I saw flashes of light and color. My face tingled. My right hand suddenly felt larger than my left—the "Alice in Wonderland" syndrome, the migraine specialist had called it. I pulled over and reached into my briefcase to get the Sumatriptan injector kit I always carried. Shit. I'd left it in my suitcase back at the motel.

I swung my car onto the road as the dull pain started on the left side of my head. I drove quickly but I'd screwed up. The Sumatriptan only worked if I took it at the first onset of symptoms. It'd be twenty minutes before I could give myself a shot. I was in for a lulu.

The headaches started about six months ago. I was seen by Dr. Stanley Ramone, a neurologist at Bellevue Hospital Center. Dr. Ramone was called "Ramone the Drone" by his medical students because of his monotonous lectures on the central nervous system. His specialty was headache research; he was a founder of the American Council for Headache Education (ACHE). Ramone was a consciousness-raising type, who called migraine sufferers *"migraineurs,"* as if adding a French suffix to their disease could make them feel better.

I told him that I felt my headaches were related to an emotional problem I was going through. He advised me to discard my ingrained, rigid, psychiatric mind-set. What I had to remember was that migraine (the word comes from the Greek *hemikrania*, meaning half the skull) was a genuine medical disorder, not something caused by psychological stress. Stress could *underlie* the headache, but it couldn't cause it. Dr. Ramone's sophistry and condescension was a migraine-trigger in and of itself, right up there with paint fumes, red wine, chocolate, foods containing sodium nitrite, MSG. . . .

"Of course," I said out loud, "MSG." *The Kung Pao Chicken. Schmuck.*

When I got back to the motel, I injected the Sumatriptan and lay down in the darkened room. *Just endure the pain, wait the monster out.* After half an hour the medication kicked in and helped. But not enough. I got up, searched in my briefcase, and found a sample packet of Nembutal. It was old but I took it anyway. As it came on, the headache started to fade, and then I conked out.

I had a strange, inchoate, disturbing dream.

Victor Janko has me cornered in his cell, slashing me over and over with his razor-sharp palette knife. I'm screaming in pain, helpless to defend myself. The blood spills from my body and runs in a crimson stream across the floor, then up into a claw foot porcelain-enameled bathtub.

Suddenly Melissa is there, twisting the hot water faucet, turning it on full blast as rising steam clouds the air. Gradually the water turns to the color of rosé wine, then to cherry Jell-O, and finally to the inflamed scarlet of arterial blood.

I awoke at dawn, my pillow soaked with sweat. My vision was bleary after a night of drug-induced sleep. But one thing was clear— I knew what I had to do about Victor Janko.

Chapter 7

"**G**in."

"Nuts," the priest said, laying down his cards on Ben's desk. "Ten . . . twenty . . . twenty-eight."

Ben took his pipe out of his mouth. "That's Game," he said. "Score is Protestants 107, Roman Catholics zippo. Looks like the Reformation all over again."

"Okay, okay," the cleric said with a moan. "I owe you a dollar seven. Put it on my tab."

I was watching from the open door, not wanting to interrupt them. The priest looked to be about sixty years old. He had a full head of snow-white hair and a florid face. His voice had the flat, sort of dimwitted tone of a hockey player in a post-game TV interview. Probably he was French-Canadian.

"Y'know, Pops," Ben said to him, "I can't believe you discarded that ace. It's almost like you wanted to lose."

"Do you come to me for confession?"

"No."

"Well, I don't come to you for psychoanalysis," the clergyman said. "So button it."

They laughed. I decided to come in.

"Hey, David," Ben said warmly. "Meet Father Emile Toussenel. He's pastor of the Roman Catholic church in town, the Church of the Incarnation. Pops . . . Dr. David Rothberg."

"I do double-duty as chaplain up here," Father Toussenel said. "The Church of the In*carcer*ation."

He chuckled at his own wit, then shook my hand. I've always felt a bit awkward around priests because I'd spent fifth through eighth grade in a Catholic school, where I was the only Jewish kid. I'd been transferred to Our Lady of Martyrs Academy to avoid what my father called "the bad element" which was beginning to overrun P.S. 189. I wasn't treated badly at the parochial school, yet I always felt like an outsider, a misfit.

As I released the cleric's hand, I recalled what I thought as a ten-year-old, when I met my first priest. *Why should I call somebody father who isn't my father?*

"These are your welcome presents," Ben said, handing me two plastic cards. "One is your keycard—it lets you use the staff entrance when you enter the prison."

"Thanks."

"You can bypass the metal detector, which is good because sometimes there's a line and like a twenty minute wait."

"Great."

"The other is your photo ID," Ben said. "Clip it to your jacket."

I looked at the picture and grimaced. "Geez. I look like Howdy Doody on a bad hair day."

"Well, your mother certainly gave you an appropriate name," the priest said amiably.

"What makes you say that?"

"In the Old Testament, David is described as a red-head."

I thought about telling him that although Renaissance artists often painted David with red hair, the Bible actually described him as ruddy. I stifled myself.

"And, of course," Father Toussenel went on, "in Hebrew, David means beloved."

"My mom told me I was named after the famous Michelangelo statue," I said. "So I always thought the name David meant young man with small pecker."

Ben laughed, the priest pursed his lips. I guess I'd made that crack to zing Father Toussenel. I was in a feisty mood, partially because of a hangover from the Nembutal, but mostly because of my plan for Victor Janko. It would force me to go *mano a mano* with Ben Caldwell.

I was about to bring it up when Ben beat me to it.

"Have you done anything on the Janko situation?"

I hesitated, not wanting to discuss a patient in front of the priest.

"Don't worry about Pops," Ben said, picking up my concern. "We talk shop all the time. We're in the same business; trying to get people to shape up."

"Well," I said, "I did meet with Janko yesterday."

"How did it go?"

"All right. It's hard to connect with him, though."

"You're talking about Victor," the priest interjected.

I nodded.

"You're right," he said. "For years I've tried to get through to him but he's a real hard case. He's Catholic, and once in a while he'll pray with me but beyond that he's, well, it's like he's put up a wall around himself."

"He's very self-protective."

"It's interesting," the priest went on. "Most of the time he strikes me as a real cuckoo, but when I see him with his girlfriend, he's as normal as blueberry pie."

"Girlfriend?" I said. "Victor has a girlfriend?"

"Quite a looker too," he said. "Name of Daisy."

Oh, the lady with the Polish name.

"Have you spoken with her?" I asked.

"A few times, in the visiting room. She's a nice, bright lady. Works in the town library."

I turned to Ben. "Did you know about her?"

"Yes, but I've never met her," Ben replied. "You seem surprised, David. You shouldn't be. Incarcerated killers attract groupies just like rock stars. Kenneth Bianchi, Richard Ramirez, Ted Bundy . . . they all had girlfriends. It's a strange phenomenon."

"I'm sure you've got some brilliant psychological theory to explain it," Father Toussenel said.

Ben put his unlit pipe back in his mouth. "Maybe these women are sexually drawn to killers out of a primal need." The pipe came out. "At one time, back in the caves, the man who was the fiercest warrior, the one most capable of brutal slaughter, was the most virile—hence, the most sexually attractive."

"Why are your theories always about sex?" the priest asked.

"What other kind of theory is there? You want Relativity? Check out Einstein."

Father Toussenel laughed.

Ben turned to me. "So, what was your take on Janko?"

"Well, he's neurotic as hell, but at this point I wouldn't bump him up to psychosis. He's got this obsession with tidiness and order, but he's channeled it into Photorealist painting, which is not unhealthy. He's thrown some bizarre defensive behavior at me, but that's not entirely inappropriate. After all, he sees me as a threat; I have the power to deny him parole."

Ben gave me the Shrink Nod; the one that means "I hear what you're saying, but I won't tell you what I think about what you're saying."

"One thing puzzles me," I went on. "When I interviewed Victor he claimed to have no memory of doing the murder. Then later, the guard, Stevie Karp, told me Victor *did* remember killing the woman—in fact he'd boasted about it in great detail."

"Which one do you believe?" Ben asked.

I shrugged.

Ben turned to the priest. "What do you think? You know Janko better than we do."

Father Toussenel hesitated. "I have no opinion."

"C'mon, Emile," Ben said. "You always have an opinion."

"Not this time."

"But you've known him for years. Haven't you tried to get him to discuss his crime? You must have . . ."

Then Ben got it. "Ah-hah," he said. "He told you about it in confession. So he's got . . . penitent confidentiality."

The priest looked at Ben without expression.

"That's a helluva poker face, Pops. You oughta use it playing cards."

Father Toussenel checked his watch. "Gotta go. Late for a meeting at the parish house."

He made for the door, then stopped. "Nice meeting you, David. See you later, Ben."

After he left Ben smiled. "Obviously Janko admitted to the murder in confession."

"We don't know that for sure."

"Look," Ben said firmly, "You don't confess to something you didn't do . . . you only confess to something you did do."

"But you're assuming there *was* a confession . . ."

Ben ignored me. "So clearly he was lying when he told you he didn't remember killing the woman. And that's reason enough to keep him in here. Which I'm sure the computer will confirm."

I wanted to discuss the confession, but Ben had brought up a more crucial issue.

"Fact is, Ben," I said in a casual voice, "I'd like to stay away from the computer for the time being."

"Why?"

"I want to find out a little more about Victor."

Ben gave me an accusing look. "You mean you want to do a *clinical* evaluation."

"I think he should be given a chance . . ."

"To do what? Convince you he's just a sweetie-pie? To swear on his mother's grave that he positively won't go out and stab a couple more mamas?"

"I'm talking about fairness, Ben. He should be examined *in person*. If he's stable enough to get out, he'll . . ."

"Are you serious?"

"I'm not saying he *should* get out. Only that . . ."

"The man lied to you."

"He may have," I said quietly, "But that doesn't prove very much. I've never had a preliminary session in which the patient didn't lie about *something*. Never."

"He lied about murder."

I tried to sound nonconfrontational. "My feeling is . . . I just need a bit more time. I've only met with him once. "

"David. You know I think a lot of you, and I'm damn happy to have you here. But you don't know what you're getting into with this Janko thing. Predicting dangerous behavior isn't only extremely difficult, it's also risky. You can put a lot of people in jeopardy by making this decision, and one of those people—who is at very serious risk—is you."

"I can handle myself."

"I'm not talking about physical risk," Ben said. "I'm talking about psychic risk."

"I can handle it. Comes with the territory."

"I'm sorry, David. I have to say no. Just use the computer."

I exploded. "I didn't come here to process data. I came here to be a doctor—to heal people, to help people. You asked me to evaluate this man. In my book that means using my professional skill to learn all I can about him. Okay. I accept the responsibility. I accept the risk. But it's gotta be *my* call. If you don't want that from me, then why the hell did you hire me?"

Ben sighed. I'd pushed the right button. He was so swamped with work he couldn't afford to lose me or make me an unhappy camper. "All right," he said quietly. "Do it your way."

"I'll need the warden's permission to be in the cell alone with Victor. I think the guard inhibits him."

"I'll arrange it," Ben said. "But you've got less than two weeks. I don't know what you can hope to accomplish."

"I'll do what I can."

"Remember, you've got a full schedule with me *here*."

"I'll do Janko on my own time."

Ben leaned forward. "David," he said, "I've been in this game for a couple few years. So, at the risk of sounding like a pretentious gray eminence, I'd like to give you a piece of advice."

He paused, then continued. "These guys are all criminals. When you deal with the complexities of the criminal mind, you gotta remember—you're never as smart as you think you are. Your judgment is never as good as you think it is."

"I understand."

"Believe me, David," Ben said, "you *don't*."

Chapter 8

The Vanderkill town library was in a gray clapboard Colonial with a front porch. I figured it had once been a private home. The house was surrounded by a white picket fence and a neat lawn. It had a flagstone entrance path flanked by carnations and hydrangeas.

I walked in through a screen door. The main reading room was a former living room; the club chairs scattered around it looked like they'd always been there.

The place was empty except for one blue-haired lady reading a newspaper attached to a wooden dowel.

At the Return Desk, I saw a young woman, also reading. She looked up and I noticed her clear gray eyes and long, uncombed blond hair.

"Can I help you?"

"Are you Daisy?"

She closed the book. It was *John Donne and the Metaphysical Poets*.

"What's this about?" she asked.

"I'm from the penitentiary. Dr. David Rothberg."

"Oh," she said. "You're the shrink."

"Yes."

"Victor mentioned you when I visited him yesterday."

"I'd like to talk to you about him, if you've got some time."

Her hand scooted up to her head and she twirled some strands of hair around a finger. "Oh, gee," she said. "I wouldn't feel right about that. You're a psychiatrist so I'm sure you understand. Like, if you treat somebody, you're not supposed to reveal what the patient tells you. Well, I believe if you *love* somebody, it's the same thing. It's not right to reveal stuff about them."

"This is different," I said. "It's part of the parole process to have Victor evaluated by a psychiatrist. The more information I have, the more accurate and fair I can be. I'm sure you want that."

"Of course, but . . ."

"I'm not asking you to betray him. But you're an important part of his life—a very positive part—so you'd really be *helping* him."

She looked at me closely, trying to figure out if she could trust me.

"Well," she said, "I can't talk to you here. Maybe we could meet somewhere."

"Fine."

"There's a diner down at the corner. I get off in about an hour.

"See you there."

Daisy bounced in to the Silver Streak Diner with a girlish smile. Her teeth were white as Chicklets, and not capped.

"Listen, in case you're interested, my last name is Leshinksi. Spelled L-e-s-z-c-z-y-n-s-k-i.

"It's Polish." She laughed. "D'ja ever think so many consonants could hang out together without touching a vowel?"

I began by asking Daisy for a little background. She came from Akron, Ohio, an orphan raised by foster parents who took her in to increase their welfare payments. As a kid she had intense feelings of loneliness and estrangement. She said her life was meaningless till her final year of high school, when she happened to see Victor Janko's beach painting in *Newsweek*.

"And I knew . . ." Daisy said, excitedly, "I just knew whoever painted that picture was special. Once, when I was little, my folks took me to Florida; it was the only vacation they ever took me on. God, I loved the beach down there. It was so beautiful and clean compared to the dirty, ugly factory town where we lived. And this painting, it seemed to totally capture the feeling of that beach. So I wrote Victor a letter telling him I admired his work. I included a copy of one of my favorite poems, which is sort've about being on a beach, and then being in prison. It goes: 'Always I climbed the wave at morning/ Shook the sand from my shoes at night./ That now am caught beneath great buildings. . . .'"

I completed the quatrain. "Stricken with noise, confused with light."

"You know Millay?"

"My mother used to read poetry to me at bedtime. She loved Millay."

"Wow. That's beautiful," Daisy said. "Did you understand the poems?"

"Not really. But I loved the sound of her voice."

"How neat. What does your mom look like? Does she have red hair like you?"

"We're getting off the subject. Please go on about Victor."

"Oh, sorry," Daisy said. "Well, Victor answered my letter. It was just a polite note really, but he said he liked the poem, except for the part about climbing the wave. He said you couldn't climb a wave — it was made out of water. I wrote back and explained about, y'know, poetic license and metaphor. And soon we became pen pals. Then gradually we started opening up with each other and sharing thoughts that were terribly personal. I realized that Victor and I were . . . kindred spirits, we were bonded together in some special way."

Her face got dreamy. Then she frowned.

"Well, my folks weren't exactly overjoyed about my corresponding with a convict and they started hassling me. But I didn't care. After I graduated high school, I decided to go visit Victor. I'd been working after school at the Public Library, so I had money for bus fare and a hotel when I got here. My folks ordered me not to go, and when I refused, they said don't bother to come back. Terrific parents, huh? Anyway, I went, and after I met Victor, I had no reason to go back. I knew I had to be near him. Been here about a year now."

I found it hard to put Daisy together with Victor. She said they were kindred spirits, but I couldn't see it. And Ben's theory about women being sexually attracted to killers—I couldn't pick that up from Daisy either. There certainly didn't seem to be an intellectual connection. Daisy was well read and articulate and Victor was . . . well, I had no real handle on Victor yet.

I asked Daisy how she felt about Victor being a convicted murderer.

"He might've been convicted," she said, "but he's certainly not a murderer."

"How do you know that?"

"I know Victor," Daisy said. "He couldn't kill anybody. He's the most gentle soul in the world."

"Did Victor tell you he was innocent?"

"He doesn't know what happened," she said. "He had a sort of blackout at the time. But I'm sure he didn't do it. I read all the newspaper articles on Victor's case—the city papers are on microfilm here at the library. The police never really investigated. The murder took place in one of New York's worst drug areas, so it could've been drug-related. And the woman had an ex-boyfriend. In the paper there was a picture of him at her funeral, looking real grief-stricken. Come over to the library and I'll show it to you. He's huge . . . and really scary-looking—y'know, the type who'd kill you just for looking at him wrong. In cases like this, everybody knows a former lover is automatically a prime suspect, but the cops never even looked into it."

"But the evidence against Victor was overwhelming."

"Maybe he was set up . . . framed," Daisy said. "I don't know. But I do know they sure as heck didn't investigate any other suspect. There was no trial, Victor never got his day in court."

"But why do you think Victor didn't respond to the police when they questioned him?"

"Because he was confused," Daisy answered with assuredness. "And afraid . . . because he couldn't remember anything."

I decided to push her a little more, to see how she'd react.

"Okay. But the fact that he didn't remember anything doesn't mean he's innocent," I said. "What if he was blocking it out because it was too disturbing to remember? And there's another possibility. Maybe Victor did know he killed the woman, but pretended to have amnesia because he had no other defense. Maybe he's still pretending."

Daisy became very agitated. "Please don't say that. You have no right to say that. You don't even know Victor."

She stopped and fought to regain self control. She blew out a whooshing breath. "I'm sorry, Doctor."

"That's all right," I said. "I understand how you feel."

Daisy sniffled, then managed a smile. "Doctor," she said, "do you mind if I ask you something?

"What is it?"

"What do you think Victor's chances are for parole?"

"I don't know."

"But you do have a say in the matter, right?"

"Somewhat."

Daisy looked across the table, gazing into my eyes. "Doctor," she said, "please, *please* help Victor get his parole. He's a good man. And I truly love him."

I looked away, signaled the waitress for the check, and told Daisy I had to get going.

As I was paying the cashier, I saw Father Emile Toussenel having coffee at the counter. He was reading a book with a yellow and black cover — *Gin Rummy for Dummies*. The priest looked up and saw us.

He smiled, winked, and then turned his attention back to the Good Book.

Suddenly I felt Daisy's hand on mine. "Thanks for the coffee," she whispered. Her fingers felt very warm and soft. I looked down and noticed she was wearing blue nailpolish.

Chapter 9

The next morning on the way to work, I stopped off at Big Bob's Sporting Goods. The night before I'd come across a JAMA article on migraines. According to an Australian study, subjects who engaged in a program of regular aerobic exercise reduced the frequency, duration, and intensity of their headaches. Those who chose jogging had the best success rates.

I'd read the piece while sitting at the Formica table in my motel room. I became aware of a slight belly-lap over my belt. When I leaned to either side, I could feel incipient love-handles. All too soon they'd be fusing with my abdominal fat to form the dreaded spare tire.

I've never thought of myself as handsome, but enough women have said I was *cute* (why is *cute* fem-speak for *good looking?*) that I must at least be in the ballpark. What I've got going for me is the curly red hair, dark brown eyes, a warm smile, and the fact that I'm over six feet tall. As for my nose, some might call it beaky, I prefer aquiline.

Cute or not, at age thirty-one I could feel myself starting a down-hill slide. I had to take steps.

I decided to get analytical. *Okay, I'm maybe ten pounds over-weight. Do the math: Running 1 mile burns 100 calories. Running 3.5 miles a day, 5 times a week (a modest goal) burns 1750 calories a week or 7000 calories a month. Since 3500 calories = 1 lb. of fat, I'll burn off 2 lbs. of fat per month. In 5 months I'll be a lean, mean machine. No diet alterations. No giving up McDonald's. Why didn't I think of this before? Plus, the aerobic exercise might help my migraines. It's a done deal. Tomorrow I buy running shoes.*

In the shoe department, the haggard, anorexic-looking salesman, obviously a marathon man, recommended Reeboks.

"They have a lively road feel," he said. "And they've got moving air cushioning."

I gave him the shrink nod.

"It reacts to your individual stride pattern. Let's get you into 'em."

He laced them up squatting on the little stool at my feet. *I wonder if he feels subservient? And why do shoe salesmen always tug the laces tighter than I do?*

"Can I take a test run?"

"You can walk around the store."

I did a couple laps. I loved the firm grip of the cleated soles, the cushy feel of the padding, the pale orange and black color insets.

"Wrap 'em up."

Driving to the prison, I thought about Victor Janko.

Judging his potential for dangerous behavior is complicated by one question—is he in fact the Baby Carriage Killer? Victor says he doesn't know, he has no memory of the murder. Stevie Karp says Victor admitted he did it, plus there's possible corroboration from the priest. And Daisy maintains he's innocent.

I'll never get to the truth unless I find a way to break down Victor's defenses. When I visit him today, I better damn well bring my A-game.

From the road, the view of Vanderkill State Correctional Facility was grim. It sat on a hill, a baleful, ominous looking structure, built of stone and concrete. Its massive walls were a lifeless gray with no architectural details. The curving, slate-shingled roofs of the guard towers gave the only hint of a human touch. The motif of chainlink fence and razorwire was everywhere—atop the prison walls, surrounding the outbuildings, and along the forest's edge on the perimeter of the penitentiary grounds. The entire complex seemed purposely designed to depress the spirit.

I was alone in the cell with Victor.

He sat on his cot, scraping the dried paint off his palette with his palette knife. The blade's shiny surface gleamed as it caught the light. Last night's dream-image of Victor attacking me flashed in my mind.

Ignoring the fear, I spoke in a soothing voice.

"Victor. I know you're worried about saying the wrong thing. But actually, talking to me can only work in your favor."

He showed no sign of hearing me.

"Let me tell you how things stand with your parole."

This grabbed his attention.

"Here's the deal," I said. "The way they usually decide on parole is—they reduce you to a bunch of statistics, and feed you into a computer. If that happens, you lose. But I've arranged to do it another way—person-to-person, just you and me. Now, I can't promise this'll give you a better shot at parole. But I guarantee if you're not totally honest me, there's no way you're getting out."

I looked directly at Victor. "You do want to get out of here, don't you?"

Victor's eyes darted. "You're not kiddin'."

"Then let's get to work. Last time you told me you had no memory of killing that woman. Was that the truth?"

"Yes."

"Remember what I said about being honest."

"Yes. I know."

"After our first meeting," I said, "I talked to Stevie Karp. He told me you were lying. He said you told him all about the murder."

"Stevie said that?"

"Yes."

"It's not true."

I watched him closely. "You're saying Stevie was lying?"

Victor hesitated, then nodded.

"Why would he do that?" I asked.

Victor didn't answer. He was starting to play defense again.

"Come on, Victor. Talk to me."

Victor got up and paced back and forth. "You think just because you say talk to me I'll be able to do it? It's not that easy."

This time I refused to respond. Victor stopped and looked at me anxiously. "Look," he said, "I know if you decide I'm . . . not, y'know, right, you're not gonna let me out of here. And I'm afraid if I tell you why Stevie lied, that's just what you're gonna think."

"You'd better tell me anyway."

Another pause. Victor started making his odd, whistling sounds again.

"Come on, Victor."

He sat back down on the cot and put his hands over his face. With his palms covering his mouth, his breathing had a stifled sound.

"Okay. Okay," Victor said. "Stevie told you I remembered the murder 'cause he wants to keep me in here. He figures if you think I lied to you, you won't trust me. And then you won't let me get paroled. He . . . he'd do anything to keep me from getting out."

"Why is that?"

"Because he hates me. He's had it in for me for years."

"He wants to keep you in here because he hates you?"

"Yes," Victor said. "And because he enjoys hating me. If I leave, he . . . won't have the pleasure of hating me anymore."

I looked at him, puzzled.

"Y'see? Y'see?" Victor went on. "You think I'm whatdyacallit? . . .
paranoid. Like I think people are against me."

"What about Father Toussenel?" I said sharply.

"Huh?"

"Your priest. Is he against you, too?"

Victor looked confused. "No," he whispered.

I had to be careful here. I couldn't suggest Father Toussenel had
violated the sanctity of confession.

"I'm puzzled about something," I said. "See, I also talked to Father
Toussenel. And I got the impression—he didn't actually say this, of
course . . . but I got the impression you confessed to him, about the
murder."

Victor looked panicky.

"Did you confess to him?"

"Pardon me?"

"Did you confess to your priest? Did you admit that you killed that
woman?"

Victor looked down at the floor. There was a long pause. Finally
he spoke without looking up. "I . . . talked about it."

"During confession?"

"Okay. Yes."

"What did you tell your priest?"

"I told him . . . I was guilty."

"Guilty of what?"

He answered so softly I could hardly hear him. "Murder."

"What?"

"Murder."

"Then you lied to me."

"No. No. No. I didn't lie to you," Victor said, staring at the floor.
Then he looked up and spoke in a shame-filled voice. "I . . . I lied to
Father Emile."

"You lied in confession?"

"I know I shouldn't have. I know it's a sin. But . . ." He broke off.

"Are you Catholic?"

"No."

"Then you probably won't understand this," Victor said. "But see, priests . . . some priests, they work on you all the time. It's like brainwashing. And Father Emile, he's like that. He's been at me for years, telling me over and over how I *had* to confess . . . How Jesus Christ would absolve me from my sin, but only if I did penance. And finally, I dunno, maybe he just wore me down. I started thinking even if I don't remember the murder, I guess I did it anyway so I better confess or else I'll be damned forever. So I did, God help me. I confessed to killing the lady. I confessed to . . . doing . . . something I don't remember doing."

Victor stopped and searched my face for a reaction. "Do you understand?" Victor said. "It's the truth. You believe me, don't you?"

Tough call. His words had an undeniable sense of veracity, suggesting two possibilities; either he was being honest or else he had a psychopathological ability to concoct stories that rang true in every detail, yet were complete fabrications . . . like his paintings.

I'd gotten Victor to talk freely so I pushed him further, saying it would help if he filled me in about his early life.

Victor said he was an only child who grew up in Washington Heights. His father deserted the family when he was born, and he was raised by his mother. He told me his childhood was "Okay, I guess," and that he got along well till he got to high school, where he became interested in painting. The other kids started tormenting him about being "an art-class fart-ass" and a faggot—"which I'm definitely not." He kept getting beaten up, and his mom had to make him sandwiches because his classmates kept stealing his lunch money. Finally, after his junior year, he dropped out. His mother approved, saying she loved having him home and he could paint all he wanted in his room. He took part-time jobs and, when he could afford it, he rode the subway down to the Art Students' League for classes in painting, life drawing, and art history.

I asked him how he felt about his mother and he answered like a child boasting.

"My mom?" he said. "Oh, she was the best mom you could ever have. She really loved me. And she believed in me. You know why she named me Victor? Because victor means winner. I bet you never thought of that, most people don't."

"Does your mother come to visit you?"

Victor's lips trembled. "My mom is dead. She passed away about a year before all this stuff happened. Heart trouble."

"I'm sorry."

"I just wish . . ." he said wistfully, "I just wish she coulda seen my painting in the *Newsweek* magazine."

"I'm curious about your paintings," I said. "How come they're always beach scenes? Tropical beach scenes?"

"No particular reason."

"Have you ever been to a beach like that?"

"No."

"Then why do you keep painting them?"

Victor shook his head back and forth as though I'd asked an unanswerable question. "Because . . . " he said, "A beach is life."

"A beach is life?"

"Yes."

"How do you mean that?"

No reply.

"I will not take *no answer* for an answer," I said.

"Look," Victor said, agitated. "The beach is just a subject matter—okay? Why did Cee-zanne paint apples? Why did Rembrandt paint . . . people? It was a subject matter. That's all. It didn't have any other meaning. Why does everything I do have to have another meaning?"

"I didn't say it did."

"You didn't *have* to say it," Victor said loudly. He was about to lose control. "I know what you're trying to do . . . You're trying to push me. You're trying to see if I'm cr . . ."

He didn't want to say the C word.

"Look," he went on, "my lawyer told me he could get me off—not guilty by reasons of insanity. But I told him no, because there's nothing wrong with me in that department. *Nothing.*"

Suddenly Victor turned dead calm, as if by his own command. He sat head down, still and silent.

"Victor," I said, "I understand what you're going through. There's so much at stake you're bound to feel pressure. If I were in your position I'm sure I'd feel the same."

My words had a soothing effect. His face showed relief.

"Doctor," Victor said, "I'd like to tell you something . . ."

We heard the sound of keys jingling. Stevie Karp entered the cell, carrying a food tray. He kicked the cell door shut with his foot and it clanged against the steel door-frame. "Suppertime," he bellowed.

"Stevie," I said, "We're not finished yet."

"Sorry," he said, setting the tray on a chair. "He has to be fed at six."

"Okay. But leave us alone, huh?"

Stevie leaned against the wall. "Rules," he said, "Guard has to be present. He's got pork chops tonight, gotta use a knife to cut his meat."

"Goddamn it," I shouted, "You have no right to . . ."

Chill, David.

"All right." I said calmly. "Victor, I'll come back tomorrow. Okay?"

"Okay."

I smiled and walked out the door. Karp locked it. Instead of leaving, I hung back and watched them.

Karp was wearing his sunglasses. He always wore them, even indoors. Guess he thought they looked cool. He also wore his guard hat at all times. Maybe he was going bald.

Stevie brought the food tray over to Victor and set it on his lap. He crossed to the wall and leaned against it. Victor unwrapped a napkin containing a knife and fork. He began to polish the utensils, inspecting for the slightest bit of dirt or grease. Then he ran his finger across the edge of the knife blade, testing its sharpness. He looked up and glared at the guard. Stevie returned his gaze steadily, while his hand slid up his side and settled on the handle of his gun. "Eat yer supper."

Victor began to eat.

"If you behave yourself, Vicky-boy, I might even let you have dessert."

Victor swallowed, then began his soft whistling, eyes fixed on the guard. From where I stood, I wasn't sure whether Victor was expressing fear or fury.

I decided to leave before they noticed me.

Chapter 10

When the alarm went off the next morning, I woke with a sense of resolve. I'd noticed a high school running track as I drove home the night before; a great place to begin my jogging program. I was pumped.

I walked to the bathroom. *Yeah, I'll drop by on my way to work, do a few laps—nice 'n' easy, enough to get my blood pumping. My endorphins will kick in, I'll start the day with a runner's high.*

I looked out the bathroom window. It was pouring rain. Running was completely out of the question. *Thank you, Lord.*

I got into the shower and thought about my ambivalence. It's funny, growing up I was a jock. I played soccer in high school and varsity lacrosse in college. But once I hit med school, work took over my life. There was no time for exercise. I devoted my spare moments to shut-eye.

Maybe I'm just plain scared to start again and face the fact that I've become a worldclass wuss.

I boiled water for coffee on the electric hot plate, which, along with the small refrigerator and puny sink, constituted the Hospitality Inn's "cooking facilities."

From the fridge I took some shredded lettuce I'd saved from a Big Mac, chopped it up and served it to Shelly.

"Come 'n' git it."

She emerged from her hide box and made a bee-line for the food.

Then I changed her water and turned on the basking light so she'd know it was daytime.

After a breakfast of instant espresso and Hostess Twinkies, I put my laptop in my shoulder bag, grabbed an umbrella, and made a dash through the downpour to my car.

When I entered my newly painted office, I felt like I was in lockdown. The walls were Post Office green and there was no window. Once there had been a window but it was cemented over, leaving only the outline of iron bars; a reminder of what the room once was. The desk was steel, battleship gray with one bent leg. For seating there were two rickety bridge chairs. There was no A/C, just an oscillating floor fan which moved the hot air around.

Ben appeared at my doorway.

He had good news. He said he was going to start shifting over some of the patients to my exclusive care.

"You don't need me looking over your shoulder any more."

"Great."

"It might be rushing it," Ben said. "But I've been watching you with the men. Like you said—you know your stuff."

I smiled.

"I can tell you care about these guys," he went on. "You really want to help them."

"That's the name of the game," I said. *Dumb response.*

"One problem," Ben said. "You've got no jailhouse smarts. I mean, every guy in here is a double whammy: he's a felon *and* a looney-tune. You might get blind-sided by some . . . situation."

"I'll stay on my toes. Before anything hits the fan, I'll come ask for help."

"Good," Ben said. "And I'd advise you to . . ."

"Enough with the help," I cut in, holding up my hand.

He laughed. I was beginning to like Ben. We'd gotten off to a rocky start, but he seemed to hold no grudge about the Victor Janko issue.

"You can start treating Bobby Sanchez this morning," Ben said. "I told him you'd be taking over for me."

"How did he react?"

"He said Lieutenant Columbo warned him not to trust nobody. I told him he could definitely trust you, and he said since he didn't trust *me*, how could he trust anybody I told him to trust?"

"Say what?"

"I've got him on Haldol," Ben said. "So he's pretty chilled out. But like I told you, this guy could be trouble. You should talk to the night nurse about him. Kim Cavanagh, have you met her?"

"Yes."

"For some reason Sanchez seems more relaxed around her. Maybe she can give you some insight."

"I'll talk to her."

If I have to I have to.

"But you better be prepared," Ben said. "Sanchez is gonna give you the Stare, bigtime."

When I went to see him I was ready for it. The patient fixed his eyes on me, scrutinizing my behavior, searching for evidence of hostility, fear, and especially harmful intent. I was familiar with the "paranoid stare" from my work at Bellevue. I had a strong urge to look away but forced myself to make eye-contact. I needed to show Sanchez that I wasn't afraid of him and that I was concerned about his well-being.

I didn't make much progress, but I hadn't expected to; it's very hard to gain the trust of a paranoid patient. When I told Sanchez he looked troubled, he narrowed his eyes and intensified his stare.

"There's a situation," he said. "As if ya didn't know."

"I *don't* know. But maybe if you tell me it I can help."

"Hey, man, you can't bamboozle me," Sanchez said. "Lieutenant Columbo told me don't tell nobody nothin'. See, I don't know who's in on it and who's not. If I tell you what I know, you might tell them. Or they might overhear me—they can listen in with their devices—then switch things around so's I can't defend myself."

"Are you saying you're in danger?"

Sanchez looked around suspiciously. "There's a situation." He watched for my reaction. I looked interested.

"Yeah. Okay," Sanchez continued. "I'm in danger. That's all I'm gonna say."

I made no comment.

"You believe me, don't you?"

"I believe you *feel* you're in danger," I said. "And it's scary. And I understand why you don't think I'm on your side. After all, you don't really know me. But maybe, as we spend more time together, we can develop a mutual trust and understanding. You willing to give that a shot?"

Sanchez looked at me guardedly. I noticed a slight softening of his stare. "Maybe," he said, looking away.

I smiled, got up and left without another word. One awkward remark or gesture could disturb the fragile connection I'd just made. But as I walked away I felt good. He'd given me a maybe.

Later that day I ran the group session while Ben observed. Everything went well till I suggested a little role playing. I told Fart-breath and the fat man to act like they were each other. Fat laughed hysterically and Fart told me to go fuck myself.

Afterwards Ben said I did well but the role playing didn't work because I was telling the men to do something.

"They feel like you're giving them an order. Don't be controlling. The guys do better when they have a feeling of freedom—'cause freedom's what they miss most in their lives."

Made sense.

After work I went over to see Victor Janko. He was uncharacteristically relaxed and showed me his progress on the new painting.

"See, I mixed a little burnt umber in with the cadmium yellow to get the sand just right. Sand is hard."

We talked about his art for a while, then I got down to business.

"Is there something you want to tell me?"

"About what?"

"Yesterday I thought you were about to tell me something, when Stevie Karp walked in."

It was like I flipped a switch; he became nervous and distant. He sat down on his cot, fidgeting.

"What did you want to say, Victor?"

He didn't respond.

"Talk to me."

"I . . . I want to. But I'm afraid."

"Of what?"

"If I tell you," he said hesitantly, "I'm afraid you'll think I'm just trying to . . . get you on my side."

"I'd expect you to try and get me on your side."

He nodded. "Okay," he said. "See, Father Emile, he told me I blocked out about the murder 'cause I couldn't face that I did it. And for a long time, I thought he was probably right. But now, well, I've got this girlfriend . . . Daisy. And she's been talking to me, telling me to look inside, and ask myself if I was really capable of killing another human being. And you know what? I realize now I could never take a person's life. Never. My girlfriend, she made me see that. So . . . for whatever it's worth, I believe I'm innocent."

I nodded.

"And Daisy believes I'm innocent too," he said. "Look, she wouldn't be my girlfriend if she didn't feel that way."

"What do you think did happen the night of the murder?"

"I don't know," he said quietly. "I wish I knew but I don't."

"What do you remember about that day? You have any memories at all?"

He closed his eyes, and swung his head slowly from side to side. "I remember . . . I was working that afternoon."

"Where?"

"At the A&P."

"Doing what?"

"Packing groceries. I was a box-boy."

"You remember anything else?"

He looked up, his eyes sweeping the ceiling as if it held the answer.

"No," he said. "Nothing."

I pressed him, urging him to dig deeper into his memory. Then he took off his glasses. By now I recognized the signal: *glasses off/ conversation over/leave me alone.*

I said we'd made some progress and I'd come back tomorrow. Victor gave me a faint smile.

I got up and left. As I walked down the hall I felt worn out; drained from a day spent trying to reach people who were uncommonly skilled at avoiding contact. I couldn't wait to get the hell outta there.

Chapter 11

Walking through the prison gate, I felt like I'd just been released from jail. The rain had stopped and the warm night air smelled of pine and fresh cut grass. As I crossed the parking area, my body relaxed, and my mind started to clear.

I turned on the car radio and pressed *scan*, hoping to pick up a New York station. There was nothing but static until WPDH Poughkeepsie—Classic Rock. Led Zeppelin was doing the mystical "Stairway to Heaven." I lowered the volume so it was background music and turned my thoughts to Victor.

I still didn't know if he was lying when he said he had no memory of the murder. Now he'd brought up a new idea—he was innocent. Was that the truth or a manipulative fabrication?

When I got home I'd decided it might help if I got a look at the NYPD file on the Janko case. I needed to learn more about what happened the night of the killing.

The newspapers had portrayed Victor as close-mouthed, but maybe he'd made statements to the cops that were never released. Or there might've been details of the crime that the police had kept confidential. But getting the file would be hard.

I got out of my working clothes and changed into shorts and my Boston Red Sox jersey. I remember when I was nine my father asked me how a New York kid could be a Red Sox fan.

"I root for 'em 'cause they never win."

He looked at me with disdain. In the '86 World Series, when Mookie Wilson's ground ball skipped between Bill Buckner's legs, causing the Bosox to lose to the Mets, I said I felt sorry for the first baseman. Dad suggested I move my sorry ass to Boston. Maybe that's why I later went to Harvard.

Thinking about my father gave me an idea. Dear old Dad had a lot of political clout in the city. He could get me the police file, and fast.

I hated to ask him for a favor. I rarely saw him; we got together at family gatherings like Thanksgiving, and an occasional wedding or *bris*. But that was it.

I'd never gotten along with my dad, but things became worse when my mom got sick. I was sixteen when she was diagnosed with cervical cancer. My father's a physician, an endocrinologist, and I had expected him to really be there for her. But he couldn't handle it. When she had chemo and lost all her hair, he hired full-time nurses' aides and started working overtime at the hospital. When he did spend time with her he had this detached "bedside manner," as if she were a clinic patient instead of his wife. The night she died, I broke down in tears, and he comforted me by saying "Don't cry, son. Your mother wouldn't have wanted that."

I couldn't forgive him for his insensitivity, and my resentment simmered. Later, when I became more psychologically hip, I saw the situation as a classic Oedipal conflict. Still later, I came to a more banal conclusion. *Oedipus-Schmoedipus, my father is just a schmuck.*

After Mom's death, Dr. Zachary Rothberg seemed to fulfill my vision of him. He wrote a bestselling diet book. He guested on talk shows, plugging his book and stoking his ego. The book was *Try a Little Slenderness—a Couple's Approach to Weight-loss.* It was no more than a compendium of the Dean Ornish low-fat diet, standard couple's therapy, and a dollop of Dr. Ruth Westheimer (the caloric expenditure of sexual intercourse, fellatio, and heavy petting.) Dr. Zach's fame enabled him to open a chic weight-loss clinic in Tribeca, and over the years he accumulated megabucks. Later he joined the committee to elect the current mayor, setting up star-studded campaign bashes and persuading some of his celebrity pals to support his candidate.

The nadir of my feelings came the night I watched my father on TV, standing next to the mayor during his acceptance speech. Dad was waving his hands in the air making the "vee" sign, grinning as if "Happy Days Are Here Again" were being played for him. Yes, he was a schmuck, but he could get me that file.

He usually worked late so I called him at the office. A chirpy voice said "Rothberg Wellness Institute. How may I direct your call?"

"Dr. Rothberg, please." *Dr. Rothberg? I'm Dr. Rothberg.*

"Dr. Rothberg's office," chirped somebody else.

"Is he there?'

"Who shall I say is calling?"

"His son."

"Does he . . . have more than one son?"

"Not that I know of."

"One moment please."

She put me on hold, and I heard synthesizer music—"I've Gotta Be Me." I moaned. Dad picked up.

"Hey, kiddo," he said. "What's happenin' at the hoosegow?"

Schmucking out already. Still I did what I had to do. I kissed Big Daddy's ass.

I steered the conversation to his favorite subject—Dr. Zachary Rothberg. After about fifteen minutes of me-me-me, Dr. Rothberg the elder was feeling we'd bonded anew. Then I said I needed his help. The prospect of his son being needy and dependent thrilled the Good Doctor. He promised to call his pal the mayor right away, who'd then call the Police Commissioner. I'd get the NYPD file ASAP. "After all, what's a father for?"

I stifled my wise-ass answer, thanked him, and hung up.

But one remark Dr. Zack made stuck with me. When I said I needed Victor Janko's police file, my father said, "Davey, you're supposed to be a shrink. Since when did you become a detective?"

Good question.

Chapter 12

"**Y**o, Doc. Check out the booty on that fox."

I was in a booth next to the visiting room, watching a closed circuit TV monitor. The VR guard was commenting on Daisy as she walked into camera range wearing tight poplin cut-offs. The day I'd interviewed her she was wearing baggy jeans and a man's shirt. Now I could see her taut, shapely legs, her nicely curved buttocks, and her small breasts poking out against her white tee-shirt.

"Kinda puts a bulge in your Calvins, know'm'sayin'?" the guard said.

I knew what he was sayin'.

Victor was waiting behind a Plexiglas window. The window had a small, perforated section in it. Daisy sat down, said a few words, then Victor began to speak. He seemed angry.

"No sound?" I asked.

"Uh-uh," the guard answered. "Law say they got the right to privacy."

Daisy looked tenderly at Victor, leaning into the perforated holes as she spoke. Suddenly Victor burst out laughing.

Watching him and Daisy was fascinating. There was an easy famil-
iarity between them, like any couple on the outside who'd been
together for long time.

"Tell me somethin', Doc," the guard said. "What's a hot lookin'
lady like that doin' with a sorry-ass wimp like Janko?"

Another good question.

"Check this out," the guard whispered. "They do this number
every time."

I watched the video screen as Victor and Daisy performed a ritual.

They placed their hands on the Plexiglas in various, seemingly
predetermined positions. Moving in slow motion, they appeared to
be touching each other through the cold plastic. They pressed their
cheeks together, and finally their lips, in a tender and passionate
expression of love.

I felt like a voyeur.

Daisy sat back in her chair, glowing like she'd just had sex.

*Is this the epitome of true love? Kindred spirits, so closely bonded
they can feel each other without even touching? Or is it self delusion—
two neuroses feeding on each other in a romantic charade?*

After work, I went over to see Victor. Right away I knew something
was wrong. He lay on his cot, staring at the ceiling, eyeglasses off. He
didn't acknowledge me. I looked at Victor's painting. The sand, with
its subtly mixed yellow pigments, was still confined to the grid he'd
filled in yesterday.

"How're things going?"

"Fine." He closed his eyes.

"You haven't done much on your painting."

"I'm . . .not in the mood, I guess."

"Something bothering you?"

"No."

He began the whistling.

"Victor," I said. "What are you doing?"

"I'm . . . just waiting for your next question."

Hard to believe this is same the man I'd watched in the visiting room, so emotionally open with Daisy.

I studied Victor's face, hoping it held a clue to his feelings. Nothing.

"Victor," I said. "I'm trying to help you, but I can't do it alone."

He picked up his blanket and started pulling at the little pills of wool. He became totally engrossed.

I said good-bye and left the cell. When I walked down the corridor I saw Stevie Karp at the guard station, hunched over a desk. His scraggly pony-tail was drooping down from his hat, like a dead spider plant.

"Hey, Doc," Karp said. He was cutting his fingernails with a nail-clipper, attached to the lanyard that held his keys. "Vic's in one of his black moods today."

"He sure didn't feel like talking."

The guard clipped away, nail snippets falling willy-nilly. "That's how he gets sometimes." *Click.* "He'll go for days without sayin' nothin.'" *Click-click.*

"Does he stop painting when he gets that way?"

"No. He paints every day." Stevie squinted his eyes. "Y'know, this ain't like him. Could be he's steppin' over the line."

"What do you mean?"

"Doc," the guard said solemnly, "I think Victor might be goin' schizo." He distorted his face to make it look demented. It wasn't much of a stretch.

"Do me a favor, Stevie," I said. "Leave the diagnosing to me."

I left the Ad Seg Unit feeling frustrated. The connection I'd made with Victor was gone. Ordinarily I wouldn't worry; it happens with deeply troubled patients and over time you can reconnect. But in this case I didn't have any time. The parole hearing was in a week. And Karp said Victor could go for days without speaking.

If I can't make him open up, I'll have no more insight than the computer program; I'll have failed my patient . . . and myself. With nothing more to go on, I'll have to assume he's dangerous and recommend against parole. All right, so be it. Except . . . what if Victor's innocent?

Is that likely? No. Is it possible? Yes.

What's my next move? Maybe the police file will tell me something. But that's a big question mark. So's my father. Who the hell knows if he'll even get it for me?

Rather than go home I decided to go back to the hospital and put a dent in my paper work.

The sun was disappearing behind the western-most guard tower. I crossed the prison yard, moving from sunlight into deep, dark shadow. Somehow I felt Victor's withdrawal was my fault. But where did I go wrong?

Ed Sorenson had drummed his dictum into me during my three year residency: *Psychiatry is the most inexact of the medical sciences. The therapist is always groping in the dark, trying to solve the most mystifying mysteries, the most puzzling puzzles. There's no room for perfectionism in psychiatry. What's required is dogged determination; the courage to follow all paths and open all doors. And the acceptance of one inescapable fact—you are going to make mistakes.*

When I got back to the hospital I felt a little better. But only a little.

Chapter 13

On the psychiatric floor, I stopped at the nurses' station.

"Hey, Kim."

"Hi." When she smiled her left cheek was indented by something you could either call a crease or a dimple. I leaned towards dimple.

"I'm going to be taking care of Bobby Sanchez," I told her. "Dr. Caldwell says you've got a good rapport with him."

"Well, I wouldn't call it a rapport. But he does tolerate me—at least enough to let me give him his injections."

"He's on Haldol?"

"Yes."

I could see where a guy might not mind being stuck in the butt by an attractive nurse like Kim, but I said nothing of the kind.

"Well," I said. "Maybe when you have time you can tell me more about him."

"I'd be glad to."

I turned to go to my office when she called out to me.

"Oh, Doctor. There's a package for you."

She held up a thick manila envelope. It was marked "Official Business — City of New York" and had a stick-on label, "By Courier."

"That's great. I've been waiting for it."

At my desk, I opened the package. It contained a copy of the NYPD file on Victor Thomas Janko.

For the first time, I had the feeling maybe my dad wasn't such a bad guy. On the other hand, he was probably just showing off, trying to prove what a big cheese he was. *Yeah, Dr. Zachary Rothberg still qualifies as a schmuck. Even a schmuck can do a good thing, only he always does it for a bad reason.*

The file had crime scene photos of 23 Dyckman Oval, Apt. 1A, noting there were no lights on in the ground floor apartment when the police arrived. The body was found in front of the living room window. The window shade was up, indicating that the crime had been committed in the dark — otherwise the killer would have risked being seen from the outside. There was a picture of the bloody murder weapon; an eight-inch long kitchen knife. There were no fingerprints anywhere except those belonging to Agnes and the child.

The housing cops and various 34th Precinct detectives all described Victor as being either in shock or in a drugged state. But the toxicology report was negative.

The case against Victor seemed airtight. One intriguing piece of evidence made the case even stronger. It was a copy of the Dr. Seuss book, *The Cat in the Hat*. Inside was a pasted-on label reading "This Book Belongs To," inscribed with the name of the victim's child, Margarita. Victor had the book with him when he was arrested. The police figured he'd taken it from the apartment after he killed the mother.

Now, why would he have done that? And what's the significance of The Cat in the Hat?

I heard a woman's voice, screaming in terror. It was coming from the nurses' station.

I raced down the hallway, but when I got there I froze. Bobby Sanchez was standing behind Kim Cavanagh. He had her in a choke-hold with his left arm. In his right hand was a hypodermic syringe. He pushed the needle against the side of Kim's neck.

Brian Cacciatti, the guard on duty, had his Magnum Special pointing at Sanchez. "I told you to drop it," he shouted.

"Fuck off."

"I'm a good shot, Sanchez," Cacciatti said. "I can put a bullet in your brain before you can blink."

"You can try it, motherfucker, but I'm tellin' ya—I'll smoke her 'fore I go dead."

Kim was looking at me, her eyes desperate. I stepped forward. "Hey, Bobby. What's up?"

"Stay away from me, Doctor."

"Okay. Okay. Just tell me what's the trouble."

"The trouble?" Sanchez said. "This place is the trouble."

"What do you mean?"

"I told you there was a situation. Well, the situation's turned real bad. There are people 'round here tryin' to kill me. They've been plottin' it . . . plannin' it . . . and now they're gonna do it."

"What makes you think that?"

"I don't think that. I know that."

"Bobby, why don't you put down the needle and we can talk about it?" I extended my hand, moved a step towards him.

"Stop," he said. "Stay where you are or I stick her."

"What's in the needle?"

Sanchez gave a sinister laugh. "Air, man. Nothin' but air."

"Air isn't gonna hurt her," I said.

"You can't run no game on me, man. I know if you shoot air in somebody, they croak."

"Where'd you hear that?"

"Lieutenant Columbo. He gave me the plan. Grab the needle from the nurse when she comes to give you your shot. Then grab her, squirt out the medicine, and the two of you can walk right on out the door."

Cacciatti shouted at the prisoner. "You're not goin' anywhere, Sanchez. Now cut the crap and drop the needle."

"I'm goin' out that door right now. Me and nursie."

"Listen, everybody," I said calmly, "Let's take it easy. We can find a way to work this out."

I turned to Sanchez. "Bobby," I said. "I'm afraid Lieutenant Columbo gave you some incorrect info. Putting air into someone's vein doesn't kill them."

"Don't be jivin' me, Doctor," Sanchez said. He pushed the needle harder against Kim's neck. It was almost breaking the skin. She whimpered.

"I'm glad you called me *Doctor*, Bobby. Because I *am* a doctor. And I can tell you that air injected into the bloodstream is just absorbed into the system. It doesn't cause an embolism or an aneurysm. . . .

"That's bullshit. Lieutenant Columbo told me . . .

"Bobby," I said. "Columbo is a television character. Death by the injection of air is just something they put in television plots. It has no scientific basis."

"You're tryin' to trick me. I'm outta here."

"Don't move, Sanchez," the guard said.

I looked around the room and spotted a tray by the nurses' station. It had some empty syringes in it. "I can prove I'm telling the truth, Bobby. Just give me a chance."

I crossed slowly over to the tray and picked up a syringe.

"Don't try nothin'," Sanchez warned me.

"No, no," I said. "Just lemme show you something."

I withdrew the plunger on the hypodermic. My mind raced over the facts. I'd been lying to Sanchez; shooting an entire syringe of air into Kim's vein would definitely be lethal—unless Sanchez hit an artery instead of a vein, which would cause a life-threatening hemorrhage. I also knew the moment Sanchez stuck Kim, the guard would kill him. I didn't want any of that to happen.

I had to inject myself, but I'd have to be very, very careful. I prayed I could still visualize the pictures in *Gray's Anatomy*.

"Okay, Bobby," I said. I opened an alcohol packet and swabbed the needle and my skin. Then I pushed the plunger in and out, "See, it's empty." Next I placed the needle point on my neck, and felt around until I was in the right spot. Well, I hoped it was the right spot.

"Now watch, Bobby." I pushed the plunger firmly, and injected the air into my sternocleidomastoid, the ropy muscle running down behind the ear to the clavicle. It hurt like hell, but I tried to look casual. I withdrew the needle and waited. Then I smiled—as much for myself as for Sanchez. I knew injecting air into a muscle would cause no damage. But I had to hit muscle only, make sure I avoided my jugular vein and carotid artery. A mistake would have caused death or a blood bath.

"So what?" Sanchez growled in anger. "Fuck you, I'm leavin' anyway. I'll cut her goddamn neck."

"You can do that, Bobby, but she won't die. She'll get medical attention right away. Meanwhile Brian'll blow your head off. Come on, put down the needle. Your threat's no good."

"Well . . . I don't know . . ." Sanchez said.

"I promise I'll help you, Bobby. I know those voices you hear are frightening. But I'll work with you, and we'll make them go away. Wouldn't you feel better if you didn't hear the voices?"

"I guess so," Sanchez said.

"Okay, put down the needle."

"The guard. He'll shoot me."

"No, he won't." I turned to Brian. "Take the bullets out of your gun."

"No way."

"It's the only way. The man's afraid and he has a right to be. He's willing to trust me, and now you have to show him he can trust *you*."

"I'm not fucking unloading my gun."

"Look," I said, "haven't we put Kim through enough? Bobby's willing to let her go now, but he's scared. I'm in charge of this ward tonight, and I'm fully responsible for what goes on. Now empty your gun, and if anything goes wrong, you can blame me."

Cacciatti hesitated, then reluctantly flipped open the chamber of his revolver. He dumped six bullets into his hand, and dropped them one by one into a waste basket. He looked at me and nodded.

"Hand me the gun, Brian," I ordered.

He didn't move.

"I said give it to me."

"Why? It's empty."

"You can still re-load," I said.

"I'll get rid of my ammo." He started to unbuckle his bullet belt. *Why doesn't he just give me the gun?*

Suddenly I understood. "Nice try, Brian. Now dump it."

"What?"

"The seventh bullet."

"Huh?"

"Don't mess with me, Brian."

The guard gave me an exasperated look.

"You're a smart guy, Doc," he said, pushing open the gun's chamber. He popped out the seventh cartridge and let it fall into the basket. "But you're also stupid. Sanchez still has the needle."

"Just gimme the gun."

Cacciatti grudgingly handed it to me. I turned to Sanchez. "I'll hold it. Unless you want to."

"That's okay," Sanchez said.

"You can let her go now, Bobby."

He released Kim, and dropped the syringe to the floor. The nurse broke down in tears of relief. She crossed to me and buried her face in my chest. My arms closed awkwardly around her, and for a moment I was aware of the yielding softness of her body. I held her for a few seconds, then signaled Brian to come over and look after her.

I walked Bobby Sanchez back to his room, and he lay down. I sedated him with Triazolam, then talked reassuringly to him for a while. Soon he drifted off.

I checked his chart—Ben had him on 50 mg Haldol, an antipsychotic. Kim must've been trying to inject him when Sanchez grabbed her. I know from experience that determining the right dosage of Haldol is tricky. Sanchez was probably getting too little so his hallucinations had really taken over. I got a syringe, increased the dosage by half, and shot it into his glute.

When I returned to the nurses' station, Kim was back at her post. "Dr. Rothberg," she said, "you were wonderful. You saved my life, and . . . and I don't know how to thank you."

"Aw, shucks," I said, doing a bad John Wayne. "Just doin' my job, ma'am."

Kim laughed.

"Listen," I said. "I'm sure you've had enough for one night. Why don't you go on home? I can handle things here."

"That's all right," she replied. "This is my job. A gal's got-ta do what a gal's got-ta do."

This lady's got guts. And her John Wayne is better than mine.

"Okay," I said. "Sanchez is locked down. He should sleep through the night. I'll be in at ten tomorrow."

"No problem, Doctor. I'll keep my eye on him."

I said goodnight, and walked down to the security door. Brian Cacciatti was sitting on a chair. He got up and opened the door for me.

"Gotta hand it to ya, Doc. You're a cool dude." He held out his hand.

I shook it firmly, and smiled without feigned humility.

Chapter 14

The next morning was a beautiful summer day, and I was stoked to get out on the running track.

I hadn't slept much because I was wired from the showdown with Sanchez. And I kept worrying about Victor Janko. I woke up feeling groggy, but after a shower, a jolt of espresso, and some leftover Ben & Jerry's, I was ready to hit the ground running.

When I fed some Masori Tortoise Diet to Shelly, she was uninterested and looked sluggish. I can usually cure that by serving her an earthworm. *Maybe I'll find one near the track.*

I parked in front of the high school. I'd planned to change into my Reeboks and shorts in the car, but when I reached into the back seat I found . . . I'd forgotten to bring my gym-bag. *Damn.*

Let's see . . . it'll take twenty minutes to go back and get it, twenty minutes to return. I can't possibly run and still be at work by 10:00.

Okay, I'm not gonna get on my case. Maybe I am subconsciously avoiding exercise, but on the other hand, maybe I'm just distracted by really important stuff. It's probably the latter, no, I mean the former, no, I mean . . . Fuck it, I'll run tomorrow.

I decided to use the time to get a copy of *The Cat in the Hat*. I drove down to Main Street—the bookstore was called "All Booked Up."

The clerk handed me the thin, blue-green volume with a picture of a cat on the cover. I was overwhelmed with a bittersweet remembrance of childhood. The funny feline with the red and white tall porkpie hat and the floppy red bowtie was smiling that goofy smile at me. *What a puss*, my mother used to say, making a pun I now understood for the first time. I don't think much about my mom these days, but every so often a memory floods back and I get a little weepy.

I turned away from the clerk, and looked again at the book cover. There was a little logo on it—*I Can Read It All By Myself*. It was too much. I paid for the book with a ten-dollar bill, and left while the bookseller was ringing it up.

I sat in the car, thinking about my mother.

I wonder why she ever married the Schmuck? The Schmuck was so selfish and unfeeling, and mom was so giving and caring. But maybe that's just the way she was with me. Maybe with her husband those traits came out as passive and dependent. I don't know. I'll never know.

One thing I do know—Mom would be proud of me, proud of the profession I've chosen, and where my work has taken me. She would've loved what I did last night, saving a damsel in distress like Don Quixote.

I used to love it when she read Don Quixote *to me. I was too young then to understand the irony and cynicism, but I did get the general idea that it's good to lead an honorable life, and help people if you can.*

These days I don't know if my life's all that honorable, but at least I'm trying to help people.

I started the car, and set off on another day searching for answers. It was a quest, I knew, that might be hopelessly quixotic.

When I sat down in my office, Ben Caldwell came in and said "Hey, nice goin' with Sanchez." Then he changed the subject.

He sounded like he was on speed. He kept touching his mustache with his index finger, combing the hairs with his fingernail. He was definitely not himself.

In rapid phrases, he said he wanted me to run the afternoon group session—he had a meeting with the warden. And I should check on a new patient—Kennealy, a body-builder who'd been having fits of violence.

"Dude says he's not on anabolics, but his freak-outs are pure 'roid rage. Oh, yeah, and somebody's gotta buy balloons for Penrose's birthday party tomorrow, or if you want you can do it yourself."

I said I'd take care of everything. But it bugged me that Ben hadn't said more about last night. And why was he acting so weird? Had I done something to upset him? Then I was upset with myself for needing his approval. *Oh well, at least Kim Cavanagh thinks I'm hot stuff.*

After work I went to my office and read *The Cat in the Hat*. Then I took out my laptop, opened the Janko file, and began to type.

If Doctor Seuss contains a clue to the mystery of Victor Janko, I sure can't see it. There's a phrase that keeps jumping out at me. . . . "He should not be here when your mother is out." Am I just reading something sinister into a nice children's story? There's got to be something in this book that . . .

There was a knock on my door. It was Father Emile Toussenel.

"Well, David," he said, in his flat French-Canadian accent. "That was quite a display of brains and courage last night. Ben told me about it."

"Thanks."

"You're a very brave man. *Grâce a Dieu.*"

I smiled.

"Not to change the subject," the priest said, "But I notice you've got a copy of *The Cat in the Hat* on your desk."

I nodded.

"Forgive me," the priest went on, "I seem to be cursed with the sin of nosiness."

"So am I," I said, trying to make nice. "Guess it's endemic to both our professions."

The priest laughed.

"Well," I explained, "The book may have something to do with Victor Janko."

"How curious."

"Tell me something, Father," I said. "Have you ever seen Victor reading it? Or has he ever mentioned it?"

"Not that I remember. What's the connection to him?"

"I'm not sure."

He was hoping I'd say more. I didn't.

"So," he said, colleague-to-colleague. "How are things going with you and Victor?"

"I'm getting to know him."

"He's an odd bird, isn't he, David?"

"That's a fair description."

"Are you going to recommend him for parole?"

"Too early to say."

"Which way are you leaning?"

I shrugged.

"Dr. Rothberg," the priest said with intensity, "y'know, I spend a lot of time with inmates, so I've got a darn good sense about 'em. Now, I'm going to use a word to characterize Victor Janko that's definitely not part of the psychiatric vocabulary. And that word is . . . *Evil.* My gut feeling is there's a demon inside him. You may label that demon Neurosis, Psychosis, Obsessive-Compulsive disorder, or whatever, but in my opinion, Victor is evil *incarnate* . . . he's dangerous and cunning as the Devil himself. You must be extremely careful about . . ."

"Excuse me, Father," I cut in, "I can handle Victor Janko. Now, if you'll excuse me, I've got a shit-load of work."

"Of course," the priest said pleasantly. He stopped at the door. "Well, if you need me for anything . . . I'm always around."

After he left, I leaned back in my desk chair. I imagined Victor's face, staring blankly at me with glazed eyes, shutting me out with his silence, challenging me to break through and reach him.

I turned back to my computer.

I've created a pattern of going to see Victor every day. If I don't show up, he'll begin wondering why. He may not trust me, but he still needs me—I'm his only chance at parole. Maybe I can use that as a tool. I'll skip two days of visiting Victor; he's bound to wonder why, and that'll put some pressure on him. It's risky because I only have a week, but it still leaves me five days. It's worth it.

While I'm away, I've got to come up with a new approach; some mechanism to break his code.

As I was leaving the ward, Kim Cavanagh looked up from her desk and waved at me.

"I want to ask you something, Doctor," she said, smiling her dimpled smile. "Last night I said I didn't know how to thank you for saving me, but today I figured the least I could do was buy you dinner. I mean, I know you're very busy, but . . . tomorrow is my day off, my night off really, so I thought . . . well, I'm inviting you."

I said yes before I gave myself a chance to think about it.

After I left I thought about it.

Yes, I'm on a no-sex regimen. But this isn't sex. It's just a date, no— it's just dinner. Dinner with a colleague who's a very nice, gutsy woman.

Plus she has excellent breasts.

Chapter 15

I came home carrying a McDonald's bag. I was cutting down—and opted for a McVeggie burger instead of a Big Mac, and medium fries instead of large. Okay, but at least I didn't get the Hot Apple Pie.

I checked my voicemail, the only electronic amenity provided by the Hospitality Inn, unless you count cable TV. A digital female voice told me I had *ze-ro mess-a-ges.*

I looked at Shelly. She still seemed out of sorts. When I scratched on her shell, she looked annoyed. *Uh-oh. I forgot to bring home a worm. So she's pissed.* I lifted her up and placed her on my forearm. Usually she likes prowling around the curly red hairs and sniffing my pores. But now she just sat there like a pet rock. I put her back down and turned off her Vita-lite. Maybe she was too hot.

I opened the screw top of an Australian cabernet and poured some into a clear plastic bathroom cup.

I bit into the McVeggie burger. It was McNauseating, so I just ate the fries. For the first time since I'd come to Vanderkill, I felt a twinge of homesickness.

God, I'd kill for an H&H bagel with nova and scallion cream cheese from Zabar's.

Turning on the motel's dinky clock radio, I couldn't pick up an NYC station so I tuned to WPDH. They were playing early Stones. For a while I sat there, sipping the fruity red wine and having a sing-along. "*. . . You can't always get what you want./But if you try some-times/well, you just might find/you get what you need. . . .*"

I heard a sharp knocking on my door.

"Who is it?"

"Um, it's Daisy. Daisy Lesczcynski. Y'know, Victor's girlfriend?"

Strange.

"Just a minute."

I clicked off the music, got up, and opened the door. Daisy was wearing tight black jeans and a pink tank top. The light outside the door made her hair appear blonder than it really was.

"I hope I haven't disturbed you, Doctor Rothberg," she said, "but I just had to see you. Is it all right if I come in?"

"I'm afraid not. It's been a long day. . . ."

"Please, Doctor. It won't take long. It's about Victor."

I let her in.

"How did you know I was staying here?" I asked.

"You told me."

"When was that?"

"When we were at the diner. Don't you remember? You said you were new in town and I asked you where you were staying and you said here."

"I don't recall that."

"Well, I guess you were more interested in hearing about me and Victor," she said in a light tone, "so you don't remember."

"What did you want to talk to me about?"

"Well, I was just wondering how things look for Victor. I've been so worried. I was hoping you could . . . just let me know if I should get my hopes up."

"I really couldn't say."

"You sound sort of negative," Daisy said fearfully.

"It's a difficult situation."

"But there's hope, isn't there?"

"There's always hope."

"Is there anything I can do to help?"

I don't trust her. She shows up here unannounced, and claims I told her where I lived, which is bullshit. On the other hand, maybe I can learn something from her.

I thought of Ed Sorenson's advice: *follow all paths and open all doors.*

"I have a question, Daisy," I said. "Has Victor ever talked to you about the book *The Cat in the Hat*? Do you know if he ever read it?"

"You mean the Dr. Seuss book?"

"Yes."

"No. He never said anything about it. But he probably did read it. Almost every kid reads *The Cat in the Hat*. We have three copies in our children's section." She looked at me quizzically. "Why do you ask?"

I didn't want to go further. "It's kind of a psychological test we use."

"Oh, I see."

There was a silence.

"Um, Doctor," she said, "there's something . . . I think you should know."

"What's that?"

She hesitated.

"What is it?"

"Well," she said, "Victor is . . . he's become sort of jealous of you."

"What do you mean?"

"The thing is . . . I told him you and I met, and it made him . . . insecure."

Jesus. No wonder Victor's shutting me out.

"I understand him feeling that way," she continued. "I mean, you really are cute. But now he says he want's nothing to do with you. And I know if he acts that way it'll hurt his chances for parole."

I did the shrink nod.

"Doctor," she said, "can I suggest something . . . something that'd make Victor feel more secure?" She twirled an errant blond curl around her finger. "The next visiting day, could you arrange for me and Victor to have contact visitation?"

"Which means what?"

"Well, in all the time I've been coming to see Victor, I've never physically touched him. Contact visitation just means we can have physical contact. They have a special room for it, where they watch you on TV. I mean, you can't make love or anything, but you can touch and hug and stuff."

"I assume you've been turned down on this?"

"Yes," Daisy said. "Because Victor's in Administrative Segregation. But maybe you could talk to them. Explain how we love each other, and maybe say that as a psychiatrist you think it would be good for Victor's mental health. Which it would."

"I'm sorry," I said. "I can't help you."

"But see, if I could just be physically close to him, he wouldn't be jealous any more. If I could hold him in my arms, he'd know he's my only love. I've told him that, but words don't seem to be enough."

"I have to say no, Daisy. . . ."

"Please, Doctor," she implored. "I know it would make Victor open up to you." Her eyes got wet and she began to cry.

I tried to remain professionally detached. She sniffled, and looked at me with needy, tear-filled eyes. It took effort to resist her.

"I'm sorry," I said, "it's not possible."

I handed her the glass of wine. She smiled weakly, and took a sip. "Thank you."

Daisy fixed her eyes on me, then covered her face with her hands. "God, I'm so confused."

"About what?"

"About everything."

She dropped her hands. "Waiting for Victor's parole," she said, "is like a nightmare. Hoping for the best, fearing the worst. Not having any control, any say about anything. You're the only hope I've got. And that confuses me even more."

"Why?"

"Because . . . because . . . "

"What is it, Daisy?"

"I . . . I can't talk about it."

"Why are you confused?"

Daisy sighed, and started twirling another curl. I noticed her fingernails were painted purple.

"Well, this is going to sound terrible," she said, "but you're a shrink
so I guess you're used to people telling you bad things without judging them. Right?"

"What is it?"

"Okay. What I want to say is . . . maybe Victor has a right to be
jealous."

She looked at me for a reaction. I gave her none. "I've been having these thoughts," she said, "thoughts about you . . . since the day
we met, when you quoted those lines from Edna St. Vincent Millay.
And you told me how your mom used to read poetry to you . . . "

*I never should've done that. I was talking about myself, instead of
listening.*

"The thing is, I've never met a man who could quote poetry," she
said. "It was just . . . it just touched me. Then that night, when I went
home, I kept thinking about you. And when I got into bed . . . I started
to get kind of hot, which isn't unusual—I'm a very sexual person. But
when I get that way, I normally start fantasizing about me and Victor.
But this time, I started imagining what it would be like if you were making love to me. And I could really feel you. I mean, I could actually feel
your lips, taste your tongue . . . "

"Daisy . . ."

"I tried to tell you I belong to Victor, but you said you didn't care
. . . you just had to have me . . . once. *One night,* that's all you wanted.
And then . . . then I felt your hands moving all over me, stroking my
neck, my breasts, your fingers touching my . . . " She broke off. Her
breath was coming in short gasps now. "I wanted to say no, but I
couldn't . . . I couldn't . . ."

"Stop it, Daisy," I shouted. She'd pulled me so deeply into her story that my erection was tenting my trousers. I folded my hands in my lap.

"I . . . I'm sorry," Daisy said. "You must think I'm terrible."

"You'd better go."

"Doctor Rothberg," Daisy said, "I love Victor with all my heart. In all the time I've been here, I've never even looked at another man. But with you, I . . ."

"That's enough, Daisy. This is completely inappropriate."

"I . . . I apologize," Daisy said. She got up and walked over to me. "Doctor, I know you really care about Victor, that you're doing all you can to help. But *please*—promise you won't give up, that you'll keep trying with him."

"I'll do what I can."

"And you won't let what I just said affect anything, will you?"

I got up, went to the door, and opened it for her. "I told you, I'll do what I can."

"Thank you for listening," she said. "I'm sorry I . . . took up so much of your time."

Daisy came close to me. She hesitated, then leaned up and kissed me lightly on the cheek. She smiled and walked out.

I sunk down in a chair, shaking my head.

That woman made me do something I swore would never happen again—she got me to lose my objectivity, and worse, she made me forget who and what I am.

I reached for the wine glass and polished if off in a few gulps. I refilled the plastic tumbler and peered through the garnet colored liquid at the glaring bulb in my bedside lamp. The rays of light broke up into distorted fractals, floating in front of me in variegated shades of redness. The light splintered and began to whirl and flash. *Headache.*

I rushed into the bathroom, found the Sumatriptan Statdose Pen and jabbed it into my thigh. I turned off all the lights and lay down on the bed.

The pain pulsed upside my head, but if I stayed very still, I knew the drug would help. Clearly the red wine triggered this attack. But

Dr. Ramone had said stress could *underlie* migraine headache. Well, if that was true, it was sure as hell underlying this one.

It was hard to think with the throbbing in my left temple, but I gave it a try.

Daisy did a number on me. But what's her game? Does she think by turning me on I'll be in her sexual thrall and do whatever she wants? Or was she really offering herself to me, for "just one night" as she said; one night in exchange for Victor's freedom?

Maybe it's something more complex. Or maybe it's pretty simple; she's got the hots for me . . . after all, I am cute . . . why do they always say cute? . . .

I was losing it; the medication muddling my brain. I drifted off into a drug-distorted sleep. My mind wandered, searching for the solution to the Daisy puzzle, traveling down dark paths and opening creaking doors, only to find *ze-ro mess-a-ges.*

Then the dream again.

I'm in Victor's cell, and he's in a murderous frenzy—slashing, slicing me with his razor-sharp palette knife. I scream a scream so loud it has no sound at all. Blood geysers out of my body. I see the clawfoot bathtub and watch my blood flow into it; turning the water bright scarlet. Suddenly, out of the water, a naked woman sits up, grimacing as the blood drips down over her matted hair, her shoulders, her hard-nippled breasts. It's Melissa—glaring at me with fury in her eyes. She begs desperately. "Please . . . Please . . . Please . . . Please . . ."

Chapter 16

I checked my watch as I pulled up to the high school running track. It was 8:14 A.M.

Perfect. Half hour run, quick shower at the penitentiary, and I'll still make my 9:30 with Ben.

The migraine and the episode with Daisy had me really shook up, but today was a new day.

I walked to the gate of the track, bouncing on my new Reeboks. I wore gym shorts and my favorite tee-shirt, with the motto *"Eschew Obfuscation."*

A sign on the gate read: Rufus Alden "Speed" Culpepper Memorial Running Facility—Summer Hours: 9 A.M to 9 P.M. There was a padlock on the gate. A chainlink fence surrounding the track made entry impossible.

Not enough time. Not my fault.

Back at the car I grabbed the baggie and fork I'd left on the front seat. I went to a nearby stand of pine trees. Sometimes under the ground cover of fallen pine needles you can find worms. I used to dig them up in Riverside Park for Shelly when I lived at the Boat Basin.

This time I didn't even find an ant. My sweet turtle was gonna be cranky.

I drove to the Silver Streak diner and wolfed down a comfort food breakfast of ham 'n' eggs and home fries. *Very nutritious. Potatoes are vegetables.*

I was worried about Victor Janko. Aside from avoiding him for a couple days, I had no real plan. Was there a clue in *The Cat in the Hat?* I was clueless. And Victor's jealousy of me made things worse. Especially after last night.

Driving up to the prison gate I wondered what fresh hell awaited me. I found out right away. I heard what sounded like women grunting, but as I drove closer the grunts became words.

"No Parole for Janko. No Parole for Janko. No Parole for Janko."

There was a crowd of demonstrators—mostly female, pushing baby carriages and strollers. Propped up inside them were Raggedy Anns, Cabbage Patch Kids, and Tickle Me Elmos; doll eyes open, staring. The mothers marched back and forth, chanting and carrying signs: CAGE THE BABY CARRIAGE KILLER; MOTHERS FOR VICTIMS' RIGHTS; END PAROLE FOR VIOLENT FELONS; PAROLE = MURDER.

Then I saw the TV remote trucks—ABC Eyewitness News, New York One, UPN 9—and the Steadicam guys shooting the action. A nasal voice echoed over a loudspeaker, and I traced its source to a platform and podium. There was Hizzoner the Mayor. I couldn't make out all the words, but I got the gist—law and order, no mollycoddling criminals, citizens' rights . . .

Jesus. This could well be the Schmuck's handiwork. I can just picture Dad bragging to the mayor—"My Son the Shrink's working on this red-hot case." The mayor's PR boys would pick up on it as a media op, generating headlines like: "Mayor Fights to Keep Psycho Killer off Streets."

I drove slowly through the line of demonstrators. They parted to let me pass, but there were angry jeers and some pounding on the hood of my car. There was a "Staff" card on my windshield. *Why do they assume I'm against them?*

At the gate, the guard, whom I now knew as Ambrose, gave me a friendly wave. Then he looked back towards the mayor, rolled his eyes, and made the jerking-off sign with his fist.

It was the first laugh I had all morning.

At my meeting with Ben, I voiced my concern about the demonstrators. "You think they'll influence the parole board's decision?"

"With the board you never know," he said. He was still speaking in nervous rat-tat-tat fashion.

"They're not immune to political pressure," Ben continued, "but they're . . . they're just kind of ornery. Can't tell you how many times I was sure they'd go one way and they went the other."

"But this isn't just political pressure," I said. "It's social pressure. I mean, these boardmembers live in communities where people will see this TV coverage. If they were to let Victor Janko out, wouldn't they worry what their family, friends, and neighbors might say?"

"No," Ben replied. "The decision to grant parole is by a three-fourths majority and secret ballot. A board member can always claim he opposed the parole but was out-voted."

"How much influence you think my input will have on their decision?"

"Well," Ben said, "in cases like this, where the prisoner has a record of good behavior and rehab, they tend to rely heavily on the prison shrink. On the other hand, sometimes they go the other way, simply because they don't like the prisoner's attitude, or his face, or . . . the color of his skin. It's an imperfect system. But that's how it goes down."

"So," I said, "in spite of that bullshit going on in the parking lot, what I say about Victor could still affect the parole board?"

"First of all, it's not bullshit," Ben said testily. "It's a serious issue — lots of folks in this country are worried about releasing violent criminals. I wish they weren't down there demonstrating—I think parole decisions are better made without emotion. But they have a right to express their point of view. As far as your input, I can only say it *might* be the deciding factor. So . . . you better be damn sure it's right."

Ben was shouting now, shaking his right fist. I noticed a small bandage on the inside of his forearm.

"Did you cut yourself?"

Ben looked at his arm. "Nicotine patch," he said. "I've quit smoking my pipe."

"Oh, that's why you've been . . . Hey, that's great."

"Dentist saw some white crap on the inside of my mouth."

"Hairy leukoplakia?" I asked, referring to pre-cancerous oral lesions.

Ben nodded. "For years my wife's been busting my chops to quit. She's banned smoking in the house, and she won't kiss me because I have ashtray breath. Plus, here I am trying to cure drug-addicted patients, and I'm hooked on one of the most dangerous drugs on earth."

"Yeah, well, Freud couldn't quit smoking cigars," I said lightly, "even when they had to replace his cancerous jaw-bone with a wooden one."

He smiled grimly. "I've tried to quit before but I always slide back. Compulsive drives are amazing. At the same time you're *consciously* deciding *not* to do something you're *subconsciously* planning *to do* it."

You talkin' ta me?

Ben turned the discussion to various patients, and then laid out the day's schedule. Right now things were calm on the ward and our tasks were fairly routine. We separated to begin work.

In mid-afternoon, I was taking a history of Hugh Kennealy, the weight-lifter. In an emotionless voice, he told me how a shower room gang-rape made him decide to bulk up. "Man's gotta protect his manhood."

"How long you doin' 'roids?"

"Never touch 'em."

"Sure, anabolics get you pumped and ripped and cut, but lemme tell you something, Hughie. You won't be so macho when your balls shrivel up to the size of raisins."

I was interrupted by an orderly. "Call for you from Kim Cavanagh."

Shit, she's calling to cancel. I excused myself, and took the call in my office.

"Hi, Doctor Rothberg," Kim said. "I'm just phoning to find out how your mom is."

"My mom?"

"Yes. Your sister called last night asking for you. She said your mom was very sick."

"That's strange," I said. "My mother is dead and I don't have a sister."

"Oh, gosh. I'm sorry," she said in a confused voice.

"Did she ask where she could find me?"

"Well, yes," Kim replied. "She sounded real upset. So . . . I gave her your number at the Hospitality Inn. I screwed up, didn't I?"

"No, no," I said. "She . . . she was from a bill collecting agency. A charge card dispute between me and Bloomingdale's. I referred her to my accountant. No biggie."

"You sure I didn't . . . ?"

"No harm, no foul."

"Oh, that's a relief. Well, I know you're busy, so I'll get off. See ya tonight."

"I'll be down to getcha in a taxi, honey."

"Why? Is your car in the shop?"

"Nope."

"Then maybe I should . . ."

"When I pick you up you'll see why. Make it seven-thirty."

"Deal."

I hung up the phone. Then I thought of Daisy.

That woman's a piece of work. She sure went through some devious machinations to find out where I lived. After the number she did last night I pegged her as a mixed-up, manipulative young woman. Better re-think that. Daisy could be a looney-tune.

And dangerous.

Chapter 17

Kim was waiting outside her town house complex, "Hudsonville Gardens," wearing a pale green silk suit—kind of dressy. I wished I'd gone home to change. I got out of the car, hitching up my khakis and buttoning my seersucker jacket. I had on my running shoes and greeted Kim with an apology.

"Don't be silly," she said. "You look very cute."

She noticed my car. "Hey, you weren't kidding about the taxi."

"Nope."

She smiled. "What kind of cab is this?"

"Checker," I said. Then I told her its history.

"What are those things in the back?"

"Jump seats," I said. "They pull down to seat two extra people. These cabs could take six passengers."

"What a great idea. Wonder why they don't make 'em anymore."

"Money. Now if there's six people, they have to take two cabs."

As I opened the car door, she commented on my shoes. "Oh, Reeboks. They're DMX's, aren't they?"

"Yes."

"*Running Magazine* says they give you great lateral support . . . especially if you pronate."

"Definitely."

"How often do you run?"

"Well, actually . . . I've . . . just gotten into it."

"I try to run every day," she said. "Especially in the summer. I love training in hot weather. There's a 10K in Albany next month, and I'm hoping to knock two minutes off my time. My ambition is to someday run the New York City marathon."

My ambition is just to set foot on the "Speed" Culpepper Memorial Running Track some time between now and the winter solstice.

It was a ten minute drive to the restaurant—Lenny and Mike's "La Bistro." The sign outside worried me because if Lenny and Mike didn't know it was *Le* bistro, how French could the food be?

The *maître d'* seated us at a corner table. It had a checkered tablecloth and a candle in a red jar with a plastic net around it. I looked at Kim in the candlelight, and found myself trying to decide if she was pretty. I saw her dark brown hair for the first time without her nurse's hat. It was short and cut in a bob. Nice. Her nose was small, her face a bit too broad, but when she smiled, her features came together beautifully. She still wasn't wearing makeup, except some pale pink lipstick.

It's like she has no vanity—which is great.

And yet, with a little eyeliner . . .

"I'd give anything to have red hair like yours," she said.

I felt like a jerk. What gave me the right to appraise her? I vowed to act like a decent human being for the rest of the evening, and if possible, for the rest of my life.

Kim ordered a glass of white wine, and I opted for Perrier.

I asked her how she got into nursing.

She said she was no Florence Nightingale type. She was a local girl, who had to work part-time during high school because her father was laid off when the tool-and-die factory closed. After graduation she enrolled in nursing school mostly because it was near her house, and she could go at night while she did full-time slave labor at McDonald's. At first the pay scale for nurses was her main inspiration.

But later Kim realized nursing was an exciting and gratifying profession. And after her first year, she'd discovered something; she was good at it.

"Y'know," I said. "I really admire your courage."

"Courage?"

"Yes. Working in a prison, with all those unstable guys; it can't be comfortable for a woman."

"Well, I've been trained for it, and over the years I've learned how to handle myself," she said. "Except of course when Bobby Sanchez put a needle to my throat. Thank God you came along. You wanna talk about courage, I think you're the bravest man I've ever known."

"Truth is, Kim, like you I was trained for it. We're taught over and over to think on our feet, to improvise. I acted reflexively. I never actually felt afraid. I think real courage is when you're facing your deepest fear and you find the strength to overcome it."

"Like what?"

"Well, for me," I said. "It would be where I had to defend myself physically. Like if I got into a fist fight. I've never hit anybody in my life, except for a kid in fifth grade who called me a dirty Jewboy."

"Well, that counts."

"I didn't exactly hit him. I swung and clipped him on the shoulder. Then he threw me down and beat the crap outta me. That was the end of my fist-fighting career. I've wondered ever since how I'd act if the situation came up again."

"I wouldn't know how to handle a fist fight either," she said.

"You wouldn't be expected to."

Kim took a swallow of wine, and then spoke with quiet introspection. "I guess I'd feel the same way about rape. It's my greatest fear, being in a situation like that, where you've got no control at all. They give you all these self-defense techniques — the knee to the groin, the fingernails in the eyes—but I wonder if I could really do it, or if I'd just be paralyzed with fear."

"Have you decided?" The *non sequitur* came from the waiter hovering over us, a Caucasian teenager with flaxen dreadlocks.

Kim said she was kind of hungry and suggested we look at the menus and order right away. I asked the waiter what the *soupe du jour* was and he said it was the soup of the day. Then he announced the house salad was "Free-zay with bacon uh . . . uh . . . uh . . . *lardons*." We both went with the seafood crêpes appetizer.

The food was a lot better than I'd expected. Kim had *sole meunière*, which was spelled on the menu as *sole menure. Oy vey.* I had *couscous*, which was thankfully spelled correctly.

As we chatted, I felt really at ease. It was fun to talk shop with Kim. She knew all the patients and everybody on the staff, and since she'd been around a long time, she had great perspective on Vanderkill. I asked what happened to the guy who had my job before me, and Kim said he'd quit because he'd found a better position. I said I found that hard to believe. We both laughed.

We were having a very good time. Later, when I thought back over the evening, I remembered two things Kim had said; one that made me laugh, and one that made me think.

I'd mentioned Rasheed Harris, the guy with drugs up his keister. Kim smiled and said Harris was always asking her for extra medication. He kept saying he was a nervous wreck, that he'd been diagnosed as suicidal, and couldn't he please have a few more tranks from her drug tray. Finally, one night he began screaming, telling her he was so freaked that if she didn't give him some Librium, he'd kill himself, and did she want that on her conscience?

"It was sort of 'Give me Librium or give me Death,'" she said. That made me laugh.

What made me think was when I brought up Victor Janko. I said I didn't understand what would make a woman fall in love with an incarcerated killer.

"What do you think the attraction is?" I said. "From a woman's point of view."

Kim spoke after a moment's thought. "Maybe it's a matter of . . . attention."

"What do you mean?"

"Well, one of the things a woman needs most and gets least from a man is attention. I know what prison life is like for a guy. It's no life at all. So he could devote one hundred percent of his attention to a woman. Every thought, every fantasy, all his words and actions could be focused on her. If a woman had a desperate craving for attention, a guy like that would fill the bill.

"That makes sense," I said. "But why are some drawn to murderers, even to convicted serial killers?"

"Well," Kim replied, "maybe it's because their crimes are so serious the guys have no chance of getting out. So the women can keep the relationship on a fantasy level; completely safe, and on a long-term basis, which is just how they want it."

Kim paused. "That's only a guess," she said. "It could be a lot of other things too."

I thought it was a damn good guess.

But then why would Daisy be working so hard to get Victor out? If he were released, she'd have to face the reality of the man, which would be quite different from the way she saw him now. . . .

The waiter put the check down in front of me. Kim raised up, reached over and grabbed the bill.

"My treat, remember?"

As she leaned over, I caught a glimpse of the swoop of her full breasts, surging forward against the pale green neckline of her blouse.

My treat.

I drove her back to the town house complex. When I parked in front of the entrance, she turned to me.

"Would you like to come in for a decaf cappucino?"

This time I said *no* before I had a chance to think it over.

"You're missing out on a good thing."

"I better not. Early meeting with Dr. Caldwell."

"Okay," she said smiling. "Well, this was fun."

"Yeah, it was."

"Feel free to save my life anytime you want."

I had no snappy comeback.

"Well, good night," she said, getting out of the car. "Maybe I'll see you tomorrow, if you work late."

"Yeah. Maybe I'll see you tomorrow."

She turned and walked away. I called after her. "Hey. Thanks for dinner."

I don't know if she heard me. She headed towards a building in the back, and disappeared into the darkness.

Driving home I asked myself why I'd turned her down, when I really wanted to be with her.

Since Melissa I've steered clear of sex. And women, picking up the vibe, haven't seemed interested in me. Now suddenly . . . last night Daisy, tonight . . . Kim. I don't get it.

Earlier this evening I vowed to act like a decent human being. Maybe that's what I'm doing.

Yeah, right.

Soon as I got home I jumped in the shower. When I soaped my crotch, my penis reared up angrily, as if to say *C'mon man, I been up, I been down, up, down, up, down . . . make up your mind.*

I started stroking it to make it feel better. In my mind I saw Kim, her womanly breasts cupped in my hands, her mouth exploring mine, her strong runner's thighs opening to receive me. I exploded in a paroxysm of pure pleasure.

But the image that tripped my trigger wasn't Kim. It was Daisy; intruding into my fantasy, touching herself and moaning my name, as her middle finger glided in and out between her slick folds. . . .

I turned off the water and stood there panting in the steamy shower stall.

What the hell am I looking for? What do I want?

Maybe the answer is in the words of Mick Jagger—"You can't always get what you want, but if you try sometimes . . . well, you just might find . . . you get what you need."

Chapter 18

Early next morning, I went into the woods behind the motel to forage for earthworms. After digging around beneath some evergreens, I turned over a rotting log. Bingo. Worm convention.

I picked one up and went back to my room.

When I dropped the worm into Shelly's vivarium, she came out of her hide box, went over and sniffed it. Then, with a quick flick of her head, she walked away.

"Yo, Shelly, whassup?"

I thought about chopping up the worm, but I had no eyes for surgery, at least not until I'd had breakfast.

I squirted mist from a spray bottle onto her shell. She scurried away. Turtles have nerve endings on their shells, that's why Shelly can feel me scratching her. But today she hated any contact. I hydrated her whole habitat with the shpritzer and let her be.

Over my morning coffee, I remembered I hadn't checked my voicemail. I picked up the phone and punched '2.' There was one message; a muffled man's voice, disguised by a guttural quality.

"Don't let Victor Janko out. Or you'll live to regret it."

I pressed the repeat key.

"*Don't let Victor Janko out. Or you'll live to regret it.*"

I listened a few more times, but had no idea who it was. I pressed three, *save*, and hung up.

It could've been one of those anti-parole demonstrators. But how would they know where I lived? Or that I'd be testifying before the parole board?

Maybe my father told them. The Schmuck could have blabbed that information to anybody.

It could've been someone in the penitentiary. Ben Caldwell and Father Toussenel both seemed opposed to Victor's release, but I can't imagine them harassing me like this.

No. No. The prime suspect is . . . Stevie Karp. He definitely wants Victor kept behind bars, and a threatening phone call is more his style. But whoever it is, what can I do about it? And how real is the threat anyway?

I've got no answers. But this only strengthens my resolve. Today I go back and face Victor Janko. I have no plan so I'll just have to wing it and hope I push the right buttons. Threat or no threat, I have a responsibility—to give Victor my best shot.

At the hospital my chance to see Victor came earlier than expected. Hugh Kennealy's session with me was cancelled because he'd gone violent again and had to be sedated. Combined with lunch break, that gave me two hours; enough time to go over and work with Victor.

As I approached the cell, I heard an odd, shuffling sound. When I got closer, I could hear the guard's voice.

"Come on, you pathetic wimp. Let's see a little elbow grease. Come on. Get into it."

It was a strange scene. Victor was on his knees, polishing the guard's shoes with a shoe brush. The prisoner wore only a pair of striped pajama bottoms, and his pale, pudgy body wobbled with the effort. Stevie sat on the bed with his feet up on a carton. I could see the cruelty in his eyes, even through his sunglasses. "Make it shine," he yelled. "Get some snap into it, you pussy."

"Okay. Okay," Victor said quietly.

"Okay, *what?*"

"Boss," Victor replied. "Okay, *Boss.*"

"Now spit," the guard ordered. "I want a real spit shine. You hear?"

Victor made a salivating sound, bent his head over and spit on both shoes.

"Atta boy. Now use the cloth. Come on. Spit 'n' polish. Spit 'n' polish."

Victor rubbed frantically. Stevie growled in disgust. "I said spit 'n' polish. You call that polish? Come on. Get into it, you piece of garbage."

Victor stopped and grabbed his elbow in pain. "It hurts," he pleaded.

"I said—*do* it, faggot."

The prisoner complied.

"Remember," Stevie said, "I wanna see my shinin' face in 'em."

"Right . . . boss."

Victor worked a few more minutes, till the pain and exhaustion forced him to stop. "Okay," he said, looking up hopefully. "They're done."

"Good," the guard said, after inspecting the shoes. "Now gimme the finishing touch."

"Please, Boss. Don't make me."

"*Now*, faggot," Stevie bellowed. "The *finishing touch.*"

In total humiliation, Victor bent over and kissed each of Stevie's shoes with his lips.

"Soul kiss," the guard demanded.

Victor stuck out his tongue and licked the boots with the tip of it. He gagged, then sat up, hanging his head in shame.

"Yessir, Vicky, it's sure nice havin' you around. You're a good boy."

Victor nodded subserviently. "Are we done now?"

"Yeah. We're done. In fact, you did such a good job, you might even get dessert tonight. You'd like to have dessert, wouldn't you?"

Victor didn't respond.

"I'll be back later with a nice banana split? That's your favorite, ain't it? A big banana split, with plenty o' whipped cream?"

Victor turned his face away. I heard a tormented whimper. Then he began to make his whistling sounds.

The sickening realization hit me: "banana split" might mean . . . the image flashed in my mind, Victor being split open, forced to submit to the guard's lecherous violation. *Plenty o' whipped cream.* I was disgusted and furious.

I fought my impulse to burst in on the scene and backed away. It would be better to return to my office and think about what I'd seen. I left quickly and returned to the hospital.

By the time I sat down at my desk, I realized I couldn't do much to help Victor—at least for the moment. If I reported the situation to Ben or the Warden, I could only accuse Stevie of forcing the prisoner to shine his shoes. The sexual aspect was speculation. And with any charge I made, it would be the guard's word against mine. I couldn't count on Victor's corroboration; he'd be afraid of being punished by Karp if the accusations didn't stand up.

And to raise this issue five days before the parole hearing would only muddy the waters. I had no choice but to do nothing—deal with it after the hearing.

I opened my laptop and began typing some notes. As I described the guard's domination and humiliation of Victor, I saw I'd learned something important.

It's now clear Victor wasn't lying when he said Karp took pleasure in hating him, that he'd do anything to keep him in prison. In fact, my guess is Karp was lying when he said Victor had boasted about doing the murder.

Also, watching these two men together has given me a different perspective on Victor. Although he's surely not a willing participant in this domination ritual, he probably has a psychological predilection for it—he'd tend to assume the passive role with an aggressive person.

I'm going to act more forcefully towards Victor. Maybe he'll respond to that. It's worth a try.

I recalled Victor's tortured whimper when Karp promised him a "banana split." I saw Victor's lips, puckered and emitting his strange, tuneless whistle.

There's another card I can play: I'm going to try and beat Victor at his own game.

Chapter 19

At 7:30 I went back to the Ad Seg Unit. Karp had gone off duty, and the night guard accompanied me to Victor's cell. As he left, he said if any shit went down to just holler and he'd be there in two seconds.

Victor barely acknowledged me. He sat on his cot, using the thumb and index finger of his right hand to stretch up the loose skin on top of his left hand. Then he let it snap back down. He seemed utterly fascinated by the pliability of his epidermis.

"Evening, Victor," I said casually. "Haven't seen you in a while."

Victor responded by switching his skin-stretching from his left hand to his right. He glanced covertly at me as he pulled the skin up, but said nothing. He let the skin drop.

"What's goin' on?" I asked.

More skin tweaking.

"How you feeling tonight?"

"Fine." Victor's voice was flat, devoid of affect.

"Is that all you have to say?"

Victor raised his eyes, and gave me a blank look. I stared back aggressively.

After a few moments of silent face-off, I grabbed a towel and walked over to the chair. I started to dust it, but then made a big show of dropping the towel sloppily on the floor. I sat down on the unsanitized chair and looked at Victor. He began to whistle.

I upset him. Good.

We stared at each other. Victor's whistling was unnerving, as if he were taunting me with the power of his anxiety.

Stay the course, remember—you're the doctor here, you're in control.

Victor had the advantage; relying on a defense mechanism which had always served him well. Silence was his comfort zone.

I maintained eye-contact, showing I wasn't going to crumble. After a while Victor's confidence began to get shaky. He squirmed. He scratched his neck in nervous, clawing gestures. Still he said nothing.

Abruptly the prisoner stared down at the floor. He looked to either side, glancing at me furtively. Then he faced forward and shut his eyes tight, like a willful child. He was pulling back inside himself; if he couldn't face me down, he could still beat me by withdrawing. *Christ, he's good. But the poor bastard doesn't understand that if he wins this battle, he loses the war.*

I came up with a counter-move.

I licked my lips and imitated Victor's whistling, pushing the air through my teeth and adjusting the tone to an irritating whoosh. Victor's body stiffened as he clamped his eyes tighter.

It was a fierce clash of wills. The tension increased, like a rubber band being stretched tighter . . . and tighter . . . until it snapped.

"Jesus Christ," Victor yelled. "What are you doing?"

"What do you mean?"

"Why are you? . . . I mean . . . I just don't get what you're doing."

"I asked you a question," I said calmly. "I'm just waiting for an answer."

"What question?"

"I asked how you were feeling."

Victor looked at me, puzzled. "Didn't I answer you?"

"No," I said. "You said you were fine. Fine is not an answer.

"Jesus Christ."

"Did you miss me?"

"Pardon me?"

"These past two days. Did you miss me?"

Victor went silent again. I waited as the tension built.

"You wanna go another round?"

He let out a long sigh. "What do you want from me?"

"Not much," I said harshly. "Y'know . . . I say something, you say something else. It's called conversation."

After a few seconds, I spoke again. "I asked you if you missed me."

Victor moved his lips, till he managed to stammer out some words. "I . . . I w-w-wondered where you were."

"Did it worry you?" I asked. "Did it make you anxious?"

"Would you please . . ." Victor moaned. "Look, just leave me alone. I'm tired."

He heaved himself back onto the bed, head propped up on a pillow. He took off his glasses, covered his eyes with his arm and answered my next questions without moving.

"Why are you tired?"

"Dunno."

"There must be a reason."

Victor said nothing.

"How have you been sleeping?" I went on.

"On my back."

I exploded with anger. "Goddamn it. I've *had* it with you, Victor. You're wasting my time. And you're acting like a fucking asshole."

Victor sat up, stunned by my profane outburst. I pressed on.

"I'm your only hope for getting out of here," I said. "And if you give me shit you're screwed. Now I'm gonna ask my question one more time, and I want a straight answer." A pause. "Why are you tired?"

"Bad dreams," Victor said acquiescently. "I've been having bad dreams. They wake me up and I can't go back to sleep."

"What do you dream about?"

"I don't remember."

"Try to remember."

Victor's brow wrinkled. He looked at me, shook his head hope-lessly.

"Do you dream the same dream every night?" I asked.

"Pardon me?"

"You're giving me shit, Victor."

"No I'm not . . ."

"*Victor.*"

"Okay . . . okay. I guess I have the same dream . . . sometimes."

"Try to remember one part of your dream," I said. "A person, a place . . . a feeling . . ."

"Scared. I feel scared."

"Of what?"

Victor shrugged. I leaned forward in my chair. "Where are you? What do you see in your dream?"

Victor thought for a moment. Then he spoke excitedly. "There's a beach."

"What kind of beach?"

The prisoner pointed to his paintings on the wall. "Like . . . my paintings. With palm trees."

"Tell me more," I urged him. "You're on this beach . . ."

"No. No. I'm not *on* it," Victor said. "I'm . . . I'm *looking* at it. I'm *looking* at the beach. And . . . and it's coming at me. The beach is coming at me."

"The beach is coming at you?"

"And there's this guy," Victor continued. "He's . . . he's got a hold of me, and I try to run away . . ." He was shouting now. "But I can't. He's hitting me . . . hitting me, and I can't get away."

He broke off, taking ragged breaths, reliving the terror.

"Who's attacking you?" I asked.

"I don't know."

"What about the beach? You said you were looking at the beach and the beach was *coming at you*. What do you mean by that?"

"I . . . I don't know," Victor responded. "A beach is life. A beach . . . is . . ."

He groaned in confusion, moving his head back and forth.

"A beach is *life?*" I said. "Do you mean . . . *life* was coming at you?"

Victor said nothing. I looked hard at him for several seconds. Then I spoke sharply.

"What about *The Cat in the Hat?*"

"Huh?"

"*The Cat in the Hat.*"

"I don't understand."

I reached into my shoulder bag, pulled out the Dr. Seuss book, and held it up. Victor stared at it in shock.

"*The Cat in the Hat,*" he whispered. "*The Cat in the Hat . . .*" His eyes widened in recognition.

I placed the book in Victor's hands.

"*The Cat in the Hat,*" Victor repeated. He looked down at the book, bewildered. Then he remembered.

"It belonged to the lady," he announced. "The lady at the A&P." He stopped, smiling as if he'd told me everything.

"Tell me about her."

Victor nodded. Then he spoke with a sense of discovery.

"She was my last customer—it was the end of my shift . . . nine to six. She was carrying the book, and she gave it to her little girl to hold while she paid for her groceries. The lady was so nice. I remember how she smiled at me when I packed her bag. I asked if she wanted delivery because it was awful heavy. But she said no. Then her kid started yelling, pointing at a carton of Tootsie Pops on the checkout counter, and having like a tantrum. The lady told her it would ruin her appetite, and if she didn't shut up, she was really gonna get it. Then the lady apologized to me for how her kid was acting—she was kind of embarrassed—and I told her I knew how kids were. Then she left."

Victor paused for a moment. "After, I noticed she'd left the book behind . . . well, I saw it laying on the floor. The kid must've thrown it out of the stroller, y'know, when she was having her tantrum. So I decided to bring the book back to the lady."

Victor smiled faintly at me.

"Go on," I said.

"Well . . . when I got to her building . . ."

"How did you know where she lived?" I asked.

"Oh. She paid by check, so I sneaked a look in the register drawer. Her check had her address printed on it."

"I see . . ."

"So . . . so . . . anyway . . . I got to her building. She lived in the project, and it took a while to find the place, because, y'know, those address numbers are hard to read in the dark. And just when I got to the entrance, I heard this horrible scream. Then I heard a kid crying, and I knew . . . I knew something really bad was going down."

"The building door opens and this guy comes running out. When he sees me he lets out a yell and comes after me. I was like paralyzed for a minute, till I saw him up close. He was all splattered with blood, and he had a bloody knife in his hand. He had it raised up over his head, ready to stab me. I turned and tried to run, but it was too late—he grabbed me from behind. I saw the knife blade coming right at my chest, and I . . . somehow I grabbed his wrist, and then I bit him on the hand, or a finger, or something . . . anyway he dropped the knife and let me go. I grabbed the knife and I slashed at him—I remember I cut him on the face . . . on his chin, but then I panicked and started to run. Only I couldn't because . . . because he jumped on me, he swung me around and bashed me in the face. He kept bashing me, and bashing me, till everything was just a red blur. And then . . . I heard a police siren and I guess I blacked out, because I don't remember anything else. Next thing I knew I was sitting on the sidewalk, and my head was hurting real bad, and the police were asking me questions. But I couldn't remember anything. All the stuff I just told you was gone from my memory . . . until now."

Victor's body suddenly slumped down, drained of all energy. His breathing was slow and deep, his face slack with relief. I let him rest for a few moments before I questioned him.

"You say you were bringing the book back to the woman?"

"Yes."

"Did you have the book with you when the police caught you?"

He thought for a moment.

"Yes," he answered. "They . . . they took it away from me."

"How could you fight this guy with the knife, with a book in your hand?"

"It wasn't in my hand. It was in my pocket. I was wearing my Army jacket from the surplus store, and it had big pockets."

I wondered about fingerprints on the knife. "What else were you wearing?" I asked.

"Umm . . . a wool cap, y'know with earflaps?"

"Anything else?"

"No." He squinted his eyes. "Wait . . . Gloves, woolen gloves. It was cold."

"What was the woman's name?"

"Pardon me?"

"The lady you were returning the book to."

"The lady?" Victor said, with disturbed look on his face. "I . . . I don't remember . . . I don't remember her name."

"You remembered everything else."

"I know. But . . . it was a long time ago. I . . . I just can't remember."

"All right" I said. "This guy with the knife . . . do you remember what he looked like?"

"He was huge . . . really huge. He looked like an Indian . . . one of those Apaches you see in the movies. He had long black hair, and . . . and he had these three red stripes on his forehead. Y'know, like Indians wear when they go into battle?"

"Warpaint?"

"Yeah. Like warpaint. And he had a funny nose."

"What do you mean?"

"It was like, off-center. Sorta squashed all over his face."

"You mean like a boxer's nose? Did he look like he might've been a boxer?"

"He coulda been."

"What was he wearing?"

Victor thought for a moment. "A sweatshirt," he answered. Then it hit him. "A sweatshirt . . ." he said slowly, "With a picture printed on it. A picture of a beach. A beach . . . with palm trees."

He clapped his hands and opened his mouth in amazement. He sat there in freeze-frame.

"There was printing above the picture. And, what it said was . . . 'Life's a Beach' . . . '*Life's a Beach.*' Get it? All I could remember was 'A Beach Is Life.'"

"That's very good, Victor."

"Oh, my God," the prisoner said. He looked at his paintings, one after the other. Victor's eyes filled with tears. He fought them back for a moment, and then gave in completely. He put his hands over his face, and began to sob.

After a time, Victor regained his composure, and looked up at me. "Doctor," he said in a quiet voice, "Thank you so much. Thank you for helping me remember."

"You had a real breakthrough, Victor," I said. Then I looked at my watch. "Well, that's enough for tonight."

I got up, and walked toward the cell door.

"Doctor Rothberg," Victor called out.

Interesting, that's the first time he's called me by my name.

"I've been praying every day," he said, "every day for as long as I been in here. And now, finally, my prayers have been answered. I know . . . I'm *sure* I didn't kill that lady."

You're sure. I'm not.

I unlocked the door. "See you tomorrow."

Chapter 20

Back at the motel, I checked on Shelly. She'd retreated into her hide box. I picked it up and dumped her out into my palm. Her claws gripped me and she edged her head out. She was mouth-breathing.

She hadn't touched her earthworm. It was all dried up.

I put Shelly back in her vivarium and took out my *Box Turtle Care* book. Under *Stops Eating* was listed "exposure to noxious chemicals, respiratory infection, environmental temperature changes." *Mouth Breathing* gave the same causes, plus "egg retention." Maybe that was it. She had eggs to lay and they were stuck.

If she's not better by morning, I'll have to find a vet.

I checked my phone for messages. There were two. The first was from Ben Caldwell.

"David, I'm calling to tell you the date of Victor Janko's parole hearing has been moved up . . . or moved back . . . I always get those two words confused. Anyway, it's coming up this Friday morning, instead of next Monday. Reason is the head of the parole board decided to take

his vacation starting Saturday . . . he's taking his kids to Disney World. Do you believe that shit? Anyhow, that's how it is. Let's meet tomorrow at the end of the day, so you can update me on your evaluation of Janko. See you then. 'Bye."

Damn. I'd been counting on having the next five days to work with Victor. Now I had just two—tomorrow and Thursday.

My second voicemail message was the now-familiar disguised voice. It was even more menacing. *"Don't let Victor Janko out. Don't even think about it . . . or you'll pay big-time."*

I pressed the button for my saved messages.

"Don't let Victor Janko out. Or you'll live to regret it."

These are odd warnings. They're threatening me, but with what? Live to regret it? Pay big-time? What does that mean? Both recordings have the same muffled, distorted voice; it sounds like a man, but I can't be certain. I'm fairly sure it's someone I know—something in the language sounds familiar, but I can't put my finger on it. Is it Stevie Karp?

I played the messages one after the other.

"Don't let Victor Janko out. Or you'll live to regret it."

"Don't let Victor Janko out. Don't even think about it . . . or you'll pay big-time."

It's in there. There's something in the rhythm of the speech, or the pronunciation, or the timbre, that's the tip-off.

I remembered how Karp talked, but not well enough to match it with the messages. After a few more listens, I gave up.

A shiver of fear went through me. I'd been so involved in figuring out the caller's identity, I'd overlooked the threat itself. What if someone intended to injure me, or kill me if I allowed Victor to walk? My old fear of physical confrontation grabbed me. I saw a guy stalking me, jumping out of dark shadows, and attacking me . . . with his fists, a baseball bat, a knife. How would I handle it?

Uh-oh. What if . . . what if someone tries to destroy me some other way . . . by attacking my character? Digging into my past and . . .

Whatever. I have a job to do. Let the chips fall.

I sat down at my computer. Carefully I wrote out what Victor

Janko had told me tonight, doing my best to put it in Victor's own words. It took over an hour; I had to get it right.

Afterwards, I scrolled back through my notes and read everything I'd written about Victor since day one. I reviewed each session, looking for inconsistencies, contradictions, and most importantly—lies.

Then I started typing again:

Victor's explanation of why he confessed his crime to the priest is believable—Father Toussenel could certainly have pressured him into it.

The shoeshining incident confirms Victor's statement that Karp would do anything to keep him from getting out.

Now the most critical issue—Victor's claim of innocence. Is it born out by the story he told me?

The details do match the police report. Victor's reaction to The Cat in the Hat *and his reason for having the book the night of the murder makes total sense. And the struggle with the knife-wielding man, wearing the "Life Is a Beach" sweatshirt, has the ring of truth. Even Victor's paintings confirm the subconscious repression of the trauma surrounding the murder.*

He couldn't remember the name of the victim, but that's understandable; the woman's name had no significance to him. It makes Victor's story less than perfect, but that only makes the story more plausible. If he had total recall, it would seem contrived.

Everything seems to point to one conclusion—Victor's been entirely truthful. And yet . . . how can I be certain?

My role has changed since I began working with Victor. At first I was to predict whether he'd behave dangerously if released. It was to be a psychiatric evaluation. Now the question is guilt or innocence. It's a mystery—not a Whodunit, a Did He Do It. As my dad said, since when did I become a detective?

It's true . . . I've gone from Shrink to Shamus in little over a week.

But every psychiatrist is a detective, because every patient is a mystery. Each patient has a psyche which can't easily be known or understood or explained. Each patient keeps secrets. Each patient presents

evidence and yields clues. The psychiatrist must solve that mystery,
sorting through the ambiguities, the complexities, the hidden agendas,
to have any chance of easing the patient's pain.

That night I dreamed of the huge, hulking, long-haired killer, with his boxer's nose and warpainted forehead, raising his knife and stabbing his victim, again and again. I saw the little girl in her stroller, crying in terror, as she witnessed the unimaginable: the murder of her own mother by a knife-flailing monster.

The final image was Agnes Rivera's bloody face, her last words coming out in desperate gasps. She was calling her daughter's name, *"Margarita . . . Margarita . . . Margarita . . ."*

Then she was still.

Chapter 21

In the morning Shelly looked bad and I got really worried. I searched in the *Yellow Pages* and found a vet in Peekskill. Then I called Ben and told him I'd be late for work.

Shelly sat on the car seat next to me, in a Baggie with holes poked in it. After a half-hour drive, we pulled up in front of the *My Pet Veterinary Clinic — Dr. Lee Wang, DVM*.

We entered a tan art deco bungalow with glass blocks across its front.

We sat in the waiting room with an English bulldog, clearly there for a drool problem, and a parrot who only seemed to know the word *rock*. Dr. Wang came out and to my surprise he wasn't Chinese. I figured then he must be Jewish because the only other Wang I knew was Wolfie Wang, a kosher butcher, who said it was a fairly common German name.

After twenty minutes the vet saw us. I described Shelly's symptoms and set her on the steel examining table. Dr. Wang picked her up with latex-gloved hands. He took out a magnifying lens and examined Shelly as if she were a diamond under a jeweler's loupe. He scrutinized her carapace and head, then turned her over and checked out her plastron, legs, and tail.

"I was wondering, Doctor," I said. "Could she possibly be egg-bound."

"No. This turtle is a male."

"You're kidding."

"No."

"You're sure?"

"Yes."

"Oh, wow."

He looked at my surprised face. "What's his name?" he asked.

"Shelly."

"Oh, that's lucky. You won't have to change it."

"How can you tell it's male?"

He put Shelly down on the table. "A box turtle's genitals are internal so you have to go by secondary sex characteristics. Mature males have red eyes, and this greenish color here on top of the head. There's more, but you may not want to know . . ."

"I want to know."

"Well," he said. "In turtles the anus is in the tail, and in males it's a bit further out. Here, look at his anus . . ."

"You're right. That's more than I want to know."

It was a joke, but humor wasn't Wang's thang.

"Has he been exposed to any chemicals? Solvents?" he asked.

"Not that I know of."

"He won't eat?"

"No. And she, I mean *he's* been breathing like that, with his mouth open."

"Any bubbles?"

"Where?"

"Coming from his mouth."

"No."

Dr. Wang looked thoughtful. "It may be a respiratory illness," he said. "You need to leave him here for a couple days. We'll put him on a round of antibiotics, see how he responds. I'll call you day after tomorrow."

"You think . . . he's gonna be all right."

"Turtles are tricky. They're so susceptible to change in their environment it's hard to figure out what's bothering them. We'll hope for the best."

Is he being negative or just cautious? I don't like this.

"Oh," Wang said, looking at my registration form, "I see you're an MD. What's your specialty?"

"Psychiatry."

"You're lucky."

"Why?"

"*Your* patients can talk to you. They can tell you what's wrong with them."

I wish.

I reached over and scratched Shelly on the shell.

"See ya later, old girl," I said.

I don't care. She'll always be a lady to me.

After work I went to Ben's office for our meeting. When I opened the door, I was engulfed in a cloud of pungent tobacco smoke. Ben was sitting at his desk, puffing on his favorite briar.

"I thought you quit," I said.

"I tried."

"No willpower?"

"I had plenty of will," Ben replied, "just not enough power."

"What about the nicotine patch? Didn't it help?"

"Not really. By the second night I'd developed a three-patch-a-day habit."

I laughed. "Well, you can always try again."

"I intend to," Ben said. "My wife usually yells at me when I slip back. This time . . . she cried."

He frowned, clearly upset with himself. He took a pipe tool and tamped down his tobacco. "Oh, by the way—Sally told me she may have a line on an apartment for you. She'll know in a few days."

"Thanks. Tell her I appreciate it."

Ben nodded. "So," he said. "Where do you stand with Victor Janko?"

"Well," I said. "I've got a pretty good sense of what's going on with him. But I need more time."

"More time? The hearing's Friday."

"I've still got tonight and tomorrow."

"David . . ."

"I want to get this right. And I'd be irresponsible if I didn't use all the time available. I'm going over to see Victor now."

"All right," Ben said with some annoyance. "We'll meet tomorrow night."

"Same time, same station?"

"Fine."

As I walked out the door Ben called after me.

"David," he said. "Objectivity. Remember, you lose your objectivity, your judgment goes right out the window."

I wanted to make some crack about his smoking addiction. I thought better of it and walked down the hall.

Kim was at the nurses' station. She waved as I approached.

"Hi."

"Hiya."

She's wearing eyeliner.

She reached under the counter. "I found something you might like. Do you know about the Checker Cab Club of America?"

"Um . . . no."

"I found this on the Internet and printed it out. It tells all about them. The local clubs are called Cab Stands, they have a theme song, "Mellow Yellow," . . . and the national meetings are in Kalamazoo, Michigan, which is where Checkers were made."

"I'd love to read it."

"If you want to join, there's an application form."

"Thanks. That's very nice of you. Listen, I'm on my way to see Victor Janko, so I can't talk. But I'll read it when I get home."

"Enjoy."

"Thanks." I put the papers in my shoulder bag and left. *She's a doll. What's my problem?*

"**R**ivera," Victor said to me excitedly. "That was the lady's name — Miss Rivera."

I pulled my chair closer to his cot. "What made you remember?"

"It was funny. This morning when I woke up . . . well, when I was half asleep and half awake, in my mind I could see this painting I once saw in an art book. It showed these Indians, with long black hair, doing like cooking and stuff. At first I figured I was thinking about the guy who, y'know, attacked me that night. But then I realized that these were *Mexican* Indians, and the painting was a mural by this famous Mexican artist, Diego Rivera. Then it hit me — the lady had the same exact last name — Rivera. Miss Rivera. Boy, I'll tell ya, your mind sure works funny sometimes, doesn't it?

"Do you remember her first name?"

"No, but maybe I will . . ." he said, "when I wake up tomorrow morning."

He gave me a smile. He'd never done that before.

"Victor, I'd like you to tell me again what happened the night of the murder . . . with all the details. Can you do that?"

"Sure," he said. He went through it all again. Unlike the night before, he recounted the events calmly, without emotion. There were no discrepancies.

"Describe the killer again for me," I said.

"Like I told you," he said. "The guy was huge . . . he reminded me of an Apache from the movies. He had long black hair . . . and like warpaint."

"Anything else?"

"No," he said. "Oh, sorry. I forgot about his nose. It was . . . like you said, like he mighta been a prizefighter."

Everything seemed to jibe. I could think of nothing else to ask. As I unlocked the cell door, he spoke to me.

"Doctor Rothberg," he said. "I want to apologize."

"For what?"

"Well, see, when my girlfriend Daisy told me you and her . . . got together, I got kinda jealous. Actually, I sorta freaked—I didn't want to even talk to you. But . . . I was wrong. That was really stupid on my part. So . . . I'm real sorry."

"No need to apologize."

"Doctor. I was wondering if you could do me a favor. I only get two phone calls a week, and I've already used 'em up. So Daisy doesn't know anything about . . . y'know, what I remembered last night. It would make her real happy if she knew I remembered. So . . . maybe you could tell her. If you've got a little time tomorrow, maybe you could go over to the library where she works?"

"I can't, Victor. I've got a really busy schedule. But I will come here and see you."

"Okay," he said. "Just asking."

As I descended the iron stairway, I thought about what Victor had told me.

He gave me no new information about the night of the murder—which is good.

But—wait a minute, actually he gave me an important new clue, one that might let me check out his story. The clue is one simple word . . . HUGE.

Back at the motel there was another menacing voicemail. It was a more specific threat than the previous ones.

"Don't let Janko out. If he walks, you won't."

So now someone was going to break my legs, shatter my knee-caps. *Terrific.*

Chapter 22

Next morning I stopped at the library. I didn't want to have any further contact with Daisy, but now I couldn't avoid it.

Daisy greeted me with a warm smile. She was wearing a baseball cap, and her unruly blond hair flowed out from the gap in back.

"Dr. Rothberg," she said. "It's so nice to see you again."

"Hello, Daisy."

"Is everything okay? I mean with Victor?"

"Everything's fine."

Daisy's expression turned fearful. "You . . . you don't sound very positive."

"Daisy, I need your help with something."

"Name it."

"You told me the library has newspaper coverage of Victor's case on microfilm. I'd like to look at it."

"Yes. Yes," Daisy said eagerly. "The viewer's back there in the research room. Why don't you go on in, and I'll dig up the film."

She indicated a small chamber to the left of her desk. I nodded and walked towards it.

"Doctor," she said, stopping me. "Would you mind my asking what this is all about?"

"I really can't discuss it."

"But . . . this is to help Victor, isn't it?"

"Look, if you don't mind, I'm kind of pressed for time."

She stared at me with a worried expression. Then she turned and went into a large walk-in closet behind her desk.

I sat down at the large, clunky-looking viewing machine, and thought about what I hoped to find. Each time Victor described his assailant, he'd used the same word — *huge*. And Daisy had used the same word to describe the victim's boyfriend, whose picture appeared in the *New York Post*. She'd said he was "*huge . . .* really scary . . ."

Daisy was standing behind me, and she reached over my shoulder to flick a toggle switch on top of the machine. The screen glowed, and a bright lightbulb went on beneath it.

"You need any help running this?" she asked.

"No. No. I used one at college . . ."

"Well, in case you've forgotten," Daisy said, "you press this green button here to unlock the threading mechanism. Then you thread the film through the slot over the lens, till it catches . . ."

"Right . . ."

"Oh, heck. Let me do it for you."

She took the microfilm out of its box, and deftly threaded it through the machine. I leaned out of the way so she wouldn't touch me, but I was aware of her scent. It was a floral fragrance, possibly jasmine. Her fingernails were now painted silver.

"All set," she said. "Oh, this lever here is to scan the film, the small knob is to rotate it, and the big knob is to scroll back and forth."

"What if I want to print a copy?"

"Just swipe your credit card through the copying machine on top, and press *Print*."

"Thanks a lot. I'll let you know when I'm done."

"Okey dokey," she said, then she was gone.

I scrolled through the editions of the *New York Post* for the month of March, until I saw the tabloid's front page headline: "BABY CAR-RIAGE KILLER—Fiend Slays Young Mother in Front of Toddler." Then I scrolled forward a few more issues, until, with a rush of excitement, I spotted exactly what I was looking for.

There, under a caption reading, "Services for Baby Carriage Victim," was a photograph of three mourners on the steps of a church. One of the mourners was a powerfully built man in his late twenties—definitely *huge*—with the battered nose of a boxer. It was hard to see if he had long, black hair because he was wearing a do-rag which hid most of his hair. The bandanna was worn unusually low—almost covering his eyebrows—and after a moment I guessed why. Victor'd said there were three red stripes on the killer's fore-head, like war paint. But maybe they had nothing to do with Indians on the warpath. The red stripes could have been scratch marks, inflicted by the victim's fingernails as she fought to save her life. And the do-rag was concealing those scratches. Then I saw what was clearly a Band-Aid on his chin. Victor had said he slashed the killer on his chin during their struggle.

The picture's caption gave the names of the female mourners (neighbors of the victim), and of the huge man, described as the dead woman's former boyfriend. His name was Leo Hagopian.

I printed the page with the picture and stuck it in my bag. Then I left the library, giving Daisy a perfunctory thank you as I passed the Return Desk. She looked upset that I wouldn't talk to her, but I said I was in a hurry.

D riving by the high school, I remembered that I'd let the whole jog-ging thing go these past few days. *But when did I have time?*

Then my mind jumped to Kim Cavanagh. I hadn't read the Checker Car Club stuff last night. And I didn't give any more thought to my ambivalence about her.

But . . . when did I have time?

At the prison gate, I saw the anti-parole demonstrators. Their num-bers had grown; now there were about fifty of them, parading in front of the entrance. In addition to the women, there was now a phalanx of men, some with bullhorns. They were down to a single chant, "No Parole Tomorrow. No Parole Tomorrow."

The satellite uplink trucks were still parked, their antenna dishes broadcasting news of this hot-button issue to the entire universe.

As I drove through the surly, shouting crowd, my heart was hammering in my chest.

Maybe I'm wrong about the threatening phone calls. Maybe it's not someone I know. It could be one of these wild-eyed demonstrators on some demented mission to save society from violent felons, by perpetrating a violent felony . . . on me.

The pressure was ratcheting up. I gripped the steering wheel so tightly it hurt my fingers.

Chapter 23

During my lunch break I went to my office and typed out a four page document summing up my evaluation of Victor Janko.

After work I handed it to Ben in his office.

"It's a condensed version of my notes," I explained. "Would you mind reading it?"

Ben nodded. His pipe had gone out and he set it in his cut-glass ashtray.

"Okay if I sit here while you read?" I asked.

"Fine," he said. "But if you see my lips move, be tolerant. Senior moment."

As he read I noticed he'd missed a spot on his chin while shaving. I saw his grumpy looking face, with its cappuccino colored skin and neat gray mustache, and I realized how much our relationship had mellowed. Despite occasional friction, I was genuinely fond of the guy.

Ben finished reading and looked disturbed. "So, you're saying Janko's been suffering from Disassociative Amnesia?"

"Localized type."

"Caused by physical trauma."

"Yes. As I say, he was punched repeatedly in the face and head and must've sustained brain and cervical damage."

"And this amnestic disorder lasted for fifteen years?"

"Yes," I replied. "Since he had no therapy, he had no way to recover those memories. Actually, with his beach paintings, he was subconsciously trying to remember, but he couldn't."

Ben nodded and thumbed through my notes. Then he closed the document and pushed it aside.

"David," he said, "y'know, Janko could've made that whole story up. Guys around here'll try anything to get sprung, and they're pretty crafty."

"No, no. Victor doesn't have that kind of imagination."

"The man's a painter," Ben pointed out. "He must have a vivid imagination."

"He only paints one subject—beaches. And he copies them from photographs."

Ben banged his pipe on the ashtray, knocking out the ashes. It sounded like a gavel rapping for order. "You say that book, *The Cat in the Hat*, triggered his memory, right?"

"Yes."

"Did anyone else know about the book?"

"No." Then I remembered that wasn't true. "Um . . . actually, I did mention it to Father Toussenel. Oh, and I also asked Victor's girlfriend about it."

"His girlfriend?" Ben said with surprise. "You interviewed her?"

"I thought it would be useful," I said. "Problem?"

"No. I'm just surprised you didn't mention her in your notes."

"I told you they were condensed."

"All right," Ben said. "But what if Janko's girlfriend told him you'd asked about the book? What if she helped him concoct this whole story?"

"I didn't tell her the book was connected to the crime."

Ben ignored me and went on.

"Maybe Janko doesn't have the imagination for it," he said, "but his girlfriend certainly does. Father Emile says she's very bright. And these women who love killers are real obsessive types. Convoluted schemes are part of their mindsets.

"That's not what happened . . . "

"And this business of the killer looking like an Indian," Ben said, "With the long black hair, and the broken nose. It's bizarre. It sounds contrived. Can't you see that?"

"What about the sweatshirt?" I retorted. "What about the palm trees . . . and 'Life Is a Beach'?"

"You didn't see any sweatshirt, did you? Janko has a fixation on painting beach scenes so it would be easy to make those two things fit together. "

"Look. We just disagree, Ben," I said. "But that's mostly because — you don't really *know* Victor Janko, not the way I do."

"You've spent one week with him. That's not . . ."

"It was long enough for me to learn that it's not in his *character* to be part of such a complex conspiracy. He's very introverted—it's hard to get him to talk at all. To think of him planning this with his girlfriend and then coming up with an acting performance like he did . . . well, it's just not Victor."

Ben began filling his pipe. "Lemme ask you one thing," he said. "Is it possible you're wrong?"

"Of course." I looked in his eyes.

He glared back implacably. "You have no proof that he was telling the truth, do you?"

I reached in my shoulder bag and took out the newspaper photo. I pushed it across his desk. He glanced at it. "What's this?"

"*New York Post* photograph. It shows the victim's ex-boyfriend, Leo Hagopian. The Band-Aid on his chin is where Victor cut him. The do-rag covers the scratch marks on his forehead. That backs up what Victor told me."

"A Band-Aid and a do-rag? I'd hardly call that corroboration."

"But the picture matches Victor's description of the killer exactly. He looks like an Apache."

"Well, if Janko knew about this photo," Ben said, "he could've made up his story to fit the picture."

"But how would he know I'd go to library to look at it?"

"I don't know. But this isn't proof . . ."

"Look, if Victor's story isn't true, then why did he have the Dr. Seuss book when the cops picked him up?"

"He stole it from the woman's apartment."

"But why?"

"Happens all the time. One guy up here took hairbrushes from the six women he killed. Turned out his mama had sexually abused him with a hairbrush."

"But why *The Cat in the Hat?*"

"I don't know," Ben said. "We may never know. We don't *need* to know."

"Of course we need to know," I said. "Look, whether you accept this photo as corroboration, I want you to consider something else."

I paused. I needed to get my words exactly right.

"Ben," I said. "What we do . . . you know it's not an exact science. In the end it's really about instinct—it always comes down to what you *feel* about something. That's all we've got going for us. Now, I've listened carefully to my patient, weighed all the evidence, looked at all the possibilities, and my instinct, my *gut feeling* is that Victor did not kill that woman."

"David," Ben said calmly, "you know I have great respect for you. But this is a life and death decision. If you're wrong and Janko's part of this elaborate construct of lies, then he's one of the most devious and dangerous convicts in this whole facility."

"But as you said—this is my call."

He held up his hand and looked directly into my eyes. "You plan to recommend Janko for parole, don't you?"

"Yes."

The battle was joined. Now each sentence would be loaded with fighting words.

"Look," Ben said. "If you give Janko the okay, there's a good chance he'll walk."

"I know that."

"If he does," Ben said, "you'd better be prepared for the worst-case scenario. You pick up the paper one morning and there's the head-line—'Paroled Psychopath Kills Again.' That blood will be on *your* hands."

I looked at Ben with irritation.

"Christ," he went on, "haven't we seen enough of those headlines in the last few years?"

"Oh, suddenly Victor is a serial killer?" I said. "Ben, he was con-victed of killing *one* person, and he's innocent."

"You say he's innocent. I say he might well be a serial killer *wannabe*, who got caught before he could kill again."

"Based on what evidence?"

Ben smiled condescendingly and began refilling his pipe. "David," he said. "I'm sorry, but I think you've lost your objectivity."

"Because I don't agree with you?"

"You're doing what I warned you against. You think your judgment is better than it really is."

I glared angrily at him. Ben took out a sheet of paper from his desk drawer. "I want you to look at something."

"What's that?"

"It's the computer read-out on Victor Janko."

"I don't have to look," I said defiantly. "I know it's a bunch of multi-dimensional contingency tables, cluster analyses of risk factors, and the RPP's percentile prediction of recidivism. Which puts Victor in the high nineties. . . . *Very High Risk.* Right?"

"Exactly."

"So that's what this is all about," I said. "It has nothing to do with my judgment. Or *your* judgment for that matter. It's all about the computer prediction."

"The computer only backs up my own opinion on Janko," Ben retorted. "And it confirms yours is way off."

"Opinion," I said. "That's the operative word, Ben. Your opinion is different than mine. I was asked to give my opinion on whether Victor is dangerous. Like you said, the parole board may concur or disagree. I don't decide if he goes free. They do. My job is to tell them what I think."

"I'm sorry, David," Ben said. He paused then spoke assertively. "I'm gonna have to overrule you on this."

I was stunned.

"Ben, we had an agreement."

"I know, but . . ."

"You gave me your word."

"I also took the Hippocratic oath," Ben said, "and swore I would 'do no harm.' There are women out there who'd suffer grievous harm if Janko goes free."

"But . . ."

Ben shouted me down. "For Chrissakes, David. You took the same oath I did. As a doctor, how can you be willing to take this risk?"

"As a doctor," I said, "how can you keep Victor Janko in here? You do that, you're not being a doctor, you're being a jailer. You're supposed to be healer—not an agent of social authority. Our job is to *treat* Victor. You just want to *punish* him—not only for a crime he didn't do, but for crimes you think he might do."

Ben rose from his chair. "You seem to think this Janko case is unique around here. Well, it's not. I've had dozens like this. And I've been wrong . . . a lot."

Ben began pacing like a caged animal.

"I'm sure I've kept some guys in here who deserved to get out," he said. "But that doesn't bother me as much as the rapist I let go, who attacked a teenager two hours after he was released. Or that nerdy guy, in here for shoplifting—I judged him borderline schiz, but not dangerous. He got paroled and a week later he shoves a homeless man in front of a subway train. *That* bothers me. So when research showed computer predictions were better than mine, hell, I was happy to accept that. In fact, I was relieved. Mistakes are still gonna be made, but if they are, let's be sure to make 'em on the conservative side. The stakes are just too high."

"You're damn right the stakes are high," I said. "I'm fighting for an innocent man's right to freedom."

Ben sat back down at his desk.

"Look," he said, "in five years, Janko will have another chance at parole. Why don't you just keep working with him, see if his story holds up over time?"

"Sure," I responded. "That's easy . . . for you. You won't be spending those five years totally cut off from the world. Ad Seg. Jesus, why not call it what it really is? *Solitary Confinement.* But that doesn't sound nice. *Confinement* . . . being penned up in an eight-by-ten cell without even a window. *Solitary* . . . being deprived of all human contact, except for a guard who . . ."

Better not to bring Karp's abuse of Victor into this.

" . . . except for guards who act like zoo-keepers, turning inmates into docile animals who are dependent on them for the smallest comforts."

"David, I'm just saying . . ."

"I know what you're saying. In five years, he'll have another parole hearing, and he'll be labeled Very High Risk again—because some IBM clone, with a microchip for a brain, scans Victor's file and reads *poor, uneducated, comes from broken home.* Conclusion—he must be a danger to society. If he were a middle-class college graduate with a father, he'd be Low Risk, and walking out the door."

I pointed a finger at Ben. "Admit it," I said. "You have no intention of ever letting Victor Janko out of here. Because you're afraid to."

I waited for him to respond. He said nothing.

"Ben, we have no right to keep Victor locked up just to be on the safe side, or because we don't want the responsibility. And we can't abdicate that responsibility to a machine, because the moment we do that, we give up our humanity."

"I don't feel the least bit inhumane," Ben said calmly. "Very simply—I cannot, in good conscience, allow Victor Janko to be roaming around in the streets."

Push had come to shove. "If you don't let me testify," I said, trying to sound unemotional, "I'm going to have to resign."

"Are you serious?" Ben asked.

"Absolutely."

"Oh, come on. You mean you'd quit over this?"

"You got it."

"Now I know you've lost your objectivity. David, this is a clinical disagreement, not a personal one."

"You went back on your word. I consider that personal."

"Okay. Okay," he said, "I made a mistake. I'm sorry. But that shouldn't make you quit. I wouldn't fire you because you made a mistake."

"This is not about mistakes," I said. "It's about a man's life."

"I know. But quitting won't solve . . ."

"Look," I said with finality. "Either I'm the one at that hearing tomorrow, or I'm outta here."

I headed for the door.

"David. Wait a minute."

I stopped. Ben had his pipe clenched between his teeth. As I watched, he appeared to move in slow motion; opening a box of wooden matches, striking one on a porcelain striker, putting the flame to his pipe bowl. Puff . . . puff . . . puff . . .

Jerk. You're using your pathetic nicotine habit to stall for time, while you try to figure your next move. Well, you've only got one move—and that's to cave.

Ben puffed rapidly. The burning tobacco gave off a bright orange glow. He exhaled a cloud of smelly smoke.

The face of this man I'd trusted and respected was now obscured by a shroud of swirling blue tobacco vapor. He looked like a soulless apparition,

"Tell you what, David," he said, kindly and avuncular. "Why don't you sleep on it tonight? Maybe you'll change your mind by morning."

"Not gonna happen," I said curtly. I left, closed the door behind me and stalked down the hall.

Kim smiled at me as I passed the nurses' station.

"How'd you like the Checker Cab stuff?"

I rushed right by her. "Sorry, I don't have time."

"Doctor," she called out.

I turned.

Her voice was tight with anger. "I don't have time either."

Shit.

Chapter 24

I opened my motel room door. There, lounging on my bed reading a book, was Daisy Lesczcynski. She looked up and smiled.

Jesus. That's all I need. "What are you doing here?"

Daisy swung her legs to the floor and moved toward me. She was wearing a man's shirt and denim shorts; I saw the play of her thigh muscles as she walked.

"I brought you a present," she said, holding the book out.

"Daisy, I don't think . . ."

"It's *Second April*, remember, the poem your mom used to read to you? It's my own personal copy. I want you to have it."

"That's very nice," I responded caustically. "But it's not appropriate. . . ."

She pressed the book into my hand. "Read the inscription," she said eagerly.

I shook my head no.

"Well, it says, 'To David Rothberg, a brilliant doctor and a sensitive . . .'"

"I said this is *not appropriate.*" I forced the book back into her hands.

"Please don't be mad," she said. Her eyes widened like a small child pleading with a parent. She grabbed a bit of blond hair at her temple and began her finger-twirl. Her nails were now orange. *What's the deal with her fingernail couleur du jour?*

"How did you get in here?"

"Oh. I told the room clerk I was your girlfriend and I wanted to surprise you. I guess I have an honest face."

Pop must've been running the desk. Probably didn't even look at her.

"Daisy," I said sternly. "You had no right to do that."

"I'm sorry. Please forgive me," she said. "I just had to see you. I was watching the 'Six O'clock News' tonight and they said Victor's parole hearing was changed to tomorrow. I didn't know. Do you *believe* that? I had to find out on TV."

"What do you want, Daisy?"

"I'm just so worried. I feel like my whole life is hanging on what that stupid parole board says. I thought maybe you could tell me . . . what's gonna happen."

I sat down heavily in a chair. Daisy looked at me anxiously.

"What?" she asked. "Is something wrong?"

I didn't respond.

"Doctor," Daisy said. "If you know something, tell me."

I looked at the floor.

"Please," she begged. "I have a right to know."

I looked up. "Yes. I guess you do."

"What?"

"I shouldn't tell you . . . because I haven't told Victor yet, But . . . okay. I'm afraid it's not going to work out."

"What do you mean?"

"Actually, I was going to recommend Victor for parole. But Dr. Caldwell, my boss, overruled me. He's convinced Victor is dangerous."

"But . . . you know he's *not.*"

"It's not my call any more."

Daisy crossed the room and knelt down beside me. "Isn't there anything you can do?"

"No."

She moved closer. "But Dr. Caldwell doesn't even know Victor," she said. "You're the one who's been . . ."

"I'm sorry," I said. "It's out of my hands."

"Oh, no."

"Now, Daisy," I said firmly, "I want you to go home."

Daisy stood up suddenly. "I can't believe this is happening."

She walked away and leaned against the far wall, her back to me.

"They can't do this to me," she said. "After all this time. All this waiting. They're taking away the one thing I've been living for. The only thing I've ever wanted."

"Daisy . . ."

She turned to me, her hands flailing. I hardly recognized her face; it was contorted with anger. She hurled the poetry book across the room.

"And they've taken away the only thing *Victor* ever wanted," she shouted. "This'll destroy him. But that's what they want. The System decided he was a murderer, but he didn't get the death penalty. So now the System is gonna kill him anyway . . . any way they can. An eye for an eye, that's what they want . . . an eye for an eye . . . an eye for an eye . . ."

She was crying bitterly. "I can't let this happen," she sobbed. "I can't. I can't . . ."

She ran to the bed and flung herself across it.

I went over to her. "Daisy," I said quietly. "I know this is upsetting. But Victor will have another chance at parole."

She turned over and looked at me tearfully. "Five years. I can't live on hope for five years."

"That's a decision you have to make," I said. "Either your love can sustain you or you can move on with your life. The important thing is—the choice is yours, and that fact can empower you . . ."

She reached up put her hand on my mouth.

"The hearing is at noon," she pleaded. "You could still talk to Dr. Caldwell in the morning."

"Everything's been said."

Daisy looked at me with determination. "No," she said. "You can still make him change his mind. I know you can."

I flinched as her fingers lightly touched my face. Her voice was an urgent whisper. "Please . . . please . . ."

She reached up, snaked both hands around the back of my head and pulled me down to her. Her mouth was ravishing; her soft lips tasted of strawberry. Her tongue darted out of her mouth, flicking, exploring.

I pushed her away, fighting the need rising in me.

"Stop it," I commanded. "And go home."

Daisy's gray eyes were moist with desire. Her hands slipped up over her breasts and moved to the top button of her shirt. She undid it, then began on the second one. I grabbed her wrists and yanked her hands away.

"No, Daisy," I said. "Victor Janko is my patient, and you're the woman in his life."

I felt the teasing caress of her hands behind my neck, then I shivered as her nails dug into me. Pulling me on top of her, she slid her hands down my back. Her fingers cupped my buttocks, holding them in a demanding grasp. She pulled me closer. Her thighs fitted against mine, and I could feel the heat of her sex seeking and finding my swelling cock. She began moving her hips, grinding herself against me. I felt her breasts, warm and firm, pressing against me through her shirt. She was wearing no bra, and suddenly I ached to see those twin mounds of woman flesh . . . to touch them . . . taste them . . .

I raised up slightly so I could open her shirt. I fumbled with the buttons till, with a choked moan, she pushed my hands away, grasped the neckline and ripped it open in one violent sweep. I saw the youthful ripeness of her beautifully formed, pearlike breasts, tipped by little pink buds.

I looked down at Daisy's face. Her skin was flushed, her eyes half-lidded, her teeth biting into her full lower lip . . . as if it were soft candy. And suddenly she was not Daisy, she was *Melissa*. She opened her eyes and she was Melissa; her eyes were blue not gray and I heard her voice, saying *please . . . please . . . please . . .* And I knew it was wrong, but here were Melissa's breasts with the hard nipples, and she was offering them, spreading herself open for me and her urgent passionate voice begging *please . . . please . . . please . . .*

This is wrong.

The desire drained out of me as quickly as it had come. I pulled away and stood up.

Daisy was breathing hard. The expression on her face changed from sexual excitement to disappointment and then to anger. We stared at other; in a few moments we'd gone from adversaries to lovers and back again.

The tension was broken by the ringing of my telephone; like a wake-up call—*br-r-ing . . . br-r-ing . . . br-r-ing . . .*

"Don't answer it."

I picked up the phone. "Hello?"

"David? This is Emile Toussenel."

"Oh . . . oh, yes," I said. "What is it?"

"I'm calling about Victor Janko," he said urgently, "He's had a bit of a breakdown. I'm in Ad Seg. Ben asked me to ring you."

"What happened?"

"You'd better get down here."

"I'll be right there." I slammed down the receiver.

"What's going on?" Daisy asked.

"It's Victor. There's a problem. I have to go."

"What do you mean? What kind of problem?"

I turned my back to her and adjusted my clothing. I noticed Daisy's poetry book on the floor.

"Can I go with you?" she asked.

"No," I answered brusquely. "Pick up your book. We're leaving . . . right now."

Chapter 25

As I ran down the Ad Seg corridor, I saw two white coated hospital workers wheeling a gurney out of Victor's cell. Victor was on his back, body strapped down with leather restraints. Eyes closed, he was breathing slowly and deeply.

"What happened?" I asked.

"He berserked," one of the men said.

Ben came out of the cell. "We had to sedate him," he explained. "He'll need hospitalization."

The orderlies took Victor away.

The cell was a wreck; furniture overturned, paints and brushes scattered around the room, all Victor's paintings slashed to shreds. The canvases hung like torn rags from their broken frames.

I saw Father Toussenel sitting on a chair. Stevie Karp was unbending one of the legs on Victor's cot so it would stand upright.

"What happened here?" I asked.

"Apparently Janko had a psychotic episode," Ben replied.

"Did anybody see him do this?"

"Yeah," Karp said. "I did."

"How did it happen?'

"It was weird. I checked on him when I came on duty around eight and he was fine."

"I thought you worked the day shift," I said.

"Usually I do, but I switched today with the night man, because I wanted to keep tabs on Victor. Y'know, this bein' thc night before his hearing, I wanted to be here . . . to like give him moral support."

Sure. Whatever this asshole tells me now will be complete bullshit.

"A little while later," Karp went on, "Father came to visit him, and he was okay—right, Father?"

"Yes," the priest said. "He wouldn't pray with me, but when I told him I was praying for him, he thanked me."

Yeah. Father Emile was asking the Lord to bless and keep this sinner in the joint for the rest of his natural life.

"Then about an hour after Father left," the guard said, "I heard Vic raisin' a ruckus. I went over, and he was stompin' around on the floor, makin' funny sounds, and mumblin' to himself. When I tried to calm him down he went ape-shit. Started yellin' and throwin' his paintin' stuff against the wall—kickin' over the chair and the easel. I tried to stop him, but—he was like ten times stronger than usual. He threw me against the wall like I weighed nothin'. Then he picked up his paintin' knife—guess he'd sharpened it on the cinder blocks— and started cuttin' his pictures. He was slashin' like a maniac, like he must've done when he killed that woman."

This guy deserves an Oscar.

The truth was obvious—it was Stevie Karp who'd destroyed Victor's work, to make it look as if Victor were dangerous. Victor had said it—*he'd do anything to keep me in here.*

"I got back up and tried to stop him," Karp said, "but he cut me." He held up the palm of his left hand. There was a gash on it. *Superficial wound.*

"Finally I managed to deck him with a rabbit punch," the guard said. "Then I cuffed him."

"He called me on my pager," Ben explained. "I was having dinner with Emile, and the two of us came right over."

"What was Victor upset about?" I asked Karp.

"I dunno."

"Sounds like he was very angry. What did he say to you?"

"Just crazy stuff."

"About what?"

Karp didn't answer. He looked uncomfortable.

"Tell me exactly what he said," I said in a demanding voice.

"You don't wanna know."

"Come on, Stevie."

"Well," the guard said tentatively. "Like Dr. Caldwell said, he started talkin' real psychotic."

"Just tell me."

Karp looked at me for a long moment. Then he let out a resigned sigh. "Well, for one thing, he accused you of humpin' his girlfriend."

His words were like a punch to my gut. "Go on," I said.

"Well, see, ever since Victor found out you spent time with his girl," Karp explained, "he's been possessed by the green-eyed monster. At first he was real casual about it—talkin' 'bout how Daisy was so pretty she could have any guy she wanted, and what the hell was she doin' in love with a moke like him? But over the last few days, he started obsessin' on the idea—sayin' how Daisy must be gettin' real horny from goin' so long without no lovin'. And that you was a cool lookin' guy, much smarter than him, and bein' a shrink and all, you knew how to do a number on Daisy and make her go for ya. Tonight I guess it all blew up in his head. When he went into his freak-out, he kept sayin' 'I know it's happenin'. I just know he's doin' her.'"

"How did you respond?" I asked.

"Respond? I responded by tellin' him he was way off base, there was no way a doctor would do a thing like that to a patient. Hell, it ain't ethical."

Jesus. It's like he saw me with Daisy tonight.

"I tried to reason with him," Karp went on. "Told him he was lettin' his imagination run away, and he should just calm down, 'cause he's got his parole hearing in the mornin'."

He shook his head in pity. "It was really sad," he said. "But I take part of the blame myself; I said a word that really set him off. He was carryin' on about Daisy bein' unfaithful and all, and I said to him, 'Victor, you're actin' real paranoid.' *Paranoid*. Sayin' that was like pushin' a button. When he heard it, he went completely wacko. I shouldn'ta said that. I shoulda known better."

He looked down at the floor, real sad.

"Don't blame yourself, Stevie," the priest said. "What Victor did was in no way your fault."

"Well," I said, "that gives us a good picture of what happened. Ben, if you don't mind, I'd like to talk to you alone."

Ben nodded, then spoke to Karp and the priest. "Gentlemen, if you'll excuse us."

Karp headed for the door. "I'll be at the guard station if you need me."

Father Emile picked up a broken frame. The remnants of a Victor Janko beach scene hung down, a mutilated, fragmentary picture. "Such a waste," he said. "It's terrible to see beauty destroyed, especially by its creator."

He paused, looking thoughtful. "But then . . . perhaps it's a parable, like the story of God's banishment of Lucifer, the beautiful yet evil angel. Like Lucifer, Victor was struck down by his Creator to keep him from perpetrating further evil. And for that we should be grateful. We should thank the Heavenly Father that Victor Janko cut up a bunch of paintings in a jail cell and not some poor woman out on the street."

He crossed to the cell door, looked back at us with a benevolent expression, then left.

"Sit down, Ben," I said, indicating the chair. "We need to talk."

I took a seat on Victor's cot. It was a little unsteady but it held my weight. I deferred to Ben. "What's your take on all this?"

"Well," Ben replied, "I don't know Janko well enough to see inside his mind. But he probably had some ambivalence about getting out of here. I've seen it before . . . guys goin' bananas when it's time for them to be released. For a variety of reasons, some inmates are afraid to leave. They feel incapable of dealing with the outside world or they feel guilty about their crimes and think they deserve more punishment. Or sometimes—and this may be true in Janko's case—they have psychological problems that cause them to act out in stressful situations. And, to a prisoner, what could be more stressful than a parole hearing?"

"But something doesn't make sense here, Ben," I said. "I know Victor—he'd never destroy his paintings. His reaction to stress is to withdraw, to put up a wall around himself. As you saw in my notes, I don't think Victor's psychotic. Oh, he's loaded with neuroses, but even if he did go over the edge, he'd follow his own psychic patterns. He might sink into protracted dysthymia, but he wouldn't act out violently, especially towards his art—that's his biggest area of security."

"Hold it," Ben said. "Are you suggesting Victor didn't destroy his paintings?"

"Yes."

"Then who did?"

"Stevie Karp," I replied.

Ben looked incredulous. "You think Karp made up his whole story?"

"Correct," I answered. "To convince us Victor was dangerous."

"That's hard to believe."

"It's true."

"But when we got here, Victor never said a word. He never blamed Karp."

"Because he was afraid to squeal on the guard," I explained. "Victor knows he has no chance for parole now, and his life here is totally in Karp's hands."

"Listen, I've known Stevie for a long time," Ben said. "He's a tough son-of-a-bitch, but he's a good guard. I can't see him doing anything like this."

"But he had a very strong motive," I said. "When I explain it to you, you'll see him differently."

"Okay. Explain."

"Well," I said, "Karp was abusing Victor. It was a sado-masochistic thing. Victor was Stevie's slave, and the guard wanted to keep things that way."

"How do you know that?"

"I saw them together. One day when I came to visit Victor, Karp was forcing him to shine his shoes."

"Okay."

"And then . . . he made Victor kiss them."

"Kiss who?"

"The shoes," I explained angrily. "He made Victor kiss his shoes."

Ben gave me a dubious look. "Look, David," he said. "Even if they were into some sort of kinky stuff, it doesn't mean Karp slashed his paintings."

"But this was about sex. Victor was 'servicing' the guard."

"You saw that?"

"No. But it was obvious. Karp was determined not to lose his sexual partner."

"Refresh my memory," Ben said. "Was there anything in your report about this?"

"Well . . . no."

"Why not?"

"I . . . I felt bringing it up before the parole hearing would only complicate things."

"Complicate things?", Ben said, his voice rising in anger. "My God, man. I ask you to tell me what's up with Janko, and you choose to leave that out? And you also left out your contact with his girl-friend. Since Janko thought you were having sex with her, don't you think that's kind of relevant?"

I had no answer.

"Let me ask you this," Ben said. "If you were sure Janko was being abused by the guard, why didn't you get him out of there?"

" . . . Get him out?"

"Why didn't you order him transferred to the hospital for observation?" Ben said. "Then we could've sat down together and figured out a course of action."

Why hadn't I thought of that?

"If Karp was sexually molesting him," Ben said sternly, "Janko surely would've been better off in the safe environment of a hospital room. Didn't you feel any responsibility to protect him?"

I had no reply. Ben looked at me, seeing my anguish. "I'm sorry, David," he said. "I didn't mean to say you were irresponsible.

"No, no," I said. "You're absolutely right. "

Ben shifted gears. "Look," he said. "I know how you feel about Janko, and what happened tonight must be very upsetting. I'd like to help if I can. You can't prove this sexual abuse, but maybe we can get Janko to bring charges . . ."

"He'd never do that," I said.

"He might if we returned him to the general population."

"He'd never survive in the main cell block," I said. "What about setting him up permanently in the hospital?"

"That's impossible. We don't have the space."

Ben looked thoughtful for a moment. "Well, maybe we can figure something out—let's discuss it again in the morning. But in the meantime, there's another issue we should address."

"What's that?"

"Your resignation. Since Janko's parole hearing is now just a formality, it doesn't matter which one of us testifies. So, when you think about it, there's really no reason for you to resign. The whole issue is moot."

He looked at me earnestly. "Look, I'm sorry about going back on my word. I know you want to help Janko, and you can't do that if you leave. And there's another reason I want you to stay. You're a damn good doctor."

"You just told me what a shitty doctor I am," I said. "And you're right. I'm a liability around here. I . . . I'm really not qualified."

"That's not true . . ."

"And don't forget, Ben. You also think my judgment stinks. I'm the guy who wanted to recommend Victor Janko for parole—an inmate who, in your opinion, is a dangerous serial killer."

I turned and walked out the cell door. Ben's voice echoed in the hallway, calling after me. "David."

I ignored him. At the guard station I saw Stevie Karp sitting with his feet up on the desk. He smiled, and I felt a surge of rage at this evil man with his dark glasses and his absurd ponytail. I remembered his admonition:

"This is a bad place, Doc, with a lotta bad people in it. You hang around here any length of time, that bad is gonna rub off on ya."

The sonofabitch was right.

Chapter 26

The morning sky was a gloomy gray over the high school running track. The weather was as depressing as my life.

I'd spent an awful night playing over and over the incidents that brought on this disaster. When I got into bed, the scent of Daisy's perfume on the pillows assaulted my senses, reminding me of my libido-driven stupidity. *The only thing that stopped me was a memory of Melissa. I wish it'd been strength of character.*

As I was falling asleep, I heard a song running around my head. It was an old Jimmy Buffett tune—"*Wastin' away again in Margaritaville / Lookin' for my lost shaker of salt / Some people claim that there's a woman to blame / But I know . . . it's my own damn fault.*"

I got out of the car and headed towards the running track.

I can't figure Daisy out. I understand her actions last night—she was desperately trying to get me to help Victor. But I still don't get it. Why did she come on to me before last night? Didn't she see that if she seduced me, I might start wanting her for myself, and actually try to block Victor's release? Maybe she knew I'd feel guilty about wanting her, and those guilt feelings would force me to work even harder to secure Victor's parole. That's pretty subtle and calculating, but that's exactly what Daisy is.

I was at the entrance to the "Speed" Culpepper Running Facility. It was 9:25 A.M. and the chainlink gate was open. I had on my Reeboks and my gym shorts. Maybe running would make me feel better. *Just do it.*

I walked over to a nearby oak tree, and began stretching my calves. I put my hands on the coarse bark of the tree, stuck my right leg back and pushed against the ground. My calf muscle was tight and felt achy. I straightened up, decided not to force it. It would be stupid to strain the muscle before I even used the damn thing.

I took a deep breath, did a couple of deep knee bends, and then started to run — to trot really. Not too fast at first, just getting the feel of using long neglected muscles. It was a cinder track and there was a definite bounce to my step as my padded running shoes struck the surface. I picked up the pace. Now my heart was pounding, arms pumping back and forth in a piston-like rhythm, the breeze blowing through my hair. It was exhilarating. I was Eammon Coughlin, the Irish whippet, breaking the record for the Wanamaker Mile during the Millrose Games. I was Kipchoge Keino, the African marathon runner, who'd built up his lung power by chasing mountain goats high in the hills of Kenya. I was Steve Prefontaine, the long-haired Oregon speedster, crossing the finish line at the Munich Olympics, while the crowd shouted, *"Pre . . . Pre . . . Pre."* I was Power, Endurance, I was a Triumph of the Human Spirit, I was — the pain shot through my lower rib cage — I was an out-of-shape, out-of-breath *putz* kneeling on the dirt track, clutching my side.

I reviewed my medical training. *No, this isn't myocardial infarction.* After a while the pain died down, and I got to my feet. I was okay.

I'm not gonna give up. If I can't run, I'll walk the course. The longest journey starts with a single schlep.

Pacing slowly around the track, my thoughts turned back to Victor Janko. Again I regretted not transferring him to the psych ward. Then it hit me—*if I'd gotten him out of his cell before last night, the guard wouldn't have destroyed Victor's art work. This tragedy would never have happened.*

After one lap, I'd had it with the exercise and introspection. I was feeling even worse.

I returned to my car, and put my khaki pants on over my running shorts. There was only one thing left to do—go back to the penitentiary and clear out my desk.

At the nurses' station Nurse Rachit said Dr. Caldwell wanted to see me right away.

When I opened the door, he was at his desk sucking on an unfilled pipe. It sounded like a dentist's saliva extractor. "'Morning," he said brightly.

"Hello, Ben."

"I quit smoking again," he said. "I think I can tolerate the loss of nicotine, as long as I don't give up the oral gratification."

"Are you wearing the patch?"

"No," Ben replied. "I'm taking Zyban this time."

"That's the same as Wellbutrin, isn't it?"

"Yes."

"So . . . it's an anti-depressant."

"Yes," Ben said.

"How's it working?"

"Well, I still miss tobacco," he answered. "But I'm not depressed about it."

Ben grinned. Ordinarily I would have laughed. I only managed a nod.

"David, I want to discuss your resignation."

"There's nothing to discuss."

"Okay, okay," Ben said, "I won't try to talk you out of it. But I wonder could you do me a favor? Just hang on for a couple weeks till I find a replacement. Otherwise I'll be really short-handed."

"I wouldn't be much help."

"Look, it's only fair. I believe two weeks notice is the customary deal."

"I don't want to hang you up," I said. "But I'd be useless."

"You're wrong, David. You've done a great job with the men around here. Just because the Janko situation didn't work out . . ."

"It was my fault."

"You're being awfully hard on yourself."

"No, I'm not," I responded firmly. "The truth is—I've been completely irresponsible."

"Come on, David," Ben said. "Why are you judging yourself so harshly?"

I didn't answer him.

"You're carrying some extra baggage," Ben said.

I averted my eyes.

"Why did you come here, anyway?" Ben asked.

"Pardon me?"

"To the State Penitentiary?" Ben said, pressing me. "Why didn't you go into private practice?"

"What does that have to do with anything?"

"Look, David," he said. "Thirty years ago, when I was starting out, African-American psychiatrists were not exactly . . . in demand. When I finished my training, I decided I should at least try to go into private practice. So I opened an office on Park Avenue . . . Park Avenue and 125th Street. Well, I soon found out Harlem wasn't ready for shrinks then, even black ones, and my practice went belly-up within a year. I ended up here because it was the best job I could find, and it offered me a measure of security. Now, it turned out to be the perfect job for me. But you—you've got a whole world of opportunity open to you. What made you choose a place like this?"

"Like I said in our interview—I thought I could do some good up here."

"You can do good in lots of places," Ben said. "And make plenty of money doing it."

"I don't look at medical care as a commodity—something you sell at the highest possible price."

"So you don't think doctors should be paid well for their work?"

"I didn't say that."

"You think treating poor, disenfranchised convicts makes you a better person? A better doctor?"

"I didn't say that either." I was getting angry.

Ben spoke harshly. "Maybe you took this job because you can't hack it in the real world. But up here in the slammer, you're surrounded by 'the dregs of humanity; misfits and losers.' And next to them, you almost feel like you've got your shit together."

He stared accusingly, but I said nothing.

"That's it, isn't it?" Ben said. "You came up here to run away."

"Jesus Christ," I shouted. "You sound just like my father."

"I do?"

"He said I was running away, too," I said. "I can still hear him; 'You've taken a job in the hoosegow? When are you going to start acting like a grown-up?' Then he accused me of behaving like some 'idealistic hippie running off to join the Peace Corps'—as if that were the ultimate insult."

"You're sounding a bit rebellious, David. Maybe coming up here was your way of pissing your father off."

"I didn't come to Vanderkill to piss anybody off," I said. "I came up here to do a job."

"Doing what?"

"Being a doctor. It just turns out I'm no fucking good at it."

"You are good at it," Ben responded. "But you're lousy at facing your problems and putting them in perspective. You've done some fine things up here; but you don't see that. All you see are your mistakes. Okay, so you mishandled some aspects of the Victor Janko case. What makes you think you've always got to be perfect? Jesus, the first time you mess up, you act like you've committed a major . . ."

"It's not the first time."

"What do you mean?"

"It's not . . ." I caught myself.

"What do you mean, 'it's not the first time?'"

I didn't want to answer. I'd been repressing the memories for so long, to dredge them up now and talk about them was too painful.

But I always knew this day would come, when I could no longer keep the past bottled up because the pain of hiding it would be worse than the pain of letting it out.

I looked at Ben, then spoke with difficulty.

"Last year," I said. "When I was finishing my residency . . ." I paused. "There was this woman . . . Melissa."

"Who was she?"

"A patient . . . at Bellevue."

Ben looked at me intently but showed no reaction. "You want to tell me about it?"

I recognized that tone—the same neutrality I used with my patients.

"I . . . I was treating Melissa for depression," I said in a pained voice. "In our sessions, she was always overtly seductive. She wore tight blouses . . . a button open that should have been closed . . . high-heeled shoes, short skirts, anything to call attention to her body . . ."

An image of Daisy flashed in my mind.

"Melissa's favorite thing," I continued, "was giving me these vivid, almost pornographic descriptions of her sexual activities—sex with men in public places, group sex, masturbation with strange objects, lesbian encounters. I think a lot them were fantasies she made up to turn me on. And I have to admit . . . sometimes she really got to me."

I stopped, feeling ashamed.

"Okay," Ben said. "A little counter-transference. Happens to the best of us."

"There's more," I said. "At one session she laid it on the line—saying she knew I was attracted to her, I was just fighting it. Then she said let's do it . . . right there in my office. I did my best to, y'know, reject the idea without rejecting the patient. But when I said no, she got furious and stormed out."

"What happened after that?"

"That night she called me at home and apologized. Then she asked me to come over to her apartment . . . saying she desperately needed someone to talk to. She said her roommate was out for the night, and she was terribly lonely and depressed. I told her I'd see her in my office the next morning. She burst into tears, and warned me that if I didn't come over, she was afraid she might kill herself. She kept begging me. . . . I'll never forget her voice crying out *please . . . please . . . please*. I told her she was strong woman, strong enough to cope, and that she should just relax—maybe take a warm bath, try to get some sleep."

I took a deep breath. "The next morning," I said. "Her roommate found her in the bathtub. She'd cut open her wrists with a razor blade."

My eyes got teary. Ben looked at me with compassion. "It must have been tough for you."

"I let her down," I said in a choked voice. "I could have helped her."

"How?"

"I could have listened to her more carefully . . . heard how much she was hurting, her desperation. And I could have gone over to see her. But I was afraid of her seductiveness . . . and my own desires."

"You did the right thing," Ben said. "It would have been inappropriate to go to her."

"But I should have recognized that her suicide threat was real," I said. "If I weren't so hung up on my own problems I would've seen that. I could've taken some kind of action—told her to meet me somewhere else, like a coffee shop . . . or had her hospitalized. "

"David," Ben said. "You had no way of knowing she'd act out. Hell, around here guys are always threatening to kill themselves. Most of the time it's bullshit. Once in a while it's not. You try to make the right call, but you're really just guessing. Like I told you—predicting dangerous behavior is impossible. "

"It can't be impossible."

"Predicting anything is impossible," Ben asserted, raising his voice for the first time. "All you can do is make your best guess. We don't know what's going to happen tomorrow, or even in the next five minutes. Do we?"

I didn't answer.

"So what makes you think you can predict anything as complex and mysterious as an act of impulsive violence?"

I nodded, acknowledging his logic. Ben spoke in an empathetic tone. "You feel guilty about Melissa, don't you?"

"Of course."

"That may have a lot to do with why you took this job," Ben said. He paused, then said softly—"What I'm suggesting is—you sent yourself to prison . . . for punishment."

Then he rephrased it. "You didn't come here to serve *people*," he said. "You came here to serve *time*."

Ben's statement stunned me.

"And there was an added benefit," he went on. "No female patients."

Yeah, but I didn't let that stop me. If I couldn't find a female patient, I'd just get involved with a male patient's girlfriend.

I wasn't sure what to say, so I was grateful when there was a knock on the office door.

"Dr. Caldwell," came the nasal voice of Nurse Rachit. "I need to talk to you. It's about Victor Janko."

I indicated I didn't mind the interruption.

"Come in, Flora," Ben called out.

"Mr. Janko's awake now," she said. "You want me to keep him sedated?"

Ben picked up his pipe, polished the bowl with his thumb, then turned to me.

"He needs to be looked at," Ben said. "You want to do it, or should I?"

The idea of coming face-to-face with Victor made me very anxious.

"David," Ben said. "Janko doesn't know me that well. I think a familiar face . . ."

"You're right," I said.

I got up and went to the door. "David," Ben said. "You *are* gonna give me the two weeks?"

I nodded a reluctant yes.

I followed the nurse to Victor's room. On the way she told me I'd had a phone call from a Dr. Wang.

My meeting with Victor was brief. After the trauma of the previous night, Victor had completely withdrawn. He lay in bed, eyes closed, silent. I told him I knew it was Stevie Karp who'd slashed his paintings, hoping he'd respond. Victor only sighed and turned his face to the wall.

I told the day nurse sedation wasn't necessary but prescribed Ativan in divided doses, which would take the edge off his anxiety and depression.

I went back to my office and returned Dr. Wang's call. He said Shelly was much better, she'd had taken food this morning. She could go home today.

Whew.

I told him I'd pick her up at 6:30.

I gently placed Shelly into her vivarium. I'd changed the water, and the sand and the pebbles. I opened the bag of organic turtle wafers Wang had given me, and placed one in her dish. The vet told me the wafers had been developed at Oklahoma State U. and that the red color and slightly fruity scent really appealed to box turtles.

Maybe so, but Shelly turned up her nose and walked away. I picked her up and put her on my forearm, expecting her to take a little walk. She took a tiny nip out of a red arm hair, then pulled her head into her shell.

She'd seemed lively enough at Wang's office, but now she was spacing out again. Maybe it was the change of environment. I put her back in the box, and gave her a good talking to.

"Hey, girl. Don't do me this way. You know I'm only minding you for little Henry Simpkins. What happens if the kid gets better and comes home looking for you? Okay, okay, I know it's a long shot but hey—ya never know. So you can't flake out on me. Now, whatever's messin' up your turtle system—*Get Over It*.

"Say what? Don't gimme any back-talk. Just shut up and eat your wafer."

I scratched her shell affectionately, and then went out to the Silver Streak for dinner.

Chapter 27

"**They're** *what?*" I exclaimed. I was sitting in Ben's office the next afternoon, when Father Toussenel stuck his head in the door.

"They're getting married," he said. "Daisy called me this morning. She and Victor want me to perform the ceremony."

"Don't we have to be consulted?" I asked Ben.

"No," Ben said. "They have to apply to the Warden's office, but it's just *pro forma*. See, the law can't forbid marriage between cons and free citizens. It would be a violation of their civil rights."

"When did Daisy and Victor decide this?" I asked Father Toussenel.

"Last night. On the phone."

This is a bad idea. Victor shouldn't take a step like this—not now when he's still fragile and in shock from everything that's happened. And as far as Daisy's concerned, why the hell does she suddenly want to marry Victor?

"I think this is a big mistake," I said.

"I agree," Father Toussenel said. "As you know, I believe Victor Janko is evil and extremely dangerous.

"Did you try to talk Daisy out of it?" I asked.

179

"As best I could," Father Toussenel said. "I reminded her it'll be five years before there's even a possibility of parole, and that given this violent episode, Victor's chances are slim to none."

"What did she say?"

The priest spoke with disdain. "She explained the marriage is more symbolic than anything else, that after everything Victor's been through, he needs the reassurance of her commitment and her love. And she's willing to give it."

"True love," Ben said cynically. "How ya gonna argue with that?"

"Are you going to perform the ceremony?" I asked the priest.

"It's my duty."

"When's this gonna go down?"

"Thursday. It'll take three days for the paperwork to get done. The wedding'll be at the prison chapel."

"So basically," I said. "All three of us think this is a bad idea. But there's nothing we can do to stop them."

"I don't think it's necessarily a bad idea," Ben said, "'though I do think it's ridiculous. But it can't cause any real harm. If it cheers Victor up, that's good. If the girl has some misguided martyr complex, and this makes her feel virtuous, so be it."

"What about their conjugal visits?" the priest asked. "Victor will be alone with Daisy, in a trailer without TV surveillance. He might . . ."

"They won't get conjugal visits," Ben said. "Janko's still considered an Ad Seg inmate. They'll be allowed contact visitations; in fact their first one will be right after the ceremony, their honeymoon if you will. But there's a video camera in that room. Janko couldn't get a weapon past the metal detectors, and if he tried to get violent some other way, the guards would see it on the monitor, and be there in a flash."

"I still don't like this," I said.

"Look," Ben responded, "There's really nothing we can do. Except, of course, David, if you want to try and convince Janko to change his mind."

"That's a good idea," I said. "I'll go talk to him now."

As I walked down the hall I heard that "Margaritaville" song going around in my head again—"*Some people say that there's a woman to blame / But I know . . . it's my own damn fault.*"

I found Victor sitting in a chair, reading *National Geographic*. He was calm and in excellent spirits, greeting me with an amiable "Hi."

He said he'd never been so happy in his life, and even made a bit of a joke, saying Daisy had "finally popped the question." Then, before I could express my misgivings, Victor made a request.

"Dr. Rothberg," he said. "Do you think you could come to the wedding? I mean you're like the only friend I got. And you, well, y'know . . . you believe in me."

I couldn't say no. I thought of suggesting Victor postpone the nuptials, but I knew he wouldn't go for it.

"Oh, and listen to this neat idea," he said. "Daisy's gotta have a wedding bouquet, so I'm gonna surprise her by calling the flower store and having them send over a big bunch of daisies. What do you think of that? Daisies for Daisy."

"That sounds great, Victor." I congratulated him and left.

At the end of the day, I walked across the prison yard. It was deserted and there was a surreal, exaggerated emptiness to the place. The looming concrete walls were grim reminders of what incarceration really meant; the abrogation of all personal freedom, the separation from the outside world, the total acquiescence of the captive to his captors. If, as Ben suggested, I'd taken the job at Vanderkill to punish myself, I'd sure chosen the right environment.

But at least I can leave whenever I want. Not like the men confined here, locked up in cages, yearning for freedom, dreaming of escape. . . .

Uh-oh. What if Daisy's come up with some elaborate escape plan for Victor. I wouldn't put it past her. Yes, that would explain this wedding. The wedding ceremony might give them an opportunity—the prison chapel can't possibly be as secure as Ad Seg, or even the hospi-

tal. The room where they'd have contact visitation might be inadequately guarded. Or . . . do they have some other scheme?

Maybe Daisy has convinced Victor escape would be a solution to all their problems, but I know it would be a disaster. They have to be stopped.

Chapter 28

The next morning I saw bubbles coming from Shelly's mouth. I called Dr. Wang, but the machine picked up. I decided to drive over there anyway.

I'd run out of Baggies, and while I was looking for something to transport Shelly in, there was a knock on the door.

"Maid service."

It was Mom (Mrs. Incaviglia) with her cart full of cleaning stuff. She was a mousy, graying woman whose kind eyes had bruise colored circles beneath them. I told her what the problem was and she handed me a disposable plastic shower cap.

"Thanks," I said. "This'll be perfect."

"Sorry she's sick. Such a cute turtle," she said. "My husband don't allow no pets, but I din't tell him."

"I appreciate that."

I poked holes in the shower cap, picked up Shelly and took her out to the car. The interior was blazing hot, so I put on the A/C and we waited till it cooled down inside.

Then I put her on the seat and returned to the room to get my shoulder bag. When I entered, I saw Mom bending over Shelly's vivarium. She had a squirt bottle of glass cleaner, and was scrubbing the inside of the turtle box's glass window. I could smell the ammonia clear across the room.

"*Stop*," I yelled. She looked up startled.

"That stuff is poison to turtles."

"Oh, I'm so sorry. I din't know. . . ."

"I think that's what's been making her sick."

"I'll wash the box out for you."

"No. No. I'll do it. Do me a favor—come back later, huh?"

"Oh, sure."

"And no more chemicals of any kind in this room. Promise?"

"Dust. I'll only dust."

"Thanks," I said. "Oh, and could you leave me a trash bag?"

When she left I poured the pebbles and dirt from Shelly's habitat into the plastic bag and put it outside the door. Then I took off my clothes and carried the turtle box into the shower with me. For a long time I let the hot water pour down on it, flushing away all chemical contaminants.

Afterwards, I filled the box with new dirt and pebbles, fresh water, and a wafer. Then I dressed and went out to get Shelly.

She took a small nibble of the wafer; a good sign. And there were no bubbles forming at her mouth. She was going to be okay.

Feeling relieved, I left her there and drove to the prison.

I went to the contact visitation room to check out its security. It was located near the visitor's entrance, making escape a lot more feasible. When I asked a guard about it, he laughed and said no way. Still, I had my doubts.

I went up to the third floor to look at the prison chapel, but the door was locked. Later I talked to Father Toussenel and he said that besides the door, the stained glass window was the only way out and it had iron bars over it.

I voiced my concerns to Ben Caldwell. He said not to worry; since the new high tech security system had been installed fifteen years ago, nobody had escaped from Vanderkill.

"But if it'll make you feel better," he said, "we'll put Janko in leg shackles. How's that?"

Chaining up a man at his own wedding seemed dehumanizing. But, given the possible danger . . . "Okay," I said grimly.

"Well, look at it this way," Ben said joking, "marriage is often referred to as 'the ol' ball-and-chain.'"

I smiled, without humor.

Chapter 29

It was Thursday, the day of the wedding. I got to the chapel a little before noon. Ben was with me—he was required to witness the marriage ceremony.

The chapel had a makeshift quality. The pews were plain wooden benches, their kneelers covered with torn vinyl padding. The walls were a nondescript beige, and the fluorescent lighting did little to set a mood for worship and prayerful contemplation.

There was a coin-operated vending machine next to the front door selling electrical votive candles: Large five day candles—$5.00, Small two hour candles—50 cents. There were several shrines against the side walls of the chapel, where a number of "candles" had been placed; the shrines were cardtables draped with black felt cloth, with garish portraits of the saints hung above them.

Two cleaning women were at work; one on her knees, scrubbing the floor, the other polishing the three-foot tall ornate bronze candleholders which flanked the altar. Ben approached the floor scrubber. "Ma'am," he said, "I know you've got a job to do but . . ."

The woman stood up and gave him a timid, apologetic look.

"*Dispensame, señor,*" she said. "*No hablamos Inglés . . . no Engleesh . . .*"

Ben nodded. "*Ustedes no pueden trabajar ahora,*" he said. "*Va a haber un matrimonio.*"

I'd never studied Spanish, but being a native New Yorker and working in a municipal hospital I'd learned enough to understand— Ben had told the women to stop working because of the upcoming wedding.

The other cleaning lady had come over to us. "*¿Podemos observar?*" she asked.

"You wanna watch? Fine with me," Ben said. He pointed to the pews; the women smiled and took seats.

Ben and I sat down in front of them. The altar was, like the shrines, a table draped in black felt. Behind it was a stained glass window. I couldn't see what it depicted at first, because the window was grimy from years of neglect, and the iron bars obscured it.

But after a while, I recognized a crucifixion; I could make out the garnet colored blood running from the hands, feet, and chest of the Savior. Then I saw the crudely lettered sign tacked onto the cross above His head. That image had puzzled me from the day I first saw it as a ten-year-old. When I transferred to Our Lady of Martyrs Academy, I was given a laminated prayer card with a crucifixion on it. It showed the mysterious sign over the head of Our Lord. It read: INRI. When I asked the priest, he explained only that it was Latin. I kept pressing him, till finally he told me it was Latin for "King of the Jews." I thought that was cool, because at age ten I hadn't yet grasped the concept that Jesus Christ was Jewish. But I couldn't figure out how INRI could possibly mean King of the Jews, even after the two semesters of Latin the school required. It was only years later at Harvard, when I asked my Comparative Religions professor.

"Oh," she said, "it's an abbreviation; *Iesus Nazarenus Rex Iudaeorum . . .* Jesus of Nazareth, King of the Jews." She explained that the Roman soldiers had stuck the sign up on the cross, to mock their victim. I smiled, remembering my exhilaration at solving the INRI mystery . . .

Victor Janko entered the chapel, accompanied by the guard Brian Cacciatti. Victor's leg shackles clanked as he walked, giving him an odd, shuffling gait. *At least they didn't make him wear handcuffs.* He had on neatly pressed army pants, a blue workshirt, and a tie I'd lent him, because, as he'd said, "I gotta look sharp." When the groom saw me, he smiled and waved. I nodded.

Then the bride entered, with Father Toussenel by her side. Daisy was wearing a simple, white suit and white leather pumps. Her blond hair, still a mass of disorderly curls, cascaded down her back. I checked her fingernails. She'd finally painted them a traditional color — red. Daisy didn't look at me. In her arms she carried a large bridal bouquet, the daisies Victor had sent her.

Father Toussenel, attired in a purple robe with an embroidered golden yoke, instructed the couple to stand opposite each other in front of the altar. The guard stood off to one side. The priest reached under the altar-table, picked up a Panasonic boom box, and placed it on a chair. He pushed the "Play" button and I recognized J. S. Bach's *First Prelude* from "The Well Tempered Clavier." After a while, a clear soprano voice began singing over it, and her melodic "*Ave Maria*" harmonized beautifully with the Bach. I was glad it was the Bach-Gounod version, and not Franz Schubert's lugubrious, sappy setting; "Ahh . . . vay — mah . . . ree . . . eee . . . ahh . . ."

Oy vey Maria.

The priest lowered the volume on the cassette player. Then he crossed and stood between the couple. He got right down to business.

"Victor," he said. "Do you take Daisy to be your wife? Do you promise to be true to her in good times and bad, in sickness and in health, to love her and honor her all the days of your life?"

"I do," Victor answered solemnly.

"And Daisy," the priest went on, "do you take Victor to be your husband? Do you promise to be true to him in good times and in bad, in sickness and in health, to love and honor him all the days of your life?"

"I do."

Father Toussenel hesitated. He reached into the pocket of his robe, searching for something. Not finding it, he started rummaging in his pockets beneath the robe. Meanwhile, I heard the two women behind us, whispering.

"¡Ay, que linda novia!"

"Si, pero ¿por qué ella carga margaritas?"

"Yo no se."

I didn't get what they were saying. My attention was on the priest, who'd found the small prayer book he was looking for and began to read aloud. It was part of the traditional Roman Catholic marriage rites, but to me the words sounded creepy.

"Children," Father Toussenel began, "be correct in your judgment of what pleases the Lord. Take no part in vain deeds done in darkness; rather condemn them. It is shameful even to mention these things people do in secret, but when such deeds are condemned, they are seen in the light of day, and all that appears is light. . . ."

I suddenly realized what the cleaning women had said—"¡Ay, qué linda novia!" . . . Oh, what a pretty bride . . .

The priest was droning on. "That is why we read: Awake o sleeper, arise from the dead, and that will give you light . . ."

"Pero ¿por qué ella carga margaritas?" . . . But why is she . . . why is she carrying . . . daisies? My God, margarita is the Spanish word for daisy. Daisy is . . . MARGARITA, THE MURDERED WOMAN'S DAUGHTER.

"You have declared your consent before the Church . . ." the priest was saying.

I jumped to my feet. "Stop," I shouted. "I know who you are, Margarita."

Daisy's body froze. Then she reached into her bouquet of daisies, and drew out a long kitchen knife. She raised it in the air and lurched towards Victor. I sprung forward, reaching for Daisy, as she plunged the knife down at the stunned bridegroom. I managed to seize her arm and jerk it away from her victim. I wrapped my other arm around her, and held her firmly. Victor tried to back away, but with his leg-chains he stumbled and fell.

Daisy was struggling in my grasp with maniacal strength. She began shouting at Victor. *"You have to die . . . An eye for an eye. You have to die . . . An eye for an eye."* The words were sing-song, like a demented nursery rhyme.

Daisy kicked back with her high-heeled pump and caught me on the shin. The sharp pain caused me to let her go, but by now Brian Cacciatti had grabbed her. He tried to pry the knife out of her hand, while she shouted at Victor, *"You have to die . . . An eye for an eye. You have to die . . ."*

The guard gave her a backhand slap across her face. Daisy dropped the knife and fell to the floor. Cacciatti twisted her onto her belly, wrenched her hands behind her and snapped on handcuffs.

Victor called over to her. "Why, Daisy?" he asked softly. "Why did you do this?"

"I saw you . . ." she said hoarsely, still in a fury. *"You were the one, Victor . . . the man who killed my mother."*

Her eyes glared at him.

"No, No," Victor cried out. "It wasn't me. I didn't do it. Just ask Dr. Rothberg."

"Liar," she raged.

"It wasn't me. Daisy, I love you. I love you. . . ."

Ben was kneeling next to the handcuffed bride. "We'll have to get her to the hospital," he said. "Brian, gimme a hand."

They hauled Daisy to her feet. She looked at Victor and released a howl out of her primal depths; the sound echoed around the chapel walls like a cry of the damned. Then her body sagged and her eyes closed. The guard lifted her in his arms and carried her away.

Ben and I went back to Victor. He was sitting on the floor with the bouquet of daisies in his arms. He was slack-mouthed and staring into space.

I saw Daisy's knife on the floor and knelt down to look at it. It was a Kyocera ceramic cook's knife with a plastic handle.

No problem with the metal detector.

Chapter 30

Daisy was placed under observation at Capital District Psychiatric Center in Albany, and would presumably be prosecuted for attempted murder. If her lawyer went with an insanity defense, I knew I'd be called to testify on her behalf.

I phoned Albany and spoke to Dr. Anvita Kapoor, who was treating Daisy. I gave Dr. Kapoor a rundown on the events leading to Daisy's attempt on Victor's life. I said I felt she was clearly psychotic, and witnessing her mother's murder as a child had surely scarred her with profound Post Traumatic Stress Disorder.

"PTSD sounds right," Dr. Kapoor said. "We've got her sedated now, but we'll ease her out of it in a few days and see how it goes."

"Ring me anytime if you have questions."

"I will, Doctor Rothberg. Thanks for calling."

I now saw the extent and complexity of Daisy's hidden agenda. At first, she was hoping for Victor's parole, so she could kill him on the outside. When that began to look unlikely, she tried to get contact visitation, figuring she'd stab him in the visitation room. When I turned her down on that, she decided to marry him, and kill him during their "honeymoon" in the visitation room. And when I exposed her during the marriage ceremony, she desperately tried to kill him on the spot.

She had no concern about being caught. Her obsessive revenge was all that mattered.

I should've guessed sooner. I wish I'd paid more attention to "Margaritaville," the song playing like a loop in my brain. I knew Daisy was disturbed and dangerous, but in the end I guess she proved Ben's contention — it's impossible to predict dangerous behavior.

The police had me accompany them to Daisy's apartment, to help them understand what brought her to this act of vengeance. Among her things we found a clipping of Victor's painting in *Newsweek*, a bundle of pen-pal letters from him, and her address book, containing the phone number of her parents in Akron, Ohio.

I jotted down the number and later called them from my office. Her father Mike answered, and when I expressed sympathy for his daughter, he told me she was always a weirdo. I asked about her name-change, and he explained they'd adopted the little girl in New York, at age five. The social worker told them Margarita was Spanish for Daisy, and a year later, when they moved to Ohio, they decided to change it — maybe it would help her forget the Baby Carriage Killer stuff. Also, Mr. Lesczcynski said, they weren't too happy about her having a Spic name.

I hung up, and thought about Daisy's accusation — *You were the one, Victor . . . the man who killed my mother.*

To Ben and the priest, I'm sure Daisy's statement was an affirmation of Victor's guilt.

But I believe she was mistaken. Daisy/Margarita was only two years old when the murder took place, and her memory would've surely been clouded by time. Besides, the NYPD report stated the apartment was dark. All the little girl could've seen was a shadowy figure.

I began to type on my computer.

My main concern now is Victor, who's in very bad shape. I've looked in on him daily, but he's always in bed; either sleeping or in a state of torpor. I've tried to engage him in conversation, but he's withdrawn into his self-protective shell. He doesn't even do his whistling.

Ben says he can't keep Victor in the hospital indefinitely; which means at some point he'll be returned to Ad Seg, back into Stevie Karp's clutches.

The next day I went to see the warden. Warden Carmichael was a tall scrawny man with a gray brush cut. He wore an ill fitting three-piece suit on a ninety degree day. I told him about Karp's abuse, and he said without proof there wasn't much he could do. And if I brought charges, the union would get into it and they were a real pain. I asked if he could at least transfer Karp out of Ad Seg, and he said he'd think about it. I knew right away that meant no.

Later Ben told me Carmichael and Karp were asshole buddies who go deerhunting together and have a weekly poker game. So I was wasting my time, which he could've told me if I'd discussed it with him beforehand.

There's only one thing I can do for Victor—get him the hell out of this place. The only way I can do that is by proving he didn't kill Agnes Rivera.

But how can I prove a negative? By finding out who the real killer is. That's the key—prove Victor's innocence by nailing the man who's guilty.

But how?

Then the doubt crept in. All I had was a newspaper photo, and my gut feeling that Victor was innocent.

What if I'm wrong?

When I left for the day, I could see Kim Cavanagh sitting at the nurse's station. I stopped to gather my thoughts.

Then I walked up to her desk.

"Hiya, Kim. Listen . . . I owe you an apology."

She looked at me without warmth. "For what?"

"For . . . being rude and insensitive."

"Actually," she said, "I owe you an apology. I was expecting more than I should've. But . . . it's not a problem."

"No. No. I've been thoughtless and . . ."

"I said it's not a problem."

"There's just been a lot going on, and I guess. . . ."

"There's always a lot going on around here, Doctor," she said coolly. "Look—I'm not mad at you. You saved my life and believe me, I appreciate it. We had a nice dinner together, two co-workers—doctor and nurse. Let's keep it that way. Now, nurse to doctor—is there anything I can do for you?"

"Well," I said. "I am concerned about Victor Janko. Could you keep an eye on him tonight?"

"Yes, Doctor."

"If he can't sleep, you can let him have some Ambien."

"10 mg?"

"Yes."

As she wrote my instructions down in a book, she spoke.

"I heard what you did at Victor Janko's wedding," She looked up. "You, uh . . . saving people's lives seems to be your *thing*."

I smiled and said I had to get going.

As I rode down in the elevator I got an idea.

Flowers. I'll send her flowers.

Chapter 31

The following day after work, I waited till 8:00, when I knew Kim came on duty. Then I shouldered my laptop bag and went down to the nurses' station.

"Got your flowers . . . apology accepted," she said. "But what I said still goes. Doctor to nurse—that's it."

"Agreed," I said. "Oh, by the way, I read that Internet stuff on the Checker Cab Club. It was great. I joined."

"Good."

"Now . . . doctor to nurse," I said. "Did Victor Janko sleep last night?"

"Not much. He shook off the Ambien like it was baby aspirin. Every time I checked on him his eyes were open, staring at the ceiling. You want to double the meds?"

"Nah. It'll just fog him up even more."

"Looks to me like he's sliding into Major Depressive Disorder."

Correct diagnosis. Impressive.

"There's something you don't know about Victor," I said.

"What's that?"

"I think he's innocent. I don't believe he killed that woman."

"He's . . . not the Baby Carriage Killer?"

I gave Kim a short version of Victor's story. I finished by showing her the *New York Post* photo of Leo Hagopian.

"So," she said, examining the picture closely, "under this guy's headcloth you say there are scratch marks . . . caused by the finger-nails of the woman he killed?"

"That's right," I answered. "And that Band-Aid on his chin is where Victor slashed him.

Kim studied the photograph again. "If there are scratches on this guy's forehead," she said, "I think you may have something."

"What do you mean?"

"You ever hear of *Advocates for the Innocent?*" she asked.

"I'm not sure."

"I was watching 'Court TV'—'the Felony Channel'—and they showed a documentary about this group of lawyers and investigators, who work to get falsely convicted people out of prison."

"Oh, yes."

"One of their cases was this guy doing life in Dannemora for killing a woman after having forced oral sex with her. Ten years later they dug up her body and found traces of semen on her teeth. Using DNA testing, they proved it didn't belong to the prisoner, and he was set free."

I looked at her with great interest.

"I'm thinking," she went on, "if the murdered woman scratched her killer, tiny particles of his skin would still be under her finger-nails. If you could get the body exhumed, maybe the DNA would prove Victor didn't do it."

"Kim," I said appreciatively, "I think that's a great idea."

She nodded.

"Where are these Advocate people?" I asked.

"I think they have offices in New York."

"The other thing I need to do," I said, "is find Leo Hagopian."

"That may not be too easy."

"Yeah. Who knows if he's even alive?"

"I'll get on the phone and call National 411," she said. "Find out if he's listed anywhere in the country."

"Thanks," I said. "I'll go talk to Victor."

I walked down to Victor's room and found him in his usual position, lying in bed on his back. He didn't respond to my greeting. I told him I had something he'd find interesting. He reacted by closing his eyes.

I took out the picture of Leo Hagopian. "Victor," I said aggressively, "I want you to look at this picture."

Victor opened his eyes and put on his glasses. It took him a few seconds to focus. Then his expression became animated. "That's him," he said. "The guy in the sweatshirt. The guy who attacked me."

"Right."

"When was this taken?" Victor asked.

"At the murdered woman's funeral. His name is Leo Hagopian. Does that name mean anything to you?"

" . . . No."

"Victor," I said. "I'm going to try and find him. But I need your help. Can you tell me anything about him? Does this picture bring back any memories, anything you haven't told me?"

"Um . . . no," Victor said apologetically. "How . . . how are you going to prove he did it?"

"There's an organization called Advocates for the Innocent . . . are you familiar with DNA?"

"It's . . . what we're all made out of, right?"

"Yes. The killer's genetic material might still be on the body of the victim. Which may prove you didn't do it."

"But this guy . . . what's-his-name? . . . Leo. You don't know where he is?"

"No," I answered.

Victor looked worried. "Gee, he could be anywhere, couldn't he? And what if he, like, doesn't want to be found?"

"It could be a problem."

Victor's body suddenly slumped. He shook his head sadly. "Ah, what's the difference?" he said. "Daisy's gone. I'll never see her again. Nothing . . . nothing matters any more."

"It matters to me, Victor. I promise you, I'll do my best to find Hagopian.

"Might as well try to look for a needle in a haystack."

"It's really not that hard to find a needle in a haystack," I said. "All you need is a magnet."

"Doctor," he said. "What did they do with Daisy?"

"She's in a hospital in Albany."

"Is it . . . y'know, a hospital like this?"

"More or less."

"What's gonna happen to her?"

"Hard to say at this point."

Victor shook his head sadly and lay back down on the bed. Glasses off, eyes closed.

I went down to the nurses' station. Kim said she'd struck out with Leo Hagopian—he wasn't listed anywhere.

"Well," I said, "there's gotta be a way to track him down. Meanwhile, I should contact Advocates for the Innocent; find out how they work, get their opinion on this case. I'll call them first thing tomorrow."

She handed me a note paper with the number on it.

She's good.

"Thanks, Kim," I said. "You've really been a big help."

"No problem," she responded, "at least we made a start."

She used the W word.

Chapter 32

My call to Advocates for the Innocent was answered by an attorney, Laura Hecht, whose languid Southern drawl belied the fact that she was knowledgeable and dedicated.

After I laid out the Victor Janko situation, she wasn't optimistic. First of all, she said, it was difficult to get a body exhumed, and second even if the DNA under the victim's fingernails wasn't Janko's, that wouldn't prove Victor was innocent. All it would prove was that she didn't scratch him. You couldn't overturn a conviction based on that.

"But I know who the killer is," I said. "The DNA will belong to Leo Hagopian."

"Same deal," she replied. "All it would prove was that he was scratched by the victim. Hagopian was the woman's boyfriend, right?"

"Ex-boyfriend, I believe."

"Doesn't matter. He knew her, so he could claim he saw her earlier in the day, and she scratched him—durin' an argument or whatever. It would be hard to prove otherwise."

"So I have no case?"

"I can't see much of one," she replied. "You'd need Hagopian's DNA on the murder weapon. But even if . . ."

"Wait a minute," I said, interrupting her. "Hagopian's blood *is* on the knife. Victor Janko slashed him with it, when he struggled with him after the murder."

"With his blood you'd definitely have somethin'," the lawyer said. "Then if we exhumed the body and the skin under the victim's fingernails was his, you'd have powerful corroborating evidence."

"Sounds encouraging."

"But what I wanted to tell you," she said, "is you'd have a problem obtainin' Hagopian's DNA. See, you can't force someone to give a genetic sample just 'cause you think he did somethin' wrong. It violates his constitutional rights—unlawful search and seizure. He'd simply refuse to submit to DNA testin'."

I sighed in frustration.

"This guy Hagopian," the lawyer said, "is he by any chance a convict, or an ex-convict?"

"I don't know. Possibly."

"'Cause New York State has a DNA database of all prisoners and parolees with violent felony convictions. So they may have his genetic profile."

"I'll look into it."

"But they only started doin' DNA testin' in '92," she cautioned me. "So if he was released before that, they'd have nothin'."

"I understand," I said.

"There's another issue. We don't know where the murder weapon is. How long ago was this crime committed?"

"Fifteen years."

"That's not real good," she said. "After conviction, the police usually hold evidence for a while, pendin' appeal. But if there is none, eventually they get rid of it."

She paused for a moment. "There's one hope, though. It was a high profile case, so the knife may still be stored in the property room at One Police Plaza. But the system's kinda slipshod. Every so often, someone up there decides to do some house-cleanin', and they throw out a lot of stuff. I sure wouldn't count on findin' it."

"How do I check on that?"

"Why don't I do it," she said. "They know me. I'm always pesterin' 'em to dig up stuff. Every year I give the property clerk an extravagant Christmas present . . . cash money."

"I'd sure appreciate that," I said. "How long you think it'll take?"

"I'll get right on it."

When I tried to thank her she cut me off, saying "My secretary will take your contact numbers; phone, fax, e-mail. Hold on, I'll transfer you."

There were a few beeps, then her secretary, Max, got on the line and took down the info.

I called Kim during my lunch break and asked if she wouldn't mind coming in early, because I needed her help.

She arrived around six. I asked if she could access the database containing all men who'd been incarcerated in New York State. She said it was on the nurses' station computer. Since I wanted it done right away, Kim told the day nurse she'd take over for her. Nurse Rachit was delighted to go home early. "You're a doll," she said.

"No problem."

Flora turned to me. "Did you get your fax?"

"No."

"Oh," she said. "It came in late this afternoon, while you were in the middle of Group. I didn't want to disturb you."

She went to the fax machine, picked up a two-page document and handed it to me. I saw the logo on the cover-sheet; AFTI—*Advocates for the Innocent.*

The fax read: *You caught a break. Last year the NYPD decided to auction off evidence from famous murder cases to collectors of crime memorabilia. Apparently there's a big market for this stuff—they sold such goodies as Son of Sam's .44 caliber pistol, a black cape worn dur-*

ing a murder by Salvador "Capeman" Agron, the gasoline can used by
Julio Gonzalez to incinerate eighty-seven people at the Happy Land
Social Club, and . . . the Baby Carriage Killer's kitchen knife. The
weapon is now in the hands of a collector, Mervyn Pratt of Bayside,
Queens. I called Mr. Pratt, and he said he'd be happy to provide the
knife if it's needed for evidence. He hopes we can reopen the Janko case
because it would jack up the value of the murder weapon. Whatta
world, huh? I was concerned he might have cleaned up and polished
the knife, but he assured me he hadn't, because the bloodstains made
it a great conversation piece. Like I said, you got lucky. But remember,
unless you've got Hagopian's DNA and can match it to what's on the
knife, you have no case. Feel free to call if you have further questions.
Laura Hecht.

Kim whizzed through the sub-directories of the computer, navi-
gating like an über-hacker. She brought up a list of inmates' names.
Leo Hagopian had indeed been sent up for violent crimes, to Elmira
and Attica. But he had been released before 1992, so there'd be no
DNA sample on file.

His record contained a glowering mug shot, his broken nose giving
him a thuggish appearance. He'd done time twice—two years for dealing amphetamines, assaulting a police officer, and weapons posses-
sion, and five years for breaking and entering, malicious wounding,
and forcible rape (what other kind is there? Kim asked). It was noted
he'd once boxed professionally as a cruiserweight, using the name Leo
"The Lion" Hagopian. His probation officer was listed as Floyd W.
Feeney, NYS Division of Parole at 314 West 40th Street in Manhattan.

"Can you print that out?"

"Sure," Kim said.

"I'll call the parole office tomorrow. If this guy Feeney is still
around, maybe he'll know where Hagopian is."

"But even if you find out where he is," she asked. "What are you
gonna do?"

"Well," I said in a determined voice. "There's only one thing I *can*
do—get a sample of his DNA."

Chapter 33

The next afternoon, I drove south on the Taconic State Parkway, making the two hour trip to New York City.

Floyd W. Feeney had been standoffish on the phone. He said Hagopian was no longer on probation but he might have an idea of his whereabouts. However, he wouldn't tell me on the telephone— I'd have to come to his office in person with proper ID.

I made an appointment with Feeney for 5:30. Then I told Ben Caldwell I needed a couple of days in New York for personal reasons.

"I understand," Ben said. "You're going through a lot and it would be good to get away, sort things out."

He also said he'd found an applicant for my job, a guy from Brigham and Womens' Hospital in Boston, so if I decided to quit at the end of these two weeks, it might work out okay. I said I wasn't sure about anything at this point. Ben said neither was he.

As the Taconic merged into the Saw Mill River Parkway, I turned on my radio and knew I was getting close to Manhattan; the sports-talk station was going full blast, and the voices of Mike and the Mad

Dog warmed my heart. I listened to the jokers who called in—
"Vinnie from Queens," "Tarik" the Farrakhan sound-alike from
Yonkers, and a bunch of first-time-caller-long-time-listeners, who
held forth on the NBA salary cap, should Yankee Stadium remain in
the Bronx, and whether bowling was a sport or not.

Now I was heading down the Henry Hudson Parkway, with its
magnificent view across the river of high, rugged, columnar cliffs—
the New Jersey Palisades. Passing under the George Washington
bridge, to my left I saw the deco towers of Columbia-Presbyterian
Medical Center, where I'd once spent my summer vacation as an
undergrad intern, mostly cleaning bedpans.

Beyond the hospital, the racially mixed urban area of Washington
Heights stretched east across Manhattan to the Harlem River. It was
there, in the grim Dyckman Street housing project, where this whole
scenario had begun—fifteen years ago.

As I swung onto the circular off-ramp at 79th Street, I saw an
uplifting sight; my houseboat moored in the Boat Basin Marina to
my right. I'd arranged with Ed Sorenson to sleep there. I was looking
forward to it.

I drove north on West End Avenue, looking for what New Yorkers
call "a spot." Somebody pulled out at 81st, and I grabbed it. As I
backed in, I reveled in the simple act of parallel parking. Vanderkill
was all parking lots.

The red and white sign on a lamp post advised me I was good till
11 A.M.

Getting out of my air-conditioned Checker, the blast of ninety
degree heat felt like a sauna. It was good to experience again the hot-
house swelter of a New York summer.

I walked over to Broadway and caught the subway at 79th Street.
It rumbled down to Times Square in five quick stops.

I rode up the sleek chrome and steel escalator (which used to be
a dank, filthy stairway) and emerged at Broadway and 42nd Street.
I walked west on the sanitized, prettified main stem. Gone were
the adult book stores, porno movie houses, S&M paraphernalia

boutiques, and head shops of my youth. Now mothers, with children in tow, and hordes of nicely dressed tourists strolled the street—once the turf of hookers, transvestites, street people, and drug dealers. I passed the restored New Amsterdam Theatre, with its yellow, back-lit marquee showing a smug-looking lion's face, and the words *"Disney Presents The Lion King—the Broadway Musical."* I remembered wistfully that years ago, the same marquee had proclaimed: *"Faster, Pussycat! Kill! Kill!"* on a double-bill with *"Cycle Sluts."*

Sic transit gloria mundi.

Walking past Madame Tussaud's I saw three sample wax figures in the window. I'd once visited the Tussaud museum in London, and behind its front glass stood Winston Churchill, Lord Laurence Olivier, and Mother Teresa. Here they featured Garth Brooks, Larry King, and Whoopi Goldberg.

I turned the corner at Eighth Avenue and walked downtown. My watch said 5:05 so I had some time to kill. I passed an electronic gizmo store. In the window was a digital mini voice recorder, with a sign saying, "Secretly record any conversation." Immediately I saw how Victor could get the goods on Stevie Karp—if he could record Karp's sexually coercive statements, we'd be able to nail him. I went in and bought the device.

Continuing down Eighth, the scent of fresh ground coffee beans lured me into a Starbuck's. Starbuck's was another thing I missed up in Vanderkill. I'd tried the local coffee shop "Perc's," but it was very Maxwell House.

I ordered a *caffe latte*, made with skim milk because I was watching my weight. And a slab of maple-frosted raisin pound cake, because I wasn't watching it all that closely.

Sitting at a table, I unwrapped the voice recorder. The Aiwa ICM 120 Voice Sensor was amazing. It weighed 1.3 oz., was voice activated and would record for 120 minutes. Victor could slip it into his jumpsuit pocket and turn it on when the guard came in. Karp's ass would be grass. I just had to remember to get AA batteries.

After my coffee break, I walked down to Fortieth Street. Looking east I saw a four-story, dirty white brick building with a New York State flag drooping from a flagpole in front. It had to be the Parole Office.

The waiting room was filled with grim, scruffy people sitting on plastic chrome-legged chairs. They were all men, except for one woman who held a squalling infant. The desk clerk and I were the only white folks in the room.

At the desk I gave my name, and said I was there to see Floyd Feeney.

"Please take a seat till your name is called," the cop said.

"He's expecting me. And I'm not a . . ."

"Please take a seat till your name is called."

The guy was stuck on automatic pilot, so I sat down. Every so often a side door opened, and a police-type called out a name. A parolee got up, trudged over to the door and was ushered inside.

I noticed a large walnut board hanging on the front wall. Mounted on it were bronze embossed plaques with the names and likenesses of men wearing police hats. Above them, in bold letters, were the words, "Parole Officers Who Died Heroically in The Line Of Duty".

Forty-five minutes later Floyd Feeney came out and called, "David Rothberg." Feeney looked more like a movie star than a parole officer. He bore a strong resemblance to Brad Pitt, and you got the feeling he knew that.

He brought me into his office. On the wall was a large calendar, displaying the days of July, with Feeney's appointments scribbled over the dates. It featured a color photo of Miss July, sitting in a beach-chair reading a newspaper, topless. There was a quotation from the nubile, busty gal, "I'm keeping abreast of recent developments."

Sic transit Gloria Steinem.

"So, what can I do for you, Dave?"

I pulled out my Vanderkill ID card and handed it to Feeney, who gave it a cursory look and slid it back to me.

"You're the one who's trying to locate Hagopian?"

"Yes."

"I'm not sure I can help you."

"You're not sure?"

"Leo doesn't have to report to me anymore. He's been off probation for a couple years now."

"But on the phone you said you might know his whereabouts."

"That's right," he said. "I *might*." He opened a desk drawer and took out an eight-by-ten framed photograph,

"Are you familiar with the Police Ath-a-letic League?" he asked.

"Sure."

"I'm very active in the Police Ath-a-letic League," Feeney said, handing me the photo. "P.A.L. That's what I am . . . a pal. Here's a picture of my guys, taken in spring training."

It was a team photo of ten-year-old baseball players. Their uniforms indicated they were the "Sound View Bombers."

"I sponsor those kids," Feeney said. "Right now we're raising money for new uniforms."

"Looks like they've already got pretty nice uniforms."

"Those are *home* uniforms," Feeney explained patiently. "They need *away* uniforms. I'm looking for three hundred dollars."

"Well, I'll be glad to help out."

"Like I said, I'm lookin' for *three hundred dollars*."

"I don't think . . ."

"Dave, Dave," he pleaded. "It would really help these kids. Plus, it would really help me . . . to remember about Leo Hagopian."

The prick is shaking me down.

"C'mon, Dave . . . be a pal," Feeney said in a cajoling voice.

"All right," I said. "Can I write you a check?"

"Cash."

I took out my money clip. "All I've got is two hundred and change."

"Well, that'll have to do," he said, sticking out his hand. "You can keep the singles." I paid him and he shoved the bills in his pocket.

For a few moments, the parole officer said nothing. Then it hit me—I might not get anything for my money.

The cop was obviously getting a kick out of my anxious expression. It pissed me off.

"Cut the crap, Feeney," I said. "Tell me what I just paid for."

"You think I'm jerkin' you around?"

"Yeah. But I also know you're gonna tell me, because you're a stand-up guy."

"What if I don't?" he said, toying with me.

I reached in my bag and pulled out the voice recorder. It wasn't running, but I waved it at him.

"Voice activated."

"Hey, lighten up, Dave," he said. "You're a pal now, and I take care of my pals."

"Glad to hear it."

"Here's the story," Feeney said. "I got Hagopian a job a few years ago. I do that for some of my guys, y'know try to give 'em a leg up, keep 'em on the straight and narrow."

Yeah, for a nice, hefty kickback from their salaries.

"He's working as bouncer in a strip club called 'The Play Pen,'" Feeney went on. "No wait . . . I forgot . . . they changed the name. Now they call it 'The Sixty-Forty Club.'"

"Sixty-Forty?"

"It's a dig at the law that says sixty percent of a sex-related business has to be used for non-sex-related purposes. Strip joints now have regular bar and grill operations in the front, and the 'forty percent' in the back is where all the tits 'n' ass is."

"Where's this place?"

"Gansevoort Street," Feeney replied. "Right off the West Side Highway."

"Gansevoort Street. That's the meat packing district, right?"

"Yeah," Feeney said. "Let's see, this is Thursday. You can find him there between eight and four in the morning."

"Thanks," I said, getting up to leave.

"Word of advice," Feeney said. "I wouldn't fuck with Hagopian. He's addicted to speed . . . and also to pounding the shit outta people."

"Appreciate the warning," I said.

"Always glad to help out a pal," Feeney said, giving me a big grin. I noted with satisfaction that Parole Officer Feeney didn't look *exactly* like Brad Pitt. He had brown teeth.

Chapter 34

I walked uptown on Eighth Avenue, trying to figure out a plan. How could I get a sample of Hagopian's genetic material?

Hair? DNA is found only in the follicle and not in the hair shaft, so I'd have to yank a hair out of Hagopian's head. Get real. Blood? That would mean provoking a physical confrontation with the bouncer, and the only blood shed would probably be mine. Skin? Same problem. Semen? Forget it. Sweat, urine, feces, ditto. That leaves saliva. Buy him a drink and steal the glass with his spit on it? Possible, but how the hell do you buy a drink for a bouncer in a strip joint? Still, that seems like the best option.

I decided to call Laura Hecht. I needed to be sure that if I surreptitiously got Hagopian's saliva, it would constitute legal DNA evidence.

I rang her from a payphone.

"Perfectly legal," she said. "In fact, in a recent case, a cop was trailin' a murder suspect and the guy hocked a loogie on the street. The cop grabbed a napkin from a hotdog stand and sopped up the evidence. Judge allowed it in court, and the DA got a conviction."

"That's good to know," I said.

"How you plannin' to get this guy's spit?"

"Well, I was thinking . . . "

"One sec," she said. I could hear a voice in the background. Then the lawyer was back on with me. "I gotta go. Are you free for dinner?"

"I have no plans."

"Why don't we grab a bite and talk about it then? You like Jewish food?"

"What's not to like?"

"You know Fine & Schapiro's?"

"On Seventy-second Street?"

"Yes. Between Columbus and Broadway. Let's make it seven-thirty."

"Okay."

"What do you look like?" she asked.

"Well. I have red hair . . ."

"Cool. I'll have no trouble findin' you. See you at seven-thirty." She hung up.

It was a now 6:30. I figured whatever plan I came up with, I'd act on it tonight. Best thing would be to go back uptown and get my car, then after dinner I could drive down to the strip club.

I decided to walk up to 81st Street. It would take about forty five minutes—but I had the time and needed the exercise. I could burn off a few ounces of the pound cake.

On the corner of Fiftieth was a bank, so I stopped at the ATM to get more cash. A few blocks further north I saw "Jake's Jiffy Copy Center." A sign advertised "Picture IDs and business cards printed While U Wait." I went in and ordered business cards.

Twenty minutes later, I walked out with a hundred, which was the minimum order.

I looked at one; it was impressive. In simple *sans serif* type it read:

David Rosemont
Executive Producer—Paramax Pictures
A Spade-Archer Entertainment Company

I put ten in my wallet and threw the rest away. Then I turned my attention back to the issue of Hagopian's DNA. There was only one task left. I had to buy a box of Baggies.

And then take a cab up to my car.

I parked at a meter right in front of Fine & Schapiro's Kosher Gourmet. The restaurant's window was festooned with six hanging salamis. They were each about three feet long, and shriveled from exposure to the sun. The best word to describe them was *elephantine*.

When I entered I looked around for Laura Hecht, but there were no single diners at the tables, except for one corpulent, bearded man schlurping a bowl of matzoh ball soup.

I sat down in a booth and looked around. I hadn't been to Fine & Schapiro's since I was a kid; my folks used to take me there for Sunday dinner. It looked pretty much the same. The walls were still covered with what appeared to be broadloom carpeting, the color of smoked salmon. The ceiling was that cottage-cheesy soundproofing material, now discolored in patches by water leaks. There were several haphazardly hung Berenice Abbott photographs of New York in the forties. Those were new.

I picked up the large, laminated menu. Across the top was the familiar red, white, blue, and yellow lettering—*Only Hebrew National Glatt Kosher meat products sold here.* Below was the Hebrew National slogan—*"We answer to a Higher Authority."*

A woman's voice said, "Y'all must be David." I looked up as she slid into the seat opposite me. She held out her hand. "Laura Hecht."

I was surprised by her age. Maybe because of her southern accent, she'd sounded fairly young on the phone. But she appeared to be in her mid-sixties, although her style was more DKNY than AARP. She wore a beige shantung business suit, and her pearly gray hair was swept up in a French knot. Although her face had its share of wrinkles and lines, it was impeccably made up, with vermilion lipstick and a subtle blusher blended into her cheeks. In her ears were small diamonds with Tiffany settings.

She heaved a bulging Louis Vuitton briefcase up onto the seat beside her. "I'm so sorry I'm late," she drawled. "I stopped at the gym to do mah half hour on the Stairmaster. I'm gonna have herring in cream sauce and stuffed derma tonight, and if I don't work out, well, lemme put it this way—did you know that *schmaltz* has the exact same molecular structure as cellulite?"

I liked her immediately; she was a dietary soulmate. "I love the way you talk," I said smiling. "Where are you from?"

"Well, I come from Alabama," she said, "but please don't say with a banjo on my knee." She went on to say she'd spent most of her life in Normal, Alabama, and again warned me against any humorous comments.

"Did you practice law down there?" I asked.

"No," she said. "I only got my law degree six years ago."

She explained that her late husband, Irving (he's the Jew, by the way; I'm not), had been a civil rights lawyer for SNCC and CORE in the early days of the struggle, and later with Morris Dees at the Southern Poverty Law Center. She'd spent most of her time raising three daughters. Then, just when the last one went away to college, and she thought she might start doing something for herself, her husband was afflicted with Alzheimer's. So she continued her role as caregiver for ten more years, until her husband passed. At that point she decided to go to law school, (U of Alabama, Tuscaloosa) partly because she wanted to be "the keeper of the flame," and also because she'd learned to love the law from helping Irving.

"My husband's life insurance left me pretty well fixed," she said, "But as far as gettin' gainful employment, no firm wanted to hire a gal who was an M&M. By M&M I'm referrin' to a woman like myself, stuck between menopause and mandatory retirement. Finally, I got this job offer from AFTI, and 'though it doesn't pay a whole helluva lot, it's the kinda work I like. So I packed myself up, came to New York, passed the bar up here, and . . . well, *nous voilá*."

The waiter came over and I recognized him from the old days. He hadn't aged a bit in the last twenty-or-so years. He'd looked eighty then and he looked eighty now.

"Vell," the waiter said, holding his order pad in one hand and his pencil poised in the other, "vot'll it gonna be?"

While Laura ordered her blintzes and derma, I scanned the menu, looking for the frankfurters I always ordered as a kid. "Don't you have the two big hotdogs any more?"

"Specials," the waiter replied.

"I don't see any specials on the menu."

The waiter leaned over and pointed to an item marked "specials." Of course—I'd forgotten; "specials" was Jewish delicatessenese for those large franks, knockwursts actually, served with baked beans and potato salad.

"I'll have that," I said. "And a side of chopped liver to start."

"To drink?" the waiter asked.

"Cream soda," Laura answered.

"A fine choice, Madame," I said to her. Then I turned to the waiter. "Celery tonic."

After the waiter left, Laura looked at me. "So," she said, "what's your plan with this guy Hagopian?"

I told her my idea about getting the bouncer to have a drink with me and somehow stealing the glass with his saliva on it.

"That's a big *somehow*," she said. "And how're you gonna get him to have a drink with you?"

I showed her my Paramax Pictures business card. "Most people are suckers for anything to do with movies," I said. "I'll tell Hagopian I'm producing a film about a New York strip club, and I'm in from Hollywood, doing research. I'll say I'd like to interview him and get his expertise, and hint that I might even put him on the picture as a technical advisor. I doubt he'll say no when I offer to buy him a drink."

"Not bad," Laura said.

The waiter arrived with our first courses. We continued our discussion over herring and chopped liver.

"Okay," she said. "Let's say you get him to have drinks with you. I assume you'll order the same thing he does, then at some point you'll switch his glass with yours."

"Exactly."

"How you gonna do that?"

"I'll just wait till he gets up and leaves."

"That's no good. What if he takes the drink with him? What if the waiter or bartender takes the glasses away?"

"That could be a problem," I responded. We both gave it a few moments thought. Then Laura spoke up.

"I think I've got the answer," she said. "But it involves me comin' down to the club with you."

"I'd never . . . "

"Hear me out," she cut in. "Once you get Hagopian drinkin' with you, you chat for a while and then tell him you've gotta make a phone call—to Nicole Kidman or somebody. Then you go to the pay phone and call me on my cell—I'll be waitin' outside . . . "

"What if there's no pay phone, or it's broken, or it's in use?"

"Then you'll ask to use the office phone. Listen, you're a big Hollywood macher. You think he's gonna say no?"

"A Hollywood macher would have a cell phone."

"You left yours back at the hotel. Anyway, after you call me, you go back to Hagopian. A few minutes later I come in and start kickin' up a fuss. The bouncer'll have to come over and deal with me. That's when you can make the switch."

"No offense," I said, "but I can't see them letting a woman like you—I mean, a woman who's well dressed and alone—into a strip joint."

"I know," she answered. "That's what I'm gonna make the fuss about. I'll accuse them of sex discrimination."

"But why the hell would you *want* to get into a strip club?"

"To ogle the babes. I'm a lesbian."

She threw me with that one. I wasn't sure whether she was describing the role she'd play, or telling me her sexual preference. I responded with the shrink nod.

"So whatd'ya think?" she asked.

"Look, Laura," I said, "I really don't want to get you involved."

"I am involved. This is what Advocates for the Innocent is all about." Her grandma's face showed the courage and determination of a gunslinger.

"All right," I said. "I've got my car, so you won't have to wait outside the club on the street."

"Good," she replied. "Oh, we better stop and buy some sort of plastic bag—to store the glass with the spit in it."

From my shoulder bag I pulled out the box of Baggies. Laura gave me a big smile. "David," she said, "we're in *bid-ness*."

The waiter served our main courses. I spooned out the mustard from a jar on the table, and put it on my plate next to the two giant knockwursts. I cut into one of them and the juice spurted out onto the potato salad. I dipped the frank into the mustard and took a bite. The tangy, garlicky flavor made me groan with pleasure.

"Good hotdogs, huh?" Laura said.

"Of course. They're Hebrew National," I said. Then I raised my eyes heavenward. *"They answer to . . . A Higher Authority."*

Laura laughed. "Yeah," she said, digging her fork into her stuffed derma, "don't we all."

Chapter 35

We parked in front of the Sixty-Forty Club. From behind the wheel, I looked down the narrow street, paved with cobblestones that must've been laid down in the early eighteen-hundreds. I could see the automobiles zooming by on the West Side Highway. Across the river in New Jersey, a delicate hint of pink faded in the night sky above Hoboken, as if God had cast a beatific glow over the birthplace of Frank Sinatra.

In front of the strip joint, a flood-lit sign showed two naked women. Underneath the words "Girls! Girls! Girls!" flashed in neon. Next to the door was another sign proclaiming a 3 1/2 Cock Rating from *Screw Magazine*. *They must've lost half a cock because of their remote location.*

The area was desolate. Both sides of the street were lined with wholesale meat markets, their entrances closed by graffiti-sprayed roll-down security doors. The sidewalk was obstructed by clusters of rusting dumpsters, overflowing with stuffed plastic garbage bags. The glaring peach-colored light from the overhead street lamps lit the scene in harsh chiaroscuro.

I pictured Leo Hagopian; huge, a speed freak, a brutal killer. The prospect of coming face-to-face with him scared the shit out of me. What if I screwed up? What if he found me out?

"Look," Laura said, noticing my anxiety, "this is dangerous. Obtainin' DNA evidence is really police work. Why don't we call it a night? Ain't no shame in it."

"No," I said firmly. "This is something I have to do."

"Then we'll do it," she said. "Actually, in case the situation gets really hairy, I brought along a friend . . . " She opened her briefcase and took out an automatic pistol. " . . . Mister Glock."

This grandma really is a gunslinger.

"Nine millimeter?" I asked.

"Ten, actually," she said. "Makes bigger holes. I got it for self-protection. I've had some death threats since I put a Mafia hit-man in the slammer."

"You, uh, actually know how to use that thing?"

"Sure. I took a course at the Woodhaven Rifle and Pistol Range. Turns out a gun's pretty much like a Kodak autofocus. Y'know— *Point 'n' Shoot.*"

I suggested we go over our plan again, make sure we were on the same page. After we reviewed it, Laura gave me a business card with her cell phone number. I stuck it in my shirt pocket.

The door of the Sixty-Forty Club opened and four Japanese men came out, cameras slung over their shoulders. They looked in our direction and started shouting.

"*Takushi. Takushi.*"

One came over to my side and called through the window.

"*Takushi.*"

"Huh?"

He pointed to the rates painted on my car door.

"No." I waved him off. "No taxi."

Meanwhile another guy was tapping on Laura's window.

"*Takushi—Hai?*"

"Hi," she replied, being friendly.

Suddenly three Japanese tourists were climbing into the back of my Checker. One pulled down the jump seat.

"No. No. No. No *takushi*," I said.

A yellow cab pulled up in front of us and three business-suited men got out.

I pointed to the real taxi. "*Takushi*," I shouted. "Over there."

Finally they got out, grinning and bowing apologetically.

Laura was smiling. "I have the feelin'," she said, "this has happened before."

"Yeah," I said. "Sometimes people think this is a gypsy cab because it's not yellow. But nobody's ever made it into the back seat before."

The three businessmen hooted at the tourists.

"Check it out," one yelled. "Chinkie lookie for nookie."

"They ain't Chinks. They're Japs."

"How can you tell?"

"Cameras."

Guffaws.

"Hey, Jappos. Wanna get laid? Go down the corner—ask fer Pearl. *Pearl Harbor*."

The three caballeros entered the club, laughing and making the raucous sounds of male bonding.

"Well, Laura, I guess it's Showtime," I said.

"You sure you're up for this?"

"No guts, no glory," I said, getting out of the car.

"David," Laura said. "Good luck. Be careful."

"*Hasta la vista, baby.*"

Inside, the Sixty-Forty was dim and cheerless. A female bartender was serving drinks to the guys who'd just come in. In one corner, lit by a spotlight, a woman in bra and panties was moving in forlorn gyrations. The music sounded tinny coming from a small RadioShack speaker. But I still recognized Whitney Houston's melismatic "I, I, I, will always love youuuuuuu,"—in a dance re-mix version, with a kick drum driving the music in double-time.

As I approached the bar, the businessmen picked up their drinks and headed for the back of the room. There, they parted a curtain and entered the tits 'n' ass section.

"What'll it be?" the bartender asked. She was a Latino woman with pink hair.

"Can I order a drink inside?"

"Yeah," she said. "But you gotta order one out here first. You can take it in with ya."

"I'll have a scotch and soda."

"That's ten dollars."

"Okay."

"J&B? Johnny Walker?"

"You call it."

The woman chatted amiably as she fixed my drink. "First time here?"

I nodded.

"Let me run the rules by ya then," she continued. "Main thing is there's no touchin'. I mean, the girls can touch you, but you can't touch them. They got a closed circuit TV camera trained on all the tables, so don't think you can cop a feel on the sly. Other than that, you can have a good time."

Thank you, Rudy Guiliani.

"Oh, and we got a ATM machine over there by the men's room. It takes like *Cirrus, NYCE,* whatever—everything here's on a cash basis."

"You have a pay phone?"

"Next to the ATM."

I saw somebody talking on it. At least it worked. So far so good.

I took a slug of the scotch. Then I picked up my glass and headed for the area behind the curtain.

The 40% portion of the club was nothing like the 60%. Bright multi-colored lights bounced off a revolving mirror globe hung from the ceiling. The music, now blasting, reverberated from surround-sound speakers. There was a bare-breasted dancer writhing on a mirrored stage, wearing only a g-string. The crotch was stuffed with paper money, which a few avid oglers were handing her from ring-side.

I'd visited a few strip joints back in my medical school days. The places were different then. There was total nudity, and the strippers accepted money by having patrons insert the greenbacks in various orifices. It was better OBGYN training than I got in class. But those days were gone. This topless temptress was accepting tips only in her hands.

"Like me to dance for you?" I turned and saw a young, plump black woman smiling at me. She was wearing a silk robe.

"Not right now," I answered. "I'm just gonna hang out for a while."

"Maybe later," she said pleasantly.

I sat down at a table and sipped my drink, trying to get a feel for my surroundings. The room wasn't large; it had maybe a dozen small tables in it. Only five were occupied. At two of them, girls were performing table dances—squirming and wiggling to the music, displaying their tits to their slack-jawed admirers. One woman was white, and the other was Asian. This place was definitely equal opportunity.

The three businessmen were at a table next to me, and the on-stage dancer stepped down from her platform to join them. They'd ordered champagne (New York State), which a waitress served in plastic flute glasses. The black woman took the stage and began to dance. When she removed her robe, I could see her thighs were a tad too Rubenesque for this type of gig. But she had a nice smile.

A male voice shouting "Yee-hah!" caused me to turn towards the businessmen. Their stripper was straddling the leg of one of them, dragging her hair back and forth across his face. Her breasts, which I now saw close-up, were silicone city—two melon-sized stationary protruberances mounted on a bony chest. There was a UV black light shining on the table, making her white g-string glow as if it were radioactive.

With his buddies urging him on, the man slid his hands onto the woman's knees. She pushed them away, and waggled her finger, "naughty-naughty." She resumed her dance, and a few moments later, the lecherous hands were back, now heading for her crotch.

"No touching," she shouted.

"Aw, baby," the man whined, "I won't tell if you won't."

"Quit it.'

"C'mon . . . there's an extra twenty in it for you."

Suddenly a dark shadow fell over the customer. I recognized Leo Hagopian instantly from his hulking form and boxer's nose. Hagopian placed a huge hand on the trapesius muscle of the male-factor and squeezed it between two fingers.

"Like the lady told ya . . . no touchin'," he said in a disarmingly gentle voice. "You get one warnin', then you're history."

The man shook his head without looking up. Hagopian removed his hand and noticed me. He gave me a crooked grin. "Howya doin', Sport?" he asked.

He was dressed in voluminous FUBU denim shorts, worn mid-hip—gangsta style. Over the shorts he wore a muscle shirt. He had shoulder length hair but was nearly bald on top. His thick, hirsute arms dangled almost to his knees. On one bulging biceps was a prison tat—a clenched fist with the slogan I AM FEAR ITSELF.

Fuck me.

He walked away before I could speak to him. I took another swallow of scotch.

"Hey, Red. You a real hunky dude. You want me dance for you?"

I winced. *Hunky dude* was okay, but I hate being called *Red*. The invitation was from the Asian girl, who'd settled her butt on the edge of my table. Her kimono flapped open, revealing small sagging breasts with the stretch marks of motherhood.

"My name Amy," she said. "I Korean . . . come from Seoul. If you want . . . I be your *Seoul*-mate."

She giggled.

"Okay, sure." I said. "How much is it?"

"Ten dollar a dance."

"How long is a dance?"

"Five minutes . . . we go by song. When song over . . . dance over. Unless we start near end of song, then you get little extra time."

"Do I pay you now?"

"Yes," she said. "Why don't you gimme twenty, thirty so no interruption?"

I handed her two tens, which went into a pocket on the front of her kimono. Then she went to work.

Whatever she was doing, my mind wasn't on it. All I could think of was groping her. Hagopian would come to break things up and give me a warning. That would be my chance to talk to him.

Amy was leaning over me, cupping her bared breasts and trying to brush her nipples across my eyes. I let my hands drift to her buttocks, and then squeezed. She pulled away.

"You stoppit, Red. Not allowed."

"Oh, okay."

She resumed her lap dance. She mounted my leg, and began pressing her thighs against my knee in rhythm to the music. After a few moments, I shot my hands around her and grabbed her ass.

"Hey," she cried out, "I told you . . . not allowed."

"Who's gonna know?" I bellowed. Then I started laughing boisterously. Amy stood up and glared at me, hands on hips. Hagopian was there like a shot.

"Hey, Sport. You know better than that."

"Oh. Hey, I'm sorry."

"I don't wanna hafta come out here again," the bouncer said menacingly.

"I didn't know the rules," I said. "I'm from the West Coast. Mind if I talk to you for a second."

"About what?"

I pulled out my Paramax Pictures business card and handed it to him. Then I made my pitch about being in town to do research for a movie about a strip club, and how would he feel about sitting down with me, giving me the benefit of his expertise?

"What kinda movie is it?" he asked.

"It's . . . a mystery," I replied. "About a stripper."

"Does she get murdered?"

"Yes."

"What's the movie called called?"

"Uh, 'The Naked and the Dead.'"

"Good title," he said. "Who's in it?"

"Sharon Stone."

"Ain't she a little old to play a stripper?"

"Sharon plays a private detective."

"A chick PI," he said. "I like it."

I offered to buy him a drink at the bar. He said fine but he'd be a while 'cause he had to go settle a dispute between "two coozes" in the dressing room.

"In the meantime, why'n'cha let Amy here wiggle on your woodie?" the bouncer suggested. "I'll meet you later in the bar." He turned and walked away.

Amy began running her fingers through my hair. "You relax," she said in a sexy voice. "I take care of you."

Again I paid little attention to her moves.

Okay, Hagopian bought my story—so I'm halfway home. Now if I can only handle the situation at the bar . . .

Suddenly my face started tingling; there was a growing numbness in my right arm. I stared at my hand; it felt like it was growing larger . . . . *Shit—Migraine.* Amy's naked breasts were dangling in front of my eyes. They broke up into zigzag patterns, shifting like forms in a kaleidoscope.

Oh God, not now.

But the aura was enveloping me, the pain throbbing in my left temple. Amy's cloying perfume wafted into my nose. I felt queasy.

"That's enough," I shouted.

"You pay one more song," she said, dry-humping my leg.

"I said that's *enough.*"

I felt a squeezing in my groin, and looked down to see Amy's hand rubbing my genitals.

"God dammit," I yelled. "Get your hands off me."

She didn't stop. "Aw, c'mon, Red . . . don't be uptight stick-in-mud. I told you . . . I your *Seoul*-mate."

Her fingernails tweaked my testicles, and reflexively I shoved her off my lap—hard. She went tumbling and landed awkwardly on her side. Coruscating lights bombarded my eyes; I couldn't get my bearings. The music was pounding so loud I feared my eardrums might burst inside my skull. I felt myself being dragged out of my chair, then a sharp pain ripped through my right shoulder muscle.

I heard Hagopian's voice. "Let's go, Sport." He had my arm jammed up my back in a hammer-lock, and was force-marching me towards the rear exit.

What happened next was a blur. I was shoved down a dark hallway and out into an alley. The hot, torpid night air made me feel like I was entering Hell. Hagopian pushed me against a brick wall, and drove his fist sharply into my gut. I collapsed to the pavement, clutching my abdomen.

"Go back to Hollywood, you piece-a-shit," he said. Then he laughed and turned to re-enter the club. Hearing Hagopian's mocking laughter, I was filled with unreasoning rage. A rush of adrenaline hit me.

"Fuck you," I yelled without thinking.

The bouncer whirled and looked at me. I struggled to my feet.

He let out a grunt and rushed me. I threw a punch but he grabbed my fist in mid-air like a baseball. Then he grinned at me and squeezed till the pain buckled my knees. His own large fist plowed into the side of my face, crushing cheek against teeth. I could feel blood filling the inside of my mouth as I fell.

I saw his fist coming again but twisted my body and rolled out of the way. Staggering up, I backed into a row of steel garbage cans. I seized one by its handles and flung it at Hagopian. He deflected it in mid-air and it crashed as he came at me.

He shot his arms under my armpits, and lifted me in a punishing bear-hug. I felt myself being swung in the air and then crashing to the pavement.

I tried to get up, but Hagopian pushed me down. He dropped on top of me, straddling my torso with his massive thighs. I reached up towards the big man's face, slashing with my fingernails like the desperate Agnes Rivera. But his arms were too long, and he laughed as my nails gouged thin air.

I felt the bouncer's hands encircling my neck. His fingers tightened, closing off my esophagus. I tried to scratch my nails into his arms, but my fingers had no strength. They fluttered softly against Hagopian's skin—a caress before dying. My vision grew dim . . .

I heard a Big Bang.

The hands around my throat loosened, and I gratefully sucked in lungfuls of air. Hagopian fell back, clutching his right shoulder and howling in pain. I heard a woman's voice, "You okay?" It was Laura Hecht.

She came into my field of vision, holding the smoking Glock in a two-handed grip. Behind her was Amy, watching in amazement.

I pulled myself up to a sitting position and said I was okay. My voice was hoarse and constricted. Laura knelt down beside me, keeping her gun trained on the writhing Hagopian.

"Lucky for you I messed up," she explained. "While I was waitin' in your car, I tried to call my answering machine, but my cell phone was out of juice. Then I realized you wouldn't be able to reach me. So I went into the club to see if you'd tried to call. When I couldn't find you, I started screamin' that I was your wife, and where the hell was that no-good red-headed jerk anyway?"

She pointed to Amy. "This nice lady directed me back here."

I saw a splash of liquid fly through the air, and looked over at Hagopian. The bouncer screamed. A geyser of bright red blood was jetting out of his shoulder.

"He's hemorrhaging," I said. "It's his brachial artery." I crawled over to Hagopian and yanked up his muscle shirt. I pressed the heel of my hand firmly against the first rib, compressing the artery against the bone. The blood stopped spurting. Meanwhile, Hagopian had passed out.

"Good work," Laura said with admiration.

"You too. You're a helluva shot," I replied, keeping pressure on the bouncer's chest bone.

She groaned and stood up; her sexagenarian lower back obviously ached from bending over. "One of my Mafia informants once told me if you wanna put a hurt on someone without whackin' him, shoot him in the knee-cap. But Hagopian was on his knees so I went for the shoulder. Same general effect."

"Laura," I said. "Thanks."

"Hey, I did what I had to do. Just like you did."

"Yeah," I said sadly. "But I screwed up. I didn't get Hagopian's DNA."

"Sure you did," Laura said. "Check out your clothes."

I looked. My jacket and shirt were covered with Leo Hagopian's blood. I grinned at Laura, who'd turned to Amy.

"Do me a favor, Hon,'" Laura said. "Call 911 and tell 'em to send a squad car and an ambulance." Amy nodded and went back inside.

I switched hands and kept pressing on Hagopian's rib. My jaw was beginning to ache, my hand hurt and I could feel my lower lip swelling. There was pain radiating from my abdomen, and my left cheek was bruised and sore. But—my headache was gone.

"You need to go to the hospital," Laura said.

"Yeah, But EMS'll go to St. Vincent's 'cause it's closer. I prefer Bellevue. Would you mind driving me?"

"No problem."

We heard a moan, and saw Hagopian was coming to. Laura pointed the gun directly at his crotch.

"Try anything, asshole, and I'll blow off yer *schwanz*."

I was sure Hagopian didn't understand Yiddish. I was also sure he knew exactly what Laura meant.

She gave me a satisfied look. "Well, David," she said, "We're in *bid-ness*."

Chapter 36

I was released from Bellevue Hospital Center late the next afternoon. Ed Sorenson had gotten me a private room and supervised my
care. I was really banged-up, but after a night on Vicodin, all I
needed now was Tylenol 3. The main discomfort came from bruised
ribs, sutures inside my cheek, and a fat lip.

In the bathroom mirror, my face was not a pretty sight. The left side
was black and purple from jawline to temple, my lip was three times
normal size, and one cheek looked like it was chock full o' nuts.

I wondered how Kim would react to my new look.

*Well, for now there's no chance of us getting beyond friendship.
Kissing is definitely out.*

Earlier in the day Laura had arrived to brief me on what to say
when the cops came to take my statement.

As she advised, I told the detectives exactly what happened at the
club. I didn't lie, or leave anything out; any half-truths or inconsistencies would weaken the prosecution's case against Hagopian when
it came to trial.

Since my behavior at the club was designed to trick Hagopian into giving me a DNA sample, the defendant's lawyer would undoubtedly argue entrapment. A weak defense, Laura said. She was willing to bet the jury would find Hagopian guilty of assault and attempted murder. He'd get the max—twenty-five to life. In any event, she could still use his DNA from my bloody clothes to nail him for Agnes Rivera's murder—what we wanted in the first place.

The detectives were satisfied with my story, and told me to send a written deposition to the DA, which would be sufficient for indictment.

Laura said she'd get right to work on obtaining Hagopian's DNA sample from my clothing, which was being held as evidence.

"There's a lotta red tape," she said, "but I got my ways."

She reached over and touched my hand.

"One day soon," she declared, "Leo Hagopian is goin' down. And Mister Janko'll be walkin' out that prison gate, free at last."

"Laura," I said, "you've been incredible. I don't know how to thank you, except . . . to say thank you."

She looked at me thoughtfully. "Well," she said, "you could thank me another way, if you're up for it."

"Name it."

"Well, the kind of cases I get often involve convicts. Sometimes I could use a psychological profile, 'specially when I think somebody's handin' me the malarkey. Could you do that for me?"

"Glad to," I said, "but I should warn you—I've been known to make mistakes about people."

Laura said she'd go down to the hospital garage and get my car, while I got ready to leave. We'd meet in front of the main Bellevue gate. On her way out, Laura handed me a Brooks Brothers shopping bag.

"This is for you," she said. She was gone before I could thank her properly.

I opened the blue and gold box inside the bag. It contained a white Oxford button-down shirt. 16-34. *Perfect.*

I got dressed in the new shirt, thinking about Laura Hecht and all she'd done for me. I felt a warmth and closeness to her that seemed strange. But the emotion wasn't entirely unfamiliar. It was just—I hadn't felt it for a long time. Since my mom died.

Bellevue is on the East Side, so I decided to drive back to Vanderkill taking the FDR Drive, then crossing the Triboro and following the Major Deegan/Route 87 north till it intersects with the Saw Mill River Parkway.

I'd thought about paying a visit to my houseboat, but it seemed pointless now, and I was anxious to get back to Vanderkill and see to my patients.

It was a cloudy afternoon. A drenching rain had cooled things off and cleansed the city's streets. There were still puddles on the highway, and my Checker rode through one with a *splish-splash*. It was a happy sound—like a child dashing through the surf at Coney Island.

As I drove past Yankee Stadium, the sun broke through the clouds. Across the Harlem River, in the brilliant sunlight, I could see the red brick housing development on Dyckman Street—where Agnes Rivera had been murdered. I thought about Victor Janko and knew he'd soon have a chance at a new life. With his painting talent, and some solid guidance, Victor would do okay on the outside.

I'd discussed his case with Dr. Sorenson. Ed said he'd work with Victor at Bellevue, if he'd return to New York when he got out. I felt sure Victor would agree.

By the time I hit the Saw Mill River, my lip and cheek began to throb; the medication was wearing off. And I was getting a dull headache; not a migraine, but a garden variety type the Tylenol could easily handle. I took two gelcaps from my shirt pocket, and swallowed them without water.

As the drug started to work, I thought about my migraines—how I hated being at the mercy of them.

I know damn well what the migraine triggers are—MSG, red wine, sodium nitrite. . . . So why don't I avoid them? That night at Fine & Schapiro, I blithely chowed down two Hebrew National hot dogs, made with "the highest quality ingredients." Yeah, they were kosher, but any rabbi knows you can't make cured meat without sodium nitrite. And so do I.

Physician, heal thyself—or at least stop screwing thyself up.

I punched in the car radio. I was back in range of the classic rock station. In plaintive harmonies Simon & Garfunkel were singing "The Boxer."

" . . . *such are promises,/All lies and jest./Still a man hears what he wants to hear and disregards the rest.*"

I sang along—"*Lie la lie, Lie la lie la, Lie la lie . . .* "

Chapter 37

"**M**y God, what happened to *you?*"

That was the general reaction of people at Vanderkill when they saw my banged-up face.

I told Ben about my encounter at the strip club. "If Hagopian's blood matches the blood on the murder weapon," I said, "my lawyer'll get an order to exhume. If the tissue under the victim's fingernails matches Hagopian's DNA, that'll prove he's the real killer."

"That's a lotta ifs."

"Ya gotta believe."

"How long till you find out if the blood matches?"

"We'll get the blood types within a week. DNA testing takes longer."

Ben asked if I'd given any more thought to my resignation. I said I wasn't sure.

"Well," he said, "the shrink from Brigham and Women's told me he'll take the job. I said I'd let him know in ten days. He's an interesting guy—a former cop."

I felt a pang of jealousy.

"Well, you've got a week and a half," Ben said. "Why don't you see how you feel being back, and how things play out with this Janko business?"

I said okay.

"You shoulda seen the other guy," I said to Kim as she looked at me in shock.

"Who *was* the other guy?"

I told her about my rumble with Hagopian.

"You got his DNA?"

"Yes," I said. "When he got shot, he hemorrhaged—his blood spurted all over me."

"And of course you tended to him, stopped the bleeding, right?"

I nodded.

"So . . . you saved *his* life too. That makes three in two weeks. What's with you, Mister Knight-in-shining-armor?"

"Tarnished armor."

She took a nurse's interest in my injuries, reminding me that ice and nonsteroidal anti-inflammatories would speed the healing.

"But emotionally, you must feel real good," she said. I mean— your greatest fear, physical confrontation. You stood up to the guy."

"Yeah, but I lost the battle. If it wasn't for pistol packin' Grandma . . . "

"But you won the war."

She's right.

I smiled, crookedly because of my fat lip. At that moment I was really sorry kissing was out.

Mom Incaviglia got a little weepy when she saw my face.

Pop didn't notice.

Neither did Shelly. But she was her regular self again, eating wafers, Kibbles, and lettuce, and taking her morning strolls on my forearm.

Father Toussenel crossed himself when he saw me. "So much evil everywhere," he said sympathetically. " . . . Like a plague visited on the world."

I felt like decking him.

Odd reaction. Has my brawl with Hagopian made me more macho?

I told my patients I'd been mugged in New York but fought off my attacker. Most seemed impressed. A few looked dubious. It didn't really matter; they had their own problems. Soon I was back at work helping them.

Victor Janko was still spending all his time in bed. I told him I had evidence I hoped would clear him, but he didn't react. I took the voice recorder out of my bag—I'd put batteries in it—and offered to show him how he could get the goods on Karp. Victor just turned his face to the wall. His depression had clearly deepened. In fact, I felt something worse was going on. It was like he'd snapped inside.

He hadn't been too stable before Daisy tried to kill him. And now . . .

PTSD. Really bad.

After a week my injuries had healed and I was feeling pretty good. Until I got Laura Hecht's phone call.

"The good news is Hagopian was indicted and he pleaded guilty. Picked up five years for the plea bargain, but it's still twenty years to life. And parole's unlikely for a three-time loser."

"Great. But . . . what's the bad news?"

"The blood doesn't match," she said.

"What?"

"There's only one type of blood on the knife. It's AB negative—has to be the victim's. Hagopian's O positive and there's none of it on the murder weapon."

"Jesus. Are you sure?"

"Yep."

"So . . . we've got no case?"

"No, we don't."

I was stunned. "What . . . where do we go from here?"

"I'm afraid nowhere," Laura said.

"But . . . maybe Hagopian's blood was on the knife, and it flaked off over time or through mishandling."

"Could be," she said. "But we can't prove that. The other possibility is Janko was lying to you, that he never did slash Hagopian on the chin."

"I . . . I don't think that's true."

"Well, I'd say you have to consider that now. Like I said, convicts can be big on malarkey"

"Listen, thanks for letting me know."

"David," she said. "I'm real sorry."

"So am I."

I hung up, devastated.

Could it be? The idea that Victor fooled me with his story is too terrible to contemplate. And yet . . . it is possible.

How can I check out Victor's story? There were no witnesses.

Except . . . Daisy/Margarita. She was certain she'd seen Victor kill her mother, I felt she was mistaken. But . . . what if she was right?

I'll have to talk to her. But who knows what shape she's in? And no matter what she says, I can't really trust her. Still . . .

I called Dr. Kapoor and arranged to visit Daisy the following evening.

I'm going to open another door, follow another path. I hope to God the door is locked, and the path is a blind alley.

Chapter 38

The next afternoon there was a small crisis at the hospital. Nigel Penrose, with whom I now played chess on a regular basis, had tried to commit suicide. He'd cut open the veins in his wrists with a chess piece—using the sharp edge of the Bishop's mitre. It couldn't have been easy sawing through his skin with the wooden piece, and it must've hurt like hell.

The nurse heard Penrose moaning and found him on his blood-soaked bed. It was obvious the attempt wasn't serious; he'd made enough noise to be discovered right away, and he kept crying out in his British accent, "Folly, all is folly." His act was a cry for help and attention.

I dressed his wounds, gave him Percodan and Valium, then talked to him for a long time. I told him I'd try to spend more time with him, and that I believed he could get well. After a while he calmed down.

As I got up to leave, he said, "Doctor . . . do you think we can play chess later this afternoon?"

"Checkers," I said.

"But I . . . "
"No sharp edges."
He managed a smile.

The phone rang in my office. It was Mrs. Lucille Simpkins.
"Hi, Lucille."
" 'Morning, Dr. Rothberg," she said. "Dr. Sorenson gave me your number. I'm calling about Henry."
"How is he?"
"Wonderful news, Doctor. I brought him home last night."
"Oh, that's great."
"At Anson/Packwell they're working miracles with autistic kids," she said. "They put Henry on some kind of experimental hormone therapy."
"Secretin?"
" . . . Yes. And he's so much better. No more hand flapping."
"What about rocking?"
"Hardly at all," she said. "They said they don't know how long it'll last, but I'm grateful for anything."
"Of course."
"The thing is, Doctor, he's asking for his turtle. Crying for it really. I don't know what to tell him. I know you took Shelly, but . . . do you still have her?"
"I . . . yes, I do. And she's fine."
"Is there any way I could get her? Maybe I could rent a car and drive up there . . ."
"No. No. I'll . . . I'll bring her down. Maybe this weekend . . ."
"Could you do it sooner? Henry keeps going on about Shelly, and . . . the stress could cause a relapse."
"Yes, all right. I can't tonight, but I'll drive down tomorrow after work. I should get there around 8:00, 8:30."
"We're at 310 Riverside Drive. Apartment 4B. Gee, Doctor, this is so nice of you. And Henry will be so happy."

That evening I went to see Daisy. It was about an hour and a half drive, crossing the Beacon Newburgh Bridge then catching the New York State Thruway north to Albany.

The hospital was adjacent to the main Medical Center. It was a three story glass and steel building resembling a midsized airport terminal. As I drove in, I saw a large spreading chestnut tree illuminated by floodlights. Under it were picnic tables, a see-saw, a junglegym.

At Reception I was told Dr. Kapoor had to leave but a nurse would take me to Daisy's room.

The nurse, Linda Haliburton, came out to greet me. She was a plump West Indian woman with silver-rimmed glasses and a gold tooth.

"Daisy off sedation now," she said as we walked to the high security section. "Doin' heavy-duty Risperidone, but you can talk to her. She just a little fuzzy."

The nurse unlocked the ward door and took me to Daisy's room.

Daisy was in bed dozing, but she opened her eyes as I entered.

"Hi, Daisy."

She struggled to focus. " . . . Dr. Rothberg? Is that really you."

"Yes."

"They've got me so dopey around here . . . I don't know when I'm dreaming or when I'm awake."

She sat up, adjusting her hospital gown.

"Lean forward," I said. "Let me fix your pillows." I reached over and piled them behind her back, one vertical over two horizontal as a nurse once taught me. There was no scent of perfume.

Disheveled as she was, Daisy still looked pretty. But there was a dull look to her eyes. And the voice was different—slurred, hoarse, and nasal.

"How're you feeling?" I asked.

"Okay. I just have this horrible cold. My throat's sore, my nose is all stuffed up . . . "

"It's not a cold," I said. "Those are side effects from your medication."

"How soon you think I can get out of here? Nobody's giving me a straight answer."

"Hard to say."

"I hope when my cold's over . . . "

"It's up to your doctor."

"Please," she said softly, " . . . Sit down."

I pulled a chair over and sat next to her bed. She twirled a lock of blond hair. Her red nailpolish was now chipping off.

"Could you hand me my water? My mouth's dry all the time." She stuck out her coated tongue.

I gave her the bedside container and she sipped from the bent straw.

"Doctor Rothberg," she said. "I had . . . an epiphany. I realize now Victor must've been insane when he killed my mother. So . . . he's not responsible. And . . . I forgive him."

"That's . . . very good, Daisy."

"*An eye for an eye*, that was all wrong. *Vengeance is mine, saith the Lord.* Let God decide about Victor. Jesus teaches forgiveness."

"I'd like to ask you something, Daisy."

She put down her water and looked at me intently.

"Are you absolutely sure it was Victor who . . . did that to your mom?"

"Yes, I'm sure."

"But, you were only two years old . . ."

"Almost three. It happened in March, my birthday's in May."

"You were still quite young. . . ."

"Doctor, you of all people should know even little babies remember awful things that happen to them."

"The lights were out in the apartment that night," I said. "How can you be sure it was Victor Janko?"

"I just remember I could see him clearly. If the lights were out, I guess light was shining in through the window from the street."

"What do you remember about how he looked?"

Her expression darkened. "Why are you asking me all these questions? I *told you* it was Victor. I thought you came here to help me, and now you're . . . you're cross-examining me like a cop or something."

Pushing too hard.

"I'm sorry, Daisy," I said. "Victor's my patient, and if there's a chance he's innocent I need to know."

"I . . . I understand."

"Just one more question, and that's it—I promise."

She nodded.

"Do you remember what he was wearing?"

She shook her head no.

"No memory at all?"

"No . . . Wait, I remember—green. He was wearing something green."

Shit. Victor said he was wearing . . . an army jacket.

I didn't want to go further, but I had to.

"What color green?" I asked.

"I dunno."

" . . . Khaki, olive-drab? Anything like that?"

"You said just one more question."

"Sorry."

"Anyway," she said after a moment, "all I remember is green. Now can we change the subject?"

"Sure."

"Doctor . . . do you think, do you think you can get me out of here?"

"You're not in my care."

"But they'll listen to you."

She put her soft hand over mine.

"I have to get out. I want to visit Victor again . . . tell him I forgive him."

Her fingers caressed me. "Please. I know you can help me."

I pulled my hand away. She was doing her sexpot number again; the seductive eyes, the moist, parted lips—almost a parody of herself. It was like meeting an old girlfriend; someone you once had the hots for but now left you feeling nothing.

It made me very sad.

I got up to leave and she seized my hand desperately.

"Promise you'll come back and see me?"

"It's hard to get over here, Daisy," I said. "And I'm very busy. But I've talked with Dr. Kapoor, and I'm sure she can help you if you work with her.

"Please, *please*, Doctor . . ."

I wrenched away. "Take care," I said as I walked out the door.

On the drive back I thought about what Daisy'd told me.

She said Victor was wearing green. If green means khaki or olive-drab—the color of an army jacket—I'm in trouble. Is she lying to me? If so why? One thing is certain—she needs to believe it was Victor she saw that night. Otherwise all her actions would have no meaning.

All right. Let's assume for the moment her memory is correct.

If Victor did kill Agnes Rivera—

It would mean every session in Victor's cell was a brilliant acting performance on his part, culminating in a totally convincing account of what happened the night of the murder.

It would suggest that Victor and Daisy were acting together—each with a distinct pathology and a different agenda, yet conjoined to form a synergy so powerful they could manipulate me with ease.

Maybe they pegged me as the perfect patsy, a shrink who'd keep an open mind about Victor; a well-trained psychiatrist who'd pick up on the clues they dropped—like their identical descriptions of Leo Hagopian as "huge."

The New York Post *picture of Agnes Rivera's ex-boyfriend, with the bandaged hand—that would be the clincher, convincing me to believe Victor's story. I remember how Daisy'd urged me to come and see Hagopian's photo.*

"If you come over to the library, I'll show it to you."

And Victor, ". . . if you've got a little time tomorrow, could you go over to the library where she works?"

What about the bandage in the photograph? Daisy could've doc-

tored the microfilm—scratching out a small section which would appear as a white strip when the light shone through it.

What if I didn't go to the library? She'd print out the picture and show it to me.

That's a very convoluted sequence of events; one that I could cook up . . . but could Victor and Daisy? And could they pull it off?

I have to admit it's possible—Victor and Daisy running a brilliant game on me, exploiting my pursuit of the truth to make me believe an absolute lie.

If Victor is a murderer, I'll have to face the fact that my gut feeling was totally worthless.

Ben Caldwell was right.

The computer was right.

Father Toussenel was right.

Daisy was right.

Even Stevie Karp was right.

And I was wrong.

One thing is clear—if I allowed myself to fall for Victor and Daisy's con job, I sure as hell don't belong in this business.

I stopped at Vanderkill on my way home, to check on Nigel Penrose. Kim told me he was resting comfortably.

"That's good," I said. "But he's very unstable; he could wig out any time. Call me at my motel tonight if there's a problem."

"I will, Doctor."

"Kim," I said, "enough already with the doctor stuff. Please call me David?"

"Okay, I will."

"Oh, and listen," I said. "I'm going into New York tomorrow night. So if something comes up while I'm gone, Doctor Caldwell will be on call."

"I'm off tomorrow night, but I'll tell Doreen," she said. "Did you say you're going to New York?"

"Yes."

"Wow. I'm going in tomorrow too. There's a race the next morning in Central Park—it'll be my first in the city. Twice around the park, 12.4 miles. It's called the Maidenform Mini Marathon."

"Sounds like I wouldn't qualify."

"No, but you could cheer me on."

"I'd love to, but I have to go back the same night."

Then I got an idea. "Hey, would you like to ride in with me?"

"Well . . . sure. I was gonna take the train," she said. "I'm staying with a girlfriend at the nurses' residence of Roosevelt Hospital. You could drop me off."

"Sure. I'll pick you up tomorrow at six."

"I'll be ready . . . *David.*"

Before I left I decided to look in on Victor. He was in pajamas, lying on his back with his arms straight. He was covered by a sheet and looked like an open-eyed corpse.

I listened to his slow breathing for a while, then spoke to him.

"Victor," I said. "I want you to know I'm still working for you, trying to find a way to get you out of prison."

No response.

"I want to ask you something. Do you remember the color of the killer's sweatshirt? Y'know, the one that said *Life is a Beach?*"

Nothing.

"Try to remember for me. It's important.

For God's sake—please say green.

It was futile.

Suddenly Victor turned to me with a blank look in his eyes. But it was different than his previous glazed stares, which were defensive, with hints of pain and sadness in them. This look was almost reptilian—cold, expressionless, devoid of emotion. It was deeply unsettling.

Victor was now very, very ill. And I had no idea how to help him.

Chapter 39

When I picked up Kim, I introduced her to Shelly, who was in her vivarium on the back seat. I explained who Shelly was and where I was taking her.

"You took care of a little boy's turtle for two years?" Kim said. "That's really sweet."

"I enjoyed it. Shelly's got a lot of personality."

"You know who she looks like?" she asked.

"Who?"

"Woody Allen."

I cracked up laughing. She was right.

I guess I hogged the conversation for most of the drive. I filled Kim in on my failure to get Hagopian's DNA, and how I was concerned about my instincts being wrong.

"Well, if your gut feeling is that Victor's innocent," she said. "I'm sure you're right."

She said it with a forthright simplicity that blew me away. I real-

ized I'd had nobody to talk to about these issues, and how great it was
to be with someone who was supportive.

"Listen," I said to Kim. "Why don't you come with me while I
drop off Shelly, then we can get a bite to eat before I take you down
to Roosevelt Hospital?"

"Okay," she said. "As long as it doesn't get too late. Remember, I
have a race tomorrow morning."

"Agreed."

I parked on Riverside Drive, and we entered the lobby of the large,
aging apartment building. It had an iron and beveled glass Nouveau
doorway flanked by limestone Corinthian columns.

"David. Going to Simpkins, 4B," I said to the doorman. He looked
at the big black plastic garbage bag I was cradling in my arms.

"Open the bag please. Gotta see what's inside," the doorman said.
"Can't be too careful since 9/11."

As I showed him the turtle, it struck me that I didn't look Middle
Eastern, but he certainly did.

Scary times.

As Kim and I walked through the vast lobby, I admired its faded
grandeur. The travertine marble floors were cracked, and the walls
were hung with discolored, frayed tapestries—St. George slaying the
dragon, and a shepherdess doing something or other with a rampant
unicorn.

We took the self-service elevator up to four and I stopped for a
moment in front of 4B.

Dejection swept over me. True, I was only Shelley's caretaker, but
I didn't think this day would ever come. Now here it was . . .

I rang the bell.

Lucille greeted me with a hug. She was a pale thirty-and-change
widow with frizzy brown hair and a weary look. She wore a floral
housecoat.

I introduced her to Kim.

Lucille took us down a long hallway into the living room. Henry was sitting cross-legged in front of the TV watching a "Rugrats" video.

He'd grown in two years. Now six, his torso was longer and he'd lost the baby look. His eyes were the same; sad, with pupils dark as black olives. He rocked from side to side, but only slightly. He was much improved.

"Henry," his mom said.

The boy looked up at us.

"Do you remember Dr. Rothberg?"

Henry shook his head no.

"He's brought you a present."

He came to full attention, like all kids when they hear that magical phrase.

I knelt down next to him and pulled off the black garbage bag. He looked down into the vivarium. For a moment he was shocked. Then a smile brightened his face like sunshine.

"Shelly," he said softly.

He picked the turtle up by the shell and pressed her against the side of his face. He giggled as the little claws tickled him.

"Did you miss me?" he asked her. "I sure missed you. I didn't know if I'd ever see you again. Gee, you look nice. Do you still like worms? I remember when they fed you worms at the hospital. Yuch . . . "

The little guy continued talking to his long lost pal, oblivious of me, Kim, and his mom. It was a good feeling, seeing the joy I'd brought to this sad-eyed kid.

Lucille walked us to the door, thanked me, and hugged me again. I said no problem and we left.

The loss hit me as we walked down Riverside Drive. That little turtle had become part of the fabric of my life; a creature to care about, worry about, even talk to. Now she was gone. I felt my heart thudding in my chest, a dull pain surrounding it. *Heartache.*

Kim picked it up. "You're gonna miss her aren't you?"

I nodded.

"You should call Mrs. Simpkins, and ask for visitation rights."

"For a turtle?"

"No. For her son. Then, of course, if you want to look in on Shelly . . ."

"Great idea," I said.

We walked a little way in silence. When we got back to the car, I told her my dinner plan.

"I know of a great place to eat," I said. "It's within walking distance, so we can leave the car here."

"Is it one of those hot West Side restaurants they wrote up in the *Times*?"

"It's a surprise. It'll be a better surprise if you don't ask any questions. You up for that?"

"Lead on."

We were at 87th Street, so we walked south on Riverside to 80th. There we turned the corner, crossed over to West End Avenue, then one block more to Broadway and Zabar's.

In the glaringly lit food emporium I led Kim past the cheeses and the appetizers till we were in the smoked fish section. I took a number from the machine but it was so late there were no other customers. The Chinese lox cutter asked me what I wanted. His name tag said Bob.

"Half a pound of nova," I answered. "And if you can, cut it from the shoulder."

Bob gave me a knowing smile, then spoke to Kim in a Chinese accent.

"Boyfriend really know fish."

He left us and went down to the other end of the counter.

"I have this friend, Wolfie," I explained to Kim. "He's a kosher butcher and all-around *feinschmecker*—uh, that's Yiddish for *Foodie*. He says the flesh near the head of a salmon is the most tender, because it's the least muscular."

Bob returned with a salmon which had only the upper portion left. He cut tissue-thin slices of the pink fish, working with the precision of a neurosurgeon. Then he put it on the scale. "It's a little over."

I said that was fine.

"Y'know," I said to Kim, "The owner of Zabar's once said he made his fortune just by using four words—*It's a little over*."

"That's very interesting," Kim said. "But enough already with the delicatessen trivia."

Busted.

I paid at the check-out counter, after picking up a container of scallion cream cheese on the way.

We stopped across the street at H&H and bought six plain bagels. And four Dr. Brown's celery tonics. I packed it all in our Zabar's shopping bag.

It was a three block walk to Riverside Park. There we followed the lamp lit asphalt path under the West Side Highway, then took the stone stairway curving around and down until it reached the Boat Basin Cafe. We heard the flute-like voice of Enya on the sound system. The restaurant was crowded, patrons dining al fresco around a circular fountain which had been covered with a platform to provide additional seating. For some reason, New York's master builder Robert Moses had decided the place should look like a medieval monastery, so it had sweeping round arches, groin vaults, and Romanesque columns.

"Wow," Kim said. "This is beautiful."

"We're not eating here."

"Oh. Then where . . . ?"

"No questions, remember?"

We walked out to the flagstone terrace, then down the stairs leading to the Hudson River promenade. In front of us was the Boat Basin marina.

It was a hot summer night. The river walk was crowded with strollers, joggers, cyclists, inline skaters. Not so long ago the park at night was dangerous; now it vibrated with joyful energy.

At the southern end of the marina was the houseboat section. The entrance gate reminded me of Vanderkill—chainlink topped by razor wire. I unlocked the gate and we walked along the wooden dock. It was good to hear the familiar sounds of lapping water, the groan of bowlines straining against their moorings.

I could see my boat down at the end. The rectangular white cabin gleamed in the moonlight. The only thing different was an American flag on the roof deck—Ed Sorenson must've raised it in a burst of patriotism.

"There's my houseboat," I said pointing to it. "That's where we're going to have dinner."

"That's yours?" Kim said, surprised.

"Yes. I lived there before I came up to Vanderkill."

As we got closer she could read the name of the boat on the bow. "*Go With The Flo?*" she said.

"Yes. It's named after my mom, Florence—everybody called her Flo."

When we reached the boat, I heard the Rachmaninoff *Second Piano Concerto—my make-out music*—and the sound of a woman laughing. There was dim light coming from the two portholes of the sleeping loft.

Damn. It's Dr. Ed and his social worker/schtupee.

"Looks like you've got some boat guests," Kim said.

"A friend of mine sometimes uses it for fun and games. I should've called first."

"So . . . we'd be interrupting."

"Exactly."

"Oh, well," Kim said. "Let's eat on one of those park benches."

We retreated to the promenade and sat down on a bench.

We had no utensils. But I worked out a system—break off piece of bagel, use bagel to scoop out cream cheese, then wrap schmeared bagel with piece of nova. Eat and repeat until stuffed. We tore up the paper shopping bag and fashioned place mats and napkins.

Between bites, and sips of celery tonic, we chatted, looking across the river to the Palisades. I pointed out what I used to call my own twin towers—two fifty story behemoth apartment houses. Next to them was a row of Victorian private homes that lined Weehawken's River Road.

There was a bright waxing moon, and we watched a red funneled tug towing a barge, slowly steaming upriver. It looked like a toy boat. Off in the distance we could see the twinkling lights of the GWB.

I let my arm rest on the bench behind Kim, wanting to hug her. But like a shy school boy I didn't.

After we'd eaten, Kim looked at her watch.

"Well," she said. "We'd better get going. I have to be up at seven, and my girlfriend's waiting up for me."

I nodded. We gathered the trash and dropped it into a waste can.

There were two bagels left. I stuck them in my shoulder bag and we walked back to the car.

I drove down West End Avenue and stopped in front of the Nurses's Residence on 61st. The street was deserted.

"Kim," I said. "How would you feel about . . . a goodnight kiss?"

"Um . . . I don't think so."

"Oh. Okay."

"The thing is," she said, "a kiss would definitely jump-start my motor, and . . . I hate starting something I can't finish."

"We could figure something out."

"David, we're in a car."

"We could get in the back."

She glanced behind her and laughed.

"Oh," she said. "Guess that's why they call 'em jump seats."

Kim leaned over and ran her very hot, wet tongue around the inside of my ear.

"Too be continued," she said softly. Then she got out of the car and went into the dormitory.

WHOA.

Chapter 40

I drove down to 57th Street, turned right and took the ramp up onto the West Side Highway.

I was jazzed about Kim; filled with fantasies of lust, love, and a possible future with her. Then the image of Victor intruded, pulling me back to the reality of my life.

Am I fit to stay at Vanderkill?

If only I could get a resolution to the mystery of Victor Janko. But how?

Just past the bridge a green and white sign caught my eye. It read: *Exit to Dyckman Street.* Without making a conscious decision, I turned the steering wheel in the direction of the sign's arrow. It was as if a powerful magnetic force were pulling my car onto the exit ramp.

I found myself driving east across Dyckman. The people of the barrio were hanging out on stoops and street corners, escaping the stifling heat of the tenements. Salsa and rap music blared out of car stereos and boom-boxes in multi-ethnic cacophony.

As I passed under the elevated tracks at Nagle Avenue a subway train clanked and clattered above me. The racket made me lose my bearings and I felt like I was in a dream. I hit the brakes.

Then the train was gone. I was breathless, feverish. I pressed hard on the accelerator pedal, crossed under the tracks and then I saw it— the lights of the Dyckman Manhattan housing project.

I was being drawn irresistibly to the scene of the crime.

I parked across the street and entered the project.

Maybe I can find Agnes Rivera's ground floor apartment. Then I can check if there's a street lamp near it, bright enough that Daisy could've seen her mother's killer.

I soon realized it would be impossible to tell. The old cobra head street lamps were now augmented by newer airfield-type fixtures, and there were floodlights shining down from the roofs. Probably they were installed in the last few years to combat urban crime.

Dyckman Manhattan was a complex of apartment houses, each fourteen stories high, built of red bricks which time and city soot had muted to the color of dried blood. The buildings were clustered around a courtyard, criss-crossed by cement pathways with unmowed lawns between them. In the center of each grassy area was a pile of gray schist rocks—some Housing Authority official's idea of abstract sculpture.

The area was notorious for gang killings and drug wars, but I had no sense of danger. A project police car passed, slowly patrolling the walkways. A sign forbidding firecrackers, loud noise, and the playing of music was being obeyed. I passed people sitting at concrete tables, playing cards or eating, teenage girls jumping in a serious game of Double Dutch, and a few elderly people, trudging along with canes or walkers. A group of four homies came towards me, dressed in red. *Were those the gang colors of the Crips? No, the Bloods. No, Tommy Hilfiger.* They were talking animated trash but paid me no mind. Then I saw a young woman pushing a child in a baby stroller. A shiver ran through me.

This is so strange. I came here without volition and with no clear purpose—just this powerful urge to see where Agnes Rivera met her death. I have no idea what that will do for me, or to me.

I came to an asphalt roadway. It ran in an oval around the interior of the project. I remembered the address in the NYPD file; something-or-other Dyckman Oval.

I decided to walk around the roadway, checking the house numbers—maybe I'd recall the exact address.

All the buildings looked the same. Their facades were scrawled with graffiti, and the windows of the ground floor apartments had metal grates over them. There were few air conditioners.

At the third building I hit paydirt, but not because of the house number. I saw a large graffito of a Cross. There were other spray-painted slogans and signatures, vying for space on the brick wall. But the area around the Cross was untouched—apparently out of respect; on the upright part of the crux had been written *R.I.P.* and on the transverse were the letters *A.R.*

Rest in Peace—Agnes Rivera. I stared at the doorway, trying to imagine the hideous murder. But my mind wouldn't allow it—I just felt a numbing sadness, which distanced me from the tragedy even as it drew me into it.

"She was a nice lady."

A wizened Hispanic woman in a wheelchair had stopped in front of me. "I seen you looking at the Cross," she said. "She was a nice lady, Agnes. And a good neighbor. Poor thing had a rotten life 'though, tryin' to raise up her *niñita* alone. And then gettin' sliced to ribbons by that punk kid who worked at the market. *Maldito cobarde.*"

"Did you know him?"

"I wouldn't say that, but I saw him sometime at services with his mother. She belong to my church."

"How did he seem to you?"

"He never look at nobody, always shiftin' his eyes around, like . . . like he was scared of somethin'."

"Scared of what?"

"How do I know? *Mira,* why you askin' me all these questions?"

"I'm . . . an investigative reporter."

"TV?"

"Newspaper."

"Well, if you want to investigate, you oughta be talkin' to Miguel Sotomayor at the A&P. He knew that Janko bastid real good. Worked with him. Miguel was a checker back then, but nowadays he's night manager of the store."

"So . . . he'd be there now?"

"Yeah. They open twenty-four seven."

"Where would I find the A&P?"

"Across the street, on Nagle."

I thanked the woman and headed for the supermarket.

Miguel Sotomayor's office was a cramped cubicle at the top of a plywood stairway. It had beaverboard walls and a large plastic window from which the manager could survey his domaine of aisles and shoppers.

Sotomayor was a short man with dyed shoe-polish black hair and a pleasant face marred by the lunar-surface residuum of adolescent acne.

I did the Hollywood producer bit again, handing him my Paramax Pictures card.

He looked at it and was visibly impressed. "You know Tom Hanks?" he asked.

"Sure, I know Tom."

"Love Tom Hanks. He's everybody."

"Everybody?"

"Yeah, like whoever he is in the movies, he's like somebody you know."

"Oh," I said. "You mean Everyman."

"Yeah. Except in 'Philadelphia,' when he was just a *maricón*."

"Mr. Sotomayor," I said. "The reason I came in from the Coast was to do research for a new film. It's called 'The Baby Carriage Killer.'"

"'The Baby Carriage' . . . Jesus," he said. "That happened right here."

"Yes. I know."

"This gonna be like that Son of Sam movie?" he asked.

"No," I said. "Son of Sam was a serial killer. Victor Janko wasn't. This film will be a psychological exploration. . . ."

"Psychological?" he said. "I love psychological. Remember 'Psycho?'"

"Of course," I said. "Listen, I understand you knew Victor Janko."

"We went to Immaculata together."

"What was he like?"

"Victor? He was a real momma's boy, a goodie-two-shoes, always actin' like he was better than you. What a joke. Up till around third grade he was still wettin' his pants, which made him smell like a piss-pot. And he kept braggin' on his mother, sayin' she was better than the Brady Bunch mom and the Partridge Family mom, which was also a joke, because half the time his knuckles were bruised and bleedin' from where she rapped him."

"You think he was physically abused by his mother?"

"I *know* he was. Sometimes he'd bunch up his jacket and sit on it, which was 'cause his ass was sore from gettin' hit."

"You think that had anything to do with what Victor did?"

Sotomayor looked like he was about to speak, then changed his mind.

"What is it?" I asked.

His face grew tense. His brow furrowed like a contestant on a TV game show.

"What?" I said, pressing him.

"Nothing."

I knew he was concealing something.

"Mr. Sotomayor," I said. "How would you feel about being a creative consultant on my film?"

"What's that?"

"Well, I want realism in this movie, so we're shooting it on location—right here, not on some Hollywood back lot. You were raised in this neighborhood, and you knew Victor Janko, so as consultant you'd be giving us info on the details of the story."

"What would I get for that?"

"Screen credit."

"What's that."

"Your name up on the screen in big letters—Creative Consultant . . . Miguel Sotomayor."

His eyes widened. "Uh . . . what about money?"

"Mmm, that depends."

"On what?"

"On how much information you give us. If you give us stuff we couldn't possibly know, that would up the price."

"How much?"

"Paramax pays top dollar, but I couldn't say till I hear what you've got."

"How do I know you won't rip me off?"

"You have my word—if this movie gets made you'll get whatever the Writer's Guild deems fair compensation."

He was hesitant. I pressed him.

"Look. If you don't tell me what you know," I said. "You can be sure you'll get nothing."

"Well . . . I do know things about the murder . . . stuff nobody knows."

"Like what?"

He held back for a moment. "The truth," he said. "I know the truth."

I faked an intense coughing fit. "Water," I choked out. " . . . please . . . water."

Sotomayor got up from his desk and put a paper cup under his office water cooler. As he did, I reached into my shoulder bag, found my digital voice recorder and pressed the ON button.

I sipped the water, then cleared my throat.

" . . . Sorry," I said. "Summer allergies really get me."

"Know whatcha mean."

"Now, Mr. Sotomayor. You were telling me about the murder?"

"Yes."

He took a deep breath.

"That day," he said, "I was workin' the checkout counter right next to Victor."

He pointed through the plastic window at the store below.

"Counter number two. There it is down there."

I nodded.

"Well, you can see I'd have a pretty good view down aisle three. I heard a guy yelling 'bitch . . . you ballbustin' bitch' and I looked up and saw this dude shakin' this woman real hard by the shoulders. It was Mrs. Rivera, I seen her in here a lot, always with her kid. Finally the guy lets her go and she comes down to Victor's checkout counter. The little girl starts cryin', freakin' out 'cause she wants some candy. Tell ya the truth, I think she was really shook about the guy hasslin' her mom. After Mrs. Rivera left, Victor found this children's book on the floor—the kid must've chucked it when she freaked. Victor went out after Mrs. Rivera but she was gone. So he came back."

Sotomayor stopped.

"Go on."

He hesitated. ". . . Listen, in *el barrio* you learn to keep your mouth shut, mind your own business. I was scared to talk then and . . . I'm scared to talk now."

"This is good stuff, Miguel. Top dollar stuff."

"I know, but . . ."

I pushed on forcefully. "Who was the guy who hassled Mrs. Rivera?"

"All right, all right," he said. "I knew the guy from the 'hood . . . he was a nasty-ass punk . . . 'Leo the Lion' they called him."

"Leo the Lion."

"Yeah. After Mrs. Rivera left, I look up the aisle . . . to the far end where we keep the housewares. I see this Leo guy boostin' a big kitchen knife, y'know one that like comes in a plastic and cardboard package. Well, he slips it into his pants pocket, ambles around for a while, and then he bops right through my checkout, givin' me a peace sign. I wasn't gonna say nothin' . . . you don't wanna fuck with a mean muthafucka like him."

"You remember what he was wearing?"

"No."

"Try."

His face went blank. "Geez, it was a long time ago . . . what twenty years?"

"Fifteen. Look, I need details. Details are what's gonna make this picture. *Now, what did he have on?*"

He shrugged.

"Do you remember a color? What color was he wearing?"

" . . . Green," he said emphatically. "I remember now, 'cause it was a couple days after St. Paddy's day, and I was thinkin' what was he wearin' green *now* for? It was bright green, like a pool table. A sweat-shirt, a heavy sweatshirt with some writin' on the front."

"What did it say?"

"I don't know. Hey, I gave you the color."

"Yes, you did."

"That's all I remember."

"What about Victor?"

"Oh, well, Victor's shift was over like twenty minutes later and he split."

"Do you know where he went?"

"I figured he went home. But then when the cops nabbed him I realized he must've gone to give Mrs. Rivera back the book. And right away he was a suspect, and y'know the cops don' wanna be bothered, they too busy eatin' donuts and takin' payoffs, so they say let's nail the bastard and be done with it."

"You're sure Leo was the killer."

"Hadda be. Like they say in the movies, he had the motive, and whatdycall it? the opportunity, and . . . he had the weapon. Look, I wasn't too crazy about Victor Janko, but hey, that little sissy was no murderer."

"Mr. Sotomayor. Thank you. You've given me a lot."

"Look, I'll be a consulter on this movie, but . . . I'd rather just take the money. Forget puttin' my name up there on the big screen. That guy Leo ever sees this flick, I don't want him comin' after me."

"No danger of that. I know who Leo is—he's Leo Hagopian. The cops just nailed him for attempted murder and he's headed for a twenty to life stretch in the Joint."

Sotomayor nodded, not completely reassured.

"I'll be in touch with you," I said. "Soon as we set up our production schedule."

"Any chance Tom Hanks'll be in the movie?"

"We're checking his availability."

We shook hands and I left.

I felt bad about scamming him, but I had to do it. Later he might have to testify, but with Hagopian in prison he'd be in no jeopardy.

Anyway, it was Miguel's moral responsibility to come forward. Had he done so fifteen years ago, Victor Janko probably would've gone free.

Chapter 41

I got in my car, took Nagle Avenue under the El tracks and followed it to the University Heights Bridge. The bright moonlight illuminated the old steel arch span, with its pot-holed pavement and ornate, turn-of-the-nineteenth century ironwork railings.

I crossed over the Harlem river into the Bronx, then took the Major Deegan north, heading for home.

I kept thinking I should feel more elated. I had solved the mystery of Victor Janko. My instinct, my gut feeling was right—Victor was not the murderer. But mostly I felt a sense of relief. Now I could get on with my life, do the job I was trained for, the work I loved doing.

Then there was Kim. I had a sense memory of her tongue fluttering around the rim of my ear and I felt a tremor of desire. Yes, there definitely was Kim.

With her, my emotional life would be back on track. And so would my running program. *Yeah—soon as Kim gets home I'll invite her to join me . . . in a little fun run.*

There were still unresolved issues.

Will my recording of Miguel Sotomayor be enough for Laura to reopen the case? Only a conviction of Hagopian for Agnes Rivera's murder will enable Victor to go free. (If Hagopian does get sent to jail as the real Baby Carriage Killer, I'd love to see how long he lasts in the general prison population.)

What about Stevie Karp? Will Victor ever be together enough to get the goods on him with my voice recorder?

And the biggest concern of all—what can I do to bring Victor out of his new, more complex illness? I can still see that blank-eyed reptilian look. What's going on in his brain now? The trauma of his beloved Daisy trying to kill him was something he couldn't handle. Add to that his already fragile psyche and there's no predicting where this new pathology will take him. . . .

I decided I needed a break from introspection.

I turned on my car radio; and by doing so I solved the one remaining mystery in the case of Victor Janko. It was a mystery I'd almost forgotten about.

On WFAN they were interviewing some hockey player from the Montreal Canadiens. The topic: How NHL salary restrictions would affect the player's upcoming contract negotiations. *Boring.*

As I started to change the station, I heard the hockey player, speaking in his flat-toned French-Canadian accent, "I got agent to deal with money," he said. "My job to shoot dot puck . . . score dot goal. *No doubt about it.*"

He pronouned it Canadian style—*"no doot aboot it."*

His accent reminded me of the threatening phone calls I'd gotten on my voicemail. There was something familiar in those speech patterns—now I knew what it was. The anonymous caller had said, "Don't let Janko *oot.* Don't even think *aboot* it." It was the French-Canadian voice of *Father Emile Toussenel.*

Of course. The priest was obsessed with the idea that Victor Janko was evil incarnate. He, like Karp, was adamant Victor should never leave prison.

I was outraged.

I'm gonna confront that bastard—tell him he's a demented, hypocritical shit-heel; the antithesis of everything his religion stands for.

I've got proof of his transgressions on my answering machine tape. I'll get him convicted of a crime—Felony Harassment, Criminal Intimidation . . .

But wait. His voice was disguised, maybe it wouldn't prove anything. And what kind of a case could I make? My word against a priest's—a man of God? Okay, maybe priests aren't quite so exhalted these days, but do I really want to go through all that legal wrangling, spend my time, my energy . . . ?

No. Inflicting punishment on Father Toussenel isn't necessary. After all, in the end he has to answer to . . . a Higher Authority.

Epilogue

Victor Thomas Janko, *wearing briefs and an undershirt, lay on his bed in the unlit cell. It was his first night back in Ad Seg, and he hated it, especially after the relative comfort of his hospital room. There, he could sleep in peaceful darkness. Here, there was always the glare of that naked bulb in the corridor, shining in on him. He stretched out his hands and turned them palms up, palms down, palms up, palms down, watching the way the light coming through the mesh door mottled his skin. Alligator hands, he always called them.*

But it was important for him to be back in Ad Seg. Because of the Plan. He'd hatched the Plan during his long days and nights in the hospital. It was easy enough for him to get moved back to his cell. He just suddenly got better.

He started talking again, saying how he wasn't depressed anymore. He fed Dr. Rothberg a bunch of baloney about Daisy; that he now realized she must've been crazy to do what she did—making believe she loved him, then trying to kill him. And how in his heart of hearts he forgave her—which was the biggest bunch of baloney of all. Then he agreed to take the recording device and get Karp on tape. Ha. Ha. Ha. Sure he would.

Dr. Rothberg told him not to give up hope, that he was working to get him out. Yeah, it would happen soon . . . on the Twelfth of Never. The only help I'm gonna get, he thought, is from the Holy Trinity—Me, Myself, and I.

One good thing about being in Ad Seg was he had his painting materials. He wasn't allowed his palette knife, but that didn't matter—he could manage without it. He'd been thinking a lot about his new painting. It wouldn't be another beach scene. No. No. No. It would be something new, something different. And he felt sure when people saw it, they would say it was Victor Janko's masterpiece.

It was all part of the Plan. The Master Plan.

Stevie Karp had served him dinner at 6:00 and promised dessert for later, which meant he'd be back with his K-Y jelly and his condom and that horrible thing of his. But Victor wasn't really worried about it. In fact he was happy because it meant he could put the Plan into effect right away.

He heard the familiar jingle of Stevie's keys down the hall. Soon he'd be unlocking the cell door, and entering with that leer on his face.

Now here he was, turning on the cell light. Victor looked at him, with his sunglasses and his guard hat and his stupid ponytail and his beer-belly. Disgusting.

Victor sat up and pointed to the empty canvas sitting on his easel. "How you like my new painting?" he asked.

The guard looked at it and turned to him with a puzzled expression. "It's blank. Ain't nothin' on it."

"Yes, there is. See, it's called 'Polar Bear in a Snow Storm,' and I painted it with all these different shades of white. You gotta look real close to pick out the polar bear."

Stevie walked over to the canvas for a closer look. "I don't see shit. What the hell . . ."

Hell was the last word Karp ever uttered. Victor had come up behind him and plunged the sharpened end of a paintbrush handle deep into the soft spot between Stevie's skull and cervical spine. The hardwood handle, honed to stiletto sharpness on the cinderblock wall, sliced cleanly through the guard's brain stem.

Stevie collapsed to the floor, making a gurgling sound as if he were trying to complete his final sentence. Victor noted with satisfaction that there wasn't too much blood. It was oozing slowly from the wound, and Victor wasted no time stripping off the guard's shirt before it became badly stained.

Working quickly, Victor removed the guard's pants and dressed himself in Karp's uniform. Of course, the pants were too large, but he had planned for that. He stuffed a pillow inside the trousers and the shirt, and he immediately took on the paunchy shape of the guard. He put on his own socks and shoes.

Victor knelt down beside the body, removed Karp's shoelaces and tied them together.

Next, with the nailclipper attached to the guard's lanyard, he snipped off Karp's ponytail, right above the point where the hair was secured by a twisted rubber band.

He tied the shoelaces to the ponytail and fastened the laces around his head like a headband. The ponytail now hung down his neck. With great excitement he put on the prison guard's hat, and then, placing his own glasses in his shirt pocket, he put on Karp's dark shades. He couldn't see well, but he could see well enough; well enough to take Karp's gun, wallet, and keys.

There was no mirror, but Victor knew his disguise was excellent. It was night and it was dark and there were no other guards in Ad Seg. Anybody who saw him would take him for Karp, and it would be a snap to walk out through the prison gate.

Victor tried to imagine what life would be like on the outside after all these years. He couldn't picture it, but he could hardly wait.

Now, before Victor departed, it was time to create his masterpiece. He switched back to his own eyeglasses, then yanked the sharpened paintbrush handle out of Karp's neck. The blood flowed freely from the wound, pooling on the floor and spreading in crimson puddles. Victor liked the color. It reminded him of Matisse.

He picked up a fresh paintbrush (his favorite, the No. 12 Grumbacher sable), knelt down, and dipped it into the pool of Karp's blood. Then he went over to the blank canvas and began to paint.

As his hand guided the brush skillfully over the canvas, he again took pleasure in the bright red color. The stuff was difficult to work with, though. It had a tendency to spatter and run, and he detested sloppy work. So he was very, very careful.

Gradually the picture took shape. It was a portrait of Dr. Suess's goofy-looking feline, depicted in monochromatic red. It was a dead-on copy, with two notable exceptions. Over the cat's eyes were a pair of dark sunglasses. And behind his head a scrawny ponytail drooped down.

Victor took a few steps back and scrutinized his work. It was perfect, he thought. His whole Plan was perfect. Then he spoke harshly, doing his best Stevie Karp imitation. "Good. Now gimme the finishing touch."

Then in his own voice—"No. No. Please, boss. Please don't make me."

"Now, faggot. The finishing touch."

"All right, boss," Victor said with a smirk. He dipped his paintbrush again into the guard's blood and with great care he painted in the hat. But instead of a high porkpie, he gave the feline the hat of a prison guard. Finally, he painted seven words on the canvas, in precise imitation of the way Dr. Seuss formed his letters. The words were:

THAT IS THAT,

THE CAT IN THE HAT.

He put the sunglasses back on and fastened the gun and gunbelt around his waist. Then the cat in the hat, who you'd've sworn was Stevie Karp, calmly left the cell, went down the Ad Seg stairs, crossed the yard, and strode unchallenged through the Vanderkill Penitentiary gate.

In the lot it was easy to find Karp's car, he'd bragged enough about it—a red Camaro.

Victor got in. He'd only driven in Driver's Ed, but he remembered *well enough to get going. He stopped at a Mobil station to get gas. When the tank was full, he signed Aaron Karp on the Visa card slip.*

The gas guy went to the office and returned a few minutes later with the receipt. As he did a cop car pulled up at the gas pump next to Victor. Victor put his hand on Stevie's gun in case there was a problem.

He smiled.

They smiled.

No problem.

"Pardon me," Victor said to the gas guy. "Could you give me directions to Albany?"